"I haven't seen anything to convince me you're guilty, Kyle," she said softly. **"Please convince me you're innocent."**

It wasn't what she had requested, he was sure, but he took a step closer to Maisie and pulled her into his arms.

Their kiss was tentative at first, but as he tasted her mouth, felt her warm, curvaceous body against him—never mind that it was in a police uniform—he wanted more.

The kiss deepened, and he was gratified to realize Maisie wasn't pulling away, but seemed as invested in it as he was. He gently put one hand at the back of her head, touching her smooth, short hair, stroking it, wanting to stroke more of her.

But not here, in his office where shelter managers could walk in at any time. And not now, in the middle of their respective workdays—and maybe not ever. They certainly hadn't known each other long.

Attempting not to let his growing attraction—and lust—for this woman get in the way, he forced himself to pull away.

Dear Reader,

Guardian K-9 on Call is the second in my Shelter of Secrets series, a spinoff from my K-9 Ranch Rescue series for Harlequin Romantic Suspense. Like its predecessor, *Her Undercover Refuge*, and the books in the K-9 Ranch Rescue series, it takes place in the town of Chance, California. And I'm sure you won't be surprised to hear it also involves dogs.

It features Dr. Kyle Kornel, a veterinarian who now runs a clinic at the very special Chance Animal Shelter. Kyle cures the limp of Griffin, the K-9 of Officer Maisie Murran, and she really appreciates it.

But also visiting the shelter is the owner of a local pet store, frustrated because she can no longer make additional money as she used to by selling pets in her shop, thanks to changes in California law. She attempts to add to her profit in other ways—and is murdered. And because Kyle happened to find her body, and he'd been arguing with her, he's the most likely suspect.

But Maisie hopes to prove otherwise...

I hope you enjoy *Guardian K-9 On Call*. Please come visit me at my website: www.lindaojohnston.com and at my weekly blog, killerhobbies.blogspot.com. And, yes, I'm on Facebook and Writerspace, too.

Linda O. Johnston

GUARDIAN K-9 ON CALL

Linda O. Johnston

HARLEQUIN®
ROMANTIC
SUSPENSE™

Recycling programs
for this product may
not exist in your area.

ISBN-13: 978-1-335-75972-6

Guardian K-9 on Call

Copyright © 2022 by Linda O. Johnston

Harlequin Enterprises ULC
22 Adelaide St. West, 41st Floor
Toronto, Ontario M5H 4E3, Canada
www.Harlequin.com

Printed in U.S.A.

Linda O. Johnston loves to write. While honing her writing skills, she worked in advertising and public relations, then became a lawyer...and enjoyed writing contracts. Linda's first published fiction appeared in *Ellery Queen's Mystery Magazine* and won a Robert L. Fish Memorial Award for Best First Mystery Short Story of the Year. Linda now spends most of her time creating memorable tales of romance, romantic suspense and mystery. Visit her on the web at www.lindaojohnston.com.

Books by Linda O. Johnston

Harlequin Romantic Suspense

Shelter of Secrets

Her Undercover Refuge
Guardian K-9 on Call

The Coltons of Grave Gulch

Uncovering Colton's Family Secret

The Coltons of Mustang Valley

Colton First Responder

K-9 Ranch Rescue

Second Chance Soldier
Trained to Protect

Undercover Soldier
Covert Attraction

Visit the Author Profile page at
Harlequin.com for more titles.

Dedication

Like *Her Undercover Refuge*, *Guardian K-9 on Call* is dedicated to all those who devote their lives to helping other people in trouble, and also to those who work for and volunteer at shelters where dogs, cats and other animals without human families are cared for. It's also dedicated to veterinarians. I once wanted to be one of them, and I really admire them.

And, as I always do, I dedicate this book to my dear husband, Fred, as well as our dog Cari, who's part of our family, as well as to Mystie, who has crossed the Rainbow Bridge.

Acknowledgment

Yet again, many thanks to my wonderful editor, Allison Lyons, and my fantastic agent, Paige Wheeler.

Chapter 1

The reception room at the Chance Animal Shelter was always welcoming—a good thing especially now, thought K-9 Officer Maisie Murran. It was reasonably large, and occasionally there were people waiting to be accompanied inside to look at pets available for adoption.

Maisie was the only person there that late afternoon, but she wasn't alone.

On the floor beside her was her wonderful K-9, Griffin, a golden retriever, standing on three legs. They had been patrolling this area of Chance, California, making sure, as they often did, that no one was sneaking around the shelter, even beyond its tall wooden fence that allowed no views from outside.

But Griffin had started limping. Maisie couldn't figure out what was wrong, so she had called the shelter's director, Scott Sherridan, and he had given her good news. Yes, the new shelter veterinarian was on duty at the moment. "Come on in," Scott had invited her.

Maisie had been here with Griffin often. Fortunately, she had been approved by Scott to visit whenever she wanted, even to come inside the shelter grounds, and she knew that kind of approval was rare.

She had also received a general okay from her superiors at the Chance Police Department to visit whenever she had time between official assignments.

Yes, it was a wonderful pet shelter, taking in homeless dogs, cats and smaller animals to help find them new, loving families. That was its publicized purpose. And now a veterinarian was available to help take care of them.

But even more important to Maisie was that the shelter's secret but primary function was to take in people escaping from danger in their lives.

The inner door finally opened. Maisie rose, placing her hand on Griffin's head to keep him calm.

A man in a blue medical jacket over dark pants walked in. He was tall, with close-cropped black hair, deep brown eyes beneath thick black brows and as great-looking a male face as Maisie had ever seen, with sharp cheekbones and a broad jaw.

"Hi. You must be Officer Murran," he said as he approached. Scott had apparently let him know who she was. "I'm Dr. Kyle Kornel."

Thanks to Scott, Maisie had known that. "Hi, Dr.

Kornel. That's right, I'm Maisie Murran. I don't know if Scott told you, but Griffin, my K-9—"

"Needs medical attention. Yes, Scott told me. Let's go back into the clinic." He bent over near Griffin. "Hi, boy. Let's figure out what's wrong and take care of it." Griffin stood and took a couple of steps, so it was obvious where he was hurting. Maisie froze as the doctor bent and picked Griffin up, K-9 vest and all—but he made it appear as if her seventy-five-pound partner was a toy dog as he used a keycard to open the door into the hallway that led to the rest of the shelter. In moments, he entered the first door on the left, the vet clinic, though Dr. Kornel was the first vet on duty here since the shelter's opening about a year ago.

Maisie followed them into the exam room. She watched Kyle lay Griffin down gently on the metal examination table in the middle of the room.

"Okay, Griffin," he said, "let's see what's wrong with your paw. And Maisie, please tell me what you know about it."

Kyle didn't wait to hear what the lovely K-9 officer had to say. He immediately arranged Griffin comfortably on the table and lifted the apparently injured leg.

Lovely? Oh, yeah, even in her standard uniform—a white tailored shirt tucked into dark pants, with badges and all. Her hair was short and blond and in a style he thought he had heard described as a *pixie cut*. She had the prettiest hazel eyes that seemed to study him even as they narrowed in concern, and her skin was smooth and lovely. And her lips? Full and pink.

He'd noticed all that even as he began immediately to concentrate on his new patient's issues.

"We were patrolling this area, as we often do," Maisie was saying. She explained that they'd been in the paved parking lot across the street when Griffin let out a shriek of pain. He started limping, holding his right front paw up. She'd sat down on the ground beside him and examined the foot, seeing a little blood but no reason for it. "I just—I wish it had happened to me, not him, but at least we were near the shelter, and when I called, Scott told me you were here. I'd wanted to meet you…but not under these circumstances."

Kyle had also heard about this K-9 cop coming often to this shelter to help keep an eye on things. He'd wanted to meet her, too. But right now, he looked at Griffin's paw and also saw the hint of blood. He grabbed his equipment and began to examine it further, believing it could be a splinter.

He was right. It was a narrow but long sliver of strong, clear glass, and it had pierced Griffin's paw between its pads—and stayed there.

Kyle quickly used tweezers to remove it, and cleaned and disinfected the puncture, also adding something to deal with any pain, and bandaged it. Then he lifted the tweezers and showed Maisie the splinter.

She gasped. "It's nearly invisible, but it hurt him so much. Will he be okay now?"

"He should." Kyle gave her instructions on how to care for it and to continue to minimize Griffin's pain.

"Thank you so much, Dr. Kornel." Maisie's lovely hazel eyes sent him a glance of gratitude. He could feel her warmth through her uniform as she stood near him while he held Griffin on the table. Oh, how he liked that warmth, that nearness! But it was a bad idea to even think that way. He was a veterinarian on duty, helping an injured dog. Who the dog's handler was and her attractiveness were irrelevant.

"You're welcome. And please, call me Kyle," he said. "Time for Griffin to get back on the floor." He hefted the dog again and, very gently, lowered him till he was standing. Griffin's hurt paw was on the ground, too, in its bandage, and the dog lifted it a bit to take weight off it, but he appeared more comfortable.

Good. Kyle felt sure he had removed the entire splinter and done what was necessary to ensure the painful area would heal and not get infected.

"My car is parked right outside the shelter," Maisie said. "But I was planning on going inside and saying hi to any staff members walking dogs. Would it be okay if Griffin and I do that if we don't walk around much? The staffers know me well enough to come over and say hi, which will be enough for today. But if it's not good for Griffin, we'll head right back to the station."

"Going into the yard should be fine," Kyle told her with a smile. She obviously cared a lot about her canine partner. "Just let Griffin tell you how much walking he wants to do."

"Of course," Maisie said with a laugh that made him want to hug her for her attitude about her dog. Bad idea—but it still sounded good.

"Great. I'll be here for about another hour, so if he

seems in a lot of pain or you have any questions, be sure to pop back in or find me in the yard."

"We will." When Maisie and Griffin left the exam room a moment later, Kyle followed but didn't go after them as they exited through the clinic's waiting room.

He did intend to go inside the shelter area soon, though, after he'd entered the info about Griffin's treatment into the computer records. He would check on the animal residents then as well as Griffin and also watch staff members for a while.

The latter was a result of his once being a cop—which was one reason Scott, who was also an undercover cop, had hired him as the shelter's part-time veterinarian. The people known as staff members were actually here under protective custody because of bad things they had escaped in their lives. Once they moved in here, they were given new identities and would eventually be resettled somewhere else. Not only the animals but also the people were cared for by the shelter managers—and now that he was here, by Kyle, too.

He entered the small office in the clinic and sat down at the computer. But before he had done more than enter Griffin's name and the fact that he was a local police K-9, his cell phone rang. He pulled it from his pocket.

"Hi, Scott," he said. "Checking on how I did with Officer Murran's dog?"

"That and more. First, how did you do?"

Kyle gave a brief summary. "It wasn't serious, fortunately, and I told Officer Murran how to continue to treat it."

"Great. Thanks for that. And now, I'd appreciate it

if you'd go back to the reception room. I'm still in that meeting I mentioned earlier, and we just got a call from our entry. An owner of a local pet shop and her employee are there to drop off some dogs. We might not want to take them in, but it's good to maintain a reasonable relationship with townsfolk—without letting them inside or telling them about this shelter's real purpose. Would you please go say hi? And if those dogs need a brief vet exam, that's okay as long as the women don't go farther into the shelter than your clinic. I'll join you as soon as I can and then we can decide whether to accept the dogs for future rehoming, if that's what they want."

"Fine." Kyle hung up. He felt good that, despite his only having been here for a matter of days, Scott trusted him to represent the shelter's managers. He pulled his keycard from his pocket. It was needed to unlock the door both into and out of the reception room, as well as some other doors, although he had a separate card for his clinic in case he chose to lock the door.

He understood why this place was kept so secure. But Kyle realized it was nearly impossible to maintain perfect security.

He held the card up to the lock and heard a click, then turned the knob and pulled the door open. He heard voices inside the reception room and looked around as he entered.

Two women sat on chairs at the room's perimeter, with a leashed dog on the floor beside each of them, near their purses. They both rose as Kyle entered, and so did the pups.

"Hi," said the older woman. "I'm Greta Styles. I'm an owner of the Best Chance Pet Store downtown. And Beth Borrigan is one of our employees. Are you Dr. Kornel, the new veterinarian? Scott told me you'd be the one to come meet us."

"Yes, I am. Glad to meet you." Kyle focused his attention on the dogs. Both were medium-sized, one an apparent purebred Australian shepherd, the other a young basset hound. Both appeared healthy, but he couldn't be sure till he'd examined them.

"Glad to meet you, too." Greta smiled as if thrilled to see him. She appeared to be in her forties, with lines making her long face look strained. Her dark brown hair was pulled into a knot on top of her head, and she wore a lacy white shirt tucked into slim blue jeans. "I'm so glad you're here. These two adorable dogs were dropped off at my store for rehoming by some strangers, and I knew they needed to be taken to a shelter. It seems perfect that this one has a new vet clinic and a new veterinarian, too."

"General exams aren't why I'm here, though," he told her.

"Oh, we know," said Beth. "But you can check whether these two are healthy, then decide if they can remain here at this shelter. That works, doesn't it? I'm new at the store but know a little about shops, shelters and all." Beth's golden hair, obviously dyed but pretty, was pulled back into a clip behind her head, and she maintained a continuous frown of concern. Her T-shirt said *Dogs Are Beautiful*, and she wore it over tight jeans.

These women were obviously familiar with California's law regarding sales of pets at stores.

"Can you at least look them over for now?" Greta asked. "The basset hound is Fido, by the way. That's what the person who dropped him off said. The Australian shepherd is Toby."

Well, Scott had said it was okay to take the dogs into the clinic for a brief exam. "Sure," Kyle said. "Let's do it." After he finished he would call and interrupt Scott and confirm whether it was okay to keep the dogs at the shelter, if that seemed appropriate. They couldn't go back to the shop, anyway—not if they might be sold there. "Please follow me and bring the dogs."

Greta gripped Fido's leash, Beth held Toby's, and both women carried their purses. Kyle unlocked the door into the shelter hallway, then immediately turned left, opening the unlocked clinic door, and waved the women into the waiting room.

"One at a time." He reached for Toby's leash, then led the shepherd into the exam room and Beth followed. He left the door ajar so he'd be aware if Greta attempted to exit the waiting area.

The exam was quick. He found nothing wrong with the neutered dog, nor did he find a microchip. If he, or the shelter, wound up in charge of this pup, he'd take him to the downtown clinic for a better exam.

Same thing regarding Fido: neutered, no obvious health issues, no microchip.

"Okay," he told the women after they had all returned to the clinic's reception room. Standing there, he faced them, still holding both leashes. The dogs sat down by his feet. "I need to get the okay from Scott to see if we can take them in for rehoming."

"Thanks." The smile on Greta's face appeared forced. "I want to leave them here but would love for you to bring them to my store for display someday soon, maybe even tomorrow, so someone will hopefully adopt them there from your shelter. Or, better yet, you can hold an adoption event at my store."

Kyle got it. He understood why they'd brought the dogs here—sort of. Greta wanted to have them sold at her shop. Under the latest California law, pet stores could no longer sell dogs, cats or rabbits, but they could allow shelters or rescue groups to sell them there if they were neutered, with no profit to the shop. So why would shops encourage it? Kyle assumed they'd hope potential adopters would appreciate them for their kindness. Still—

"I don't think that's how we work here." Kyle could check with Scott, but Kyle believed he knew the limited ways animals could be brought to this shelter for rehoming—to keep it more secure.

And he might be wrong, but with Greta's enthusiasm about bringing the dogs to this shelter, he wondered if she was attempting to find a way to manipulate the system. For a while, the law had permitted pet shops to sell only animals they had gotten from a shelter, but a lot of stores had played games with that to make money and even tried turning themselves into shelters of sorts. The law had been further changed to prevent that. Pet stores could no longer profit from animals being sold there. Only rescue groups could, on a limited basis.

"Have other shelters sold pets at your shop?" he asked.

"Yes. But... Well, I need to develop a relationship with a different shelter from the one we've had contact with before, and this seemed like a good one."

Beth took a step sideways, causing the dogs to move beside Kyle. "Our shop is so wonderful that a lot of people just bring in stray animals or ones they say they can't keep and leave them with us. Sort of like they would do at a shelter, only that's not what we're about, of course."

Kyle noted Greta's glare at her employee, but she didn't say anything. "I see," Kyle said. "So you do take them in, then you bring them to a shelter."

"Yes, and usually try to work things out so that the shelter displays in our shop and sells them from there." Greta crossed her arms and glared at Kyle as if expecting him to criticize her. "And we even encourage the adoptions by giving discounts on our merchandise to the adopters."

Interesting. Well, he supposed her way of doing things worked under the law. And maybe it increased the number of customers at her shop and got them to buy more. Could she make a lot of money somehow, after those discounts?

Maybe it was her way of dealing with the most recent change in the law, especially if she had found a way around the prior version, as so many pet stores had, and made a profit from selling pets supposedly brought in from shelters.

He had a feeling that the profit on her merchandise now must be good enough for her to encourage those adoptions directly from shelters. But was there another reason she was enthusiastic about it?

"So by the time they're displayed in your shop, they've been given medical exams and checked for microchips and they're spayed or neutered and all," he said, as if that was a given. "They're ready then for the shelter to sell them."

"Sure," Greta said. "The shelters take care of all that. But you aren't the one we should be talking to about this. Please let Scott know I want to talk with him. I know this is a very special shelter, so I bet he'll cooperate with me. And I can tell him about some additional benefits."

So she apparently knew what this shelter was really about. Maybe. In any case, she was right in a way. Kyle didn't make that kind of decision. But he thought enough of Scott to believe he'd handle this well. And additional benefits? "He's in a meeting, but I'll try calling him." Kyle pulled his phone from his pocket and tapped in Scott's number on his Contacts list.

The director answered right away. "Hi, Kyle. Everything okay?"

"Is your meeting over—and could you come to the clinic? Some questions have arisen—"

"Sorry," Scott said. "I won't be able to get away for a while. What's up?"

Kyle quickly explained how Greta and her associate had brought a couple of dogs she wanted to leave here—maybe just overnight—then bring them back to display in her shop until Chance Animal Shelter sold them there. And Greta had mentioned additional benefits but hadn't elaborated.

"Tell her no. We rehome the animals we bring in to rescue right here. But if you've examined these dogs and they seem all right, we could make room and keep them here till we find appropriate adopters."

"Got it." Kyle felt relieved. He would take in those two dogs…and let Maisie, the K-9 cop, know of his suspicion the shop owner might somehow be skirting the law with other dogs. But now, after hanging up, he turned to Greta. "Sorry," he said. "Scott can't break away from his meeting. But he said you could leave the dogs here—this time—as long as they passed my initial exam, which they did."

"But we can't come back and pick them up?" Greta demanded.

"No," Kyle answered. "You can be sure, though, we'll only release them if we find them good homes."

"That's all well and good, but not what I want. I'll need to take them back right now and bring them to another shelter that will cooperate with us."

"Sorry. I've taken in the dogs, so they're now protected by this shelter." A bit of an exaggeration, but so what? Kyle was growing concerned about what would happen to these poor dogs if this woman left with them.

"Give them back!"

At her shouting, and the way she now stood confrontationally before him, the dogs began moving around on their leashes, which Kyle still held. He reached down to pat them, attempting to calm them.

If nothing else, her attitude convinced him there was

something going on here that she wasn't revealing. And he would do what he needed to protect the dogs.

"No," he said firmly. "You've brought stray dogs to this shelter, so now we'll take care of them."

"But that other shelter we worked with—they co-operated. Sold the dogs we brought them at our shop." Beth appeared a lot calmer than her boss, but she still looked upset.

"Then, you should have taken these dogs there." But Kyle was glad, for the dogs' sake, that they had been brought here.

"They stopped cooperating, I think." Beth's voice was low, and she hazarded a sideways glance at Greta, who glared at her again.

Kyle could guess why that had happened...

"Let me put these guys into the back room, then I'll accompany you out," he said.

"Not without the dogs!" Greta said, still shouting.

But Kyle, worried about the dogs, started heading out of the reception area with them.

"Leave them here!" Greta yelled. "They're not yours."

"They're not yours, either," Kyle yelled back. "Now, wait here for a minute."

But Greta maneuvered around him and grabbed the leashes. "Let go, you horrible thief!" When he didn't, she elbowed him sideways, though not particularly hard.

Kyle resisted the urge to fight back, but he didn't release the dogs. Things were getting out of control. He knew a cop was present at the shelter, but he couldn't let go of those leashes to call her.

But almost as if he had somehow managed to call her, Maisie, Griffin at her side, opened the veterinary clinic's door. He'd never been more relieved to see anyone in his life.

Chapter 2

Maisie heard loud voices as she reached the door to the waiting room. What was going on here?

It was getting late in the day. After spending some enjoyable time with staff members and the dogs they walked, Maisie had planned to leave the shelter and take Griffin back downtown to the police station.

But first she'd intended to stop in and see Kyle briefly and let him take one more look at Griffin's paw, although her wonderful K-9 hadn't been favoring it as much. Which she believed meant Kyle had done a good job. Still…it never hurt to be careful.

But now she heard shouts, including Kyle's. Who was he arguing with? She turned the knob and walked in, holding Griffin's leash so he followed behind her.

Kyle, holding two dogs' leashes, seemed to be confronting a couple of women Maisie recognized from a downtown pet store. She took her special canine there frequently to get food and treats.

One was part-owner Greta Styles, whose nephew Jackson was also a Chance PD officer. The other was one of the clerks, Beth, a newcomer there Maisie believed.

"You're a cop," Greta said to Maisie right away without even saying hello. No surprise that she'd have figured that out, even if they hadn't met before—which they had. Maisie was in her uniform, after all, and Griffin wore his vest.

"That's right," she said anyway.

"So you know the law, right?" Before Maisie could answer, Greta looked at Kyle and continued. "I think this vet believes you should arrest me." She turned back to Maisie. "I've been trying not to break the law, but he doesn't like the way I do it. He doesn't want to work with me." She was clearly miffed.

"What's going on?" Maisie asked.

"I don't think you need to arrest anybody," Kyle said, shaking his head. "And I am attempting to figure out a way to ensure no laws will be broken, okay, Officer?" He pursed his lips, then said before Maisie could respond, "I understand that Greta allowed some strangers to drop these dogs off at her pet store, and I gather this wasn't the first time. She's looking for a shelter to take them in, then return them to her shop and display them there for adoption. That's fine, as far as it goes, but I get the impression there may be more to it, maybe in product sales since she said she gives discounts to adopters. She has to comply with California law or suffer the legal consequences. The animals must be neutered, a rescue organization has to be the seller, and even they can't charge more than five hundred dollars. And…well, I think it would be better for her to leave the dogs here to be adopted out."

"I am complying with the law," Greta shouted, then turned toward Maisie. "Isn't this the best way for the dogs? They sometimes keep them here a long time, but we'll use our best efforts to encourage their adoption from our shop, probably a lot faster than this shelter could."

"Maybe, and maybe not," Kyle said, and Greta pivoted to face him again, which allowed Maisie to utter a brief sigh. She wondered if Kyle really was leading up to requesting her to threaten the shop owner with arrest, even though there was no evidence a crime was being committed. "The way I understand it from talking with the director, Scott," Kyle continued, "this shelter finds new homes for the animals we take in here. And since these two have passed their initial health exam, you could just leave them, and that would be that— also with Scott's okay. It's safer for the dogs, and that's what matters."

"That's not that," Greta said angrily. "We have a lot of people come in and out of our store, and it usually doesn't take us much time at all to find people to adopt dogs or cats. How long does it usually take you here?"

"I don't know, but it doesn't matter," Kyle said. "I'm sure they're well taken care of no matter how long they're here, and possible new owners are well vetted."

"And your shelter would still make the final decision and collect any money for the adoption," Beth said.

"So just leave them here now," Kyle responded, earning a glare from Greta. "And you've been talking like you do this a lot," he continued. "Bringing in animals to get them adopted from your shop. I know the latest law hasn't been in effect long. The idea for its predecessor law was to make sure stores didn't wind up selling dogs that are purposely bred with no concern for their health, and therefore encouraging that kind of cruel but often profitable breeding. But when they still could sell pets, some stores found ways to make a lot of money by doing so, which encouraged that bad breeding. That's why the law was changed again and stores can't sell dogs, cats or rabbits and make money from it. I take it you're aware of that. But why are you being so insistent?"

"Because we care about the animals," Greta shouted. "We know the new law. We ask potential adopters all kinds of questions that we then tell the shelter sponsoring the pets. And we encourage adoptions by our merchandise discounts. Besides, it's none of your business what we've been doing recently."

"What we've been doing is just helping the animals, right, Greta?" Beth interjected. She had drawn closer to her boss and touched her gently on the arm, as if trying to calm her down.

"Of course. But the shelter we were working with before isn't helping anymore. We were hoping you would. Why don't you get Scott to come talk to us, damn it?"

"He'll get here when he gets here," Kyle said. "Hopefully after you're gone and the dogs are still here. And what you do with dogs dumped at your shop is my business." He took a step forward. "I'm concerned not just with making sure the law's complied with but also because I care about the animals' health and safety."

"So do we, you...you horror of a vet. And I'll bet you only care about the money you make as a doctor, no matter what goes on with your animal patients and their health."

Maisie knew a lot better than that. She believed it was the opposite: Greta only cared about the money she made at her store, even though she couldn't sell most pets. And Maisie had been listening closely to the argument. So far, there'd been no real reason for her to intervene. There was a lot of anger in the room, but she'd seen nothing illegal or violent. But she wanted to calm them all down.

Especially because Kyle took yet another step closer to Greta and stared down at her angrily. "I care about the animals' health a lot more than I care about yours," he said. "And you'd better continue to obey the law, or I'll find a way to make you do it, for the dogs' sake."

Instead of backing down, Greta drew even nearer to Kyle.

"Okay," Maisie said. "Enough of this. I think it's time for you to go, Greta and Beth. I assume the dogs can stay here at the shelter, right, Kyle?"

"Yes," he said. "Scott agreed to it, since their initial medical exam went well." Kyle pulled the two leashes gently so the dogs came closer to him.

"No, they can't," Greta yelled. "They're coming back

to the store with me, since I gather this damn shelter won't let me display them on their behalf."

Fortunately, Scott entered the room just then. "What's going on?"

"Since you apparently won't let me keep these dogs in my shop to get them adopted as your shelter dogs," Greta said, now approaching the director, "I want to take them back with me now. I'll find another shelter."

But would she? If she really cared about the dogs, she could just leave them here to be adopted, maybe check on their status once in a while.

What was her real motive?

Maisie's gaze remained on Scott, but Kyle was the one to respond. "Since you haven't convinced us it would be in the dogs' best interests, the answer should be no. You can just leave them here, and—"

"No way," Greta said. Her voice was lower now, but it seemed to ooze malice. "We brought them here, and we're taking them back. I'll find another shelter and even let them hold an adoption event at my store. Unless you want to do it."

"Sorry," Scott said. "That's not something we do."

Greta took a deep breath but somehow seemed to relax for a moment. "I could give your shelter discounts on some of our merchandise, like I do with adopters, if you cooperate with me."

"You must mark that merchandise up a lot if you can give discounts that con people into cooperating with you and maybe buying a lot of supplies when bringing a new pet into their homes." Kyle had crossed his arms and had a challenging grin on his face.

Ah, that had to be it. Although some stores in Chance also sold pet products, the Best Chance was the only pet store in town, and Maisie knew it was popular, even though its prices tended to be high.

But maybe a bit less when they were discounted. And if she got new adopters to buy a lot, those sales could be Greta's motivation to have pets from rescue organizations adopted through her business.

Right now, Greta's hands fisted, and she took a step toward him, then stopped herself. "Okay, then," she spat. "Those dogs are coming back with us." And with that, she reached over and grabbed the leashes below the loops.

Maisie prepared to step in if things got physical—especially if the dogs might get hurt. But Scott held out his hand, and Kyle released the leash loops to him.

Looking at Kyle, Scott said, "I gather that the dogs did arrive in her possession."

"That's right," he responded.

"Then…" Scott looked next at Maisie "…we can fight about it, but I suppose her argument could win."

"Possibly," Maisie said, wishing she could say otherwise. "I gather they had custody before. If they're taking the dogs to another shelter, unless we have evidence they're being abused, I'm not sure this shelter has any standing to keep them."

"They won't be abused," Beth said. "I'd definitely tell you, Officer, if that ever happened." The store clerk smiled tentatively, and her brown eyes appeared quizzical as she looked at Maisie, maybe wanting reassurance that her watching over the animals' care would be enough.

"Then, we're going." Greta yanked the leashes from Scott so that the dogs startled.

"So you're going to abuse them right in front of us?" Kyle demanded.

"Of course not." And with that, Greta bent to pick up her purse, patted the dogs' heads and gently led them to the clinic's door, maneuvering around Maisie and Griffin.

"I'll go with you and let you out," Scott said, and Maisie was glad about that—but not glad that woman would remain in charge of those poor dogs.

Beth didn't immediately follow. "Really," she said to Maisie and Kyle. "I'll keep an eye on them. And... Well, would it be possible for me to go see some of the animals here? Maybe even volunteer to help care for them?"

Clearly, Beth didn't know what the Chance Animal Shelter was all about. Did Greta? Maybe, but if so, she must not have told her employee. All the better, since it was supposed to remain as secret as possible.

"Unfortunately, I don't think that would work out," Maisie said. "The volunteers here are quite different from most places." Maisie then described them as homeless people who exchanged their help for living quarters and food. But she didn't mention they were actually staff members under protective custody.

"Oh. Well, that's not me." Beth appeared disappointed. "But, well, I'd love to come back, maybe bring more dogs or other pets to stay in the shelter, if people continue to dump them at our store and Greta says this shelter's okay to take them in. I'll talk to her. See if I can get her to be more reasonable."

"We'll see," Maisie said, sharing a glance with Kyle, who didn't appear at all convinced.

"Guess I'd better catch up with Greta and the dogs," Beth said, picking up her large purse from the floor beside her. "If any more dogs are dropped off at the shop, you might see me here again, at least if I can convince Greta."

"Good," Maisie said and watched the store clerk headed to the door of the reception area after her boss and Scott.

Then she returned to talk with Kyle about what had just occurred. He was clearly rattled.

So was she.

But she did like his attitude. Still. And how he gave a damn about abandoned dogs.

And that wasn't all she liked about the handsome vet she had just met...

She had an idea. He was still in the reception area, and she asked him, "Are you okay with what happened?"

"Nope. Are you?"

"Well, I'm hoping Greta's aware our eyes will be on her, so she should take good care of these dogs, at least. But I don't understand why she was so adamant. Sure, displaying the dogs at her shop might be of some benefit to her if people come in to look and maybe take advantage of her discounts if they adopted, but... I wouldn't mind talking to you more about the law and your perception of it. It's nearly evening. Would you care to join me for dinner?"

His formerly angry face lit up. "Sounds great. Let's do that."

Scott rejoined them then, and Kyle figured it wouldn't be a good thing to discuss dinner in front of his sort-of boss, so instead he talked with both Maisie and Scott about what had just transpired. They sat in the clinic's reception for a few minutes, and Kyle took the opportunity to calm down a bit by petting Griffin, who seemed to enjoy it despite being an apparently excellent K-9 remaining on duty, even with a sore paw.

"Maisie's our only apparent cop here," Scott said. "Not everyone knows I'm still part of the Chance PD and am undercover at this shelter, although of course you do." He looked at Kyle, who nodded. "And I know you're a former cop, Kyle. I'm sure we all wish we could have taken that woman in for questioning to find out what's on her mind—and prevent her from potentially harming any dogs."

"That's for sure." Kyle's calmness threatened to disappear once more, but he caught himself.

"Well, there's always the possibility she's sincere and trying to benefit the dogs. But she seems to be the kind of person who looks out for her own interests first." Maisie looked unhappy, which wasn't surprising. "I'll talk to some of my colleagues, see if we can figure out a way to ensure she properly complies with the law."

Officer Maisie was definitely not only a gorgeous

cop, she also had the right attitude, which Kyle appreciated.

And that wasn't all he appreciated about the wonderful, good-looking—sexy—woman. He looked forward to some one-on-one time with her that evening as they got together for dinner.

"That's great," Scott said. "I'm of course concerned about those poor dogs. This place is mostly about taking care of people, but when it comes to the animals, we give a damn about them, too. We really study possible adoption situations to try to make sure they're best for those pets, even turning away potential adopters when they don't seem right. We even said no at least once to people who claimed the dog was already theirs. No guarantees of a perfect fit, of course, but we try. That Greta might ask potential adopters the right questions—or not—and notify whatever shelter is involved. But with her attitude, I suspect profit is her real motivation, no matter what happens to the animals." He shook his head. "Do I regret letting her take those dogs? Sure, but under these circumstances I didn't think we could keep them."

Kyle wasn't so sure, but he wasn't going to argue—even though his concern for the dogs continued.

"I understand," Maisie said. "Do you turn people away often?"

"Not really, but we've had a few pretty irate folks stomp away empty-handed...or empty-leashed."

Scott soon left to return to his office. When he'd gone, Kyle removed his scrubs jacket, hung it up so he just wore his blue button-down shirt over his navy slacks and said, "Okay. Let's discuss this evening."

"Great idea."

They decided that, since Maisie didn't have to go back to the station that night, she would go home, change clothes and leave her K-9 to relax rather than heading to the station as she said she'd originally planned. She clearly didn't want to appear on duty during their evening out. And that way, she could leave her car, too. Both of them were fine with eating at the Joint Restaurant.

Maisie gave Kyle her address, and though he programmed it into his GPS, he followed her. Her vehicle was an official-looking black SUV, and if he wasn't wrong, he believed he saw her glance often into the rearview mirror. To make sure he was actually there?

Of course he was. He looked forward to this evening, to their dinner and conversation.

And more? Well, he might wish that, but it was too soon and certainly inappropriate.

Maisie soon pulled onto another road that led out of town, then up to the small house in the suburbs of Chance where she and Griffin must live. She parked, got out from the driver's door and opened one in the back as Kyle, who'd also parked, exited his vehicle, too. He joined her as she unhooked Griffin, who carefully exited the car.

"Let's go inside, and you can have dinner," she said to her still-leashed dog, although she did allow him to take his time heading to the front door.

"Nice house," Kyle said, admiring it. It was small,

resembling an ornate cottage, with an attractive lawn in front. He figured there was an adequate backyard, too, for Griffin. And it went well with other similar houses on the street.

"Thanks," she said, then added, "So tell me, where do you live?"

"For now, a nice apartment downtown. I'm assuming I'll want to stay here permanently, so I'm keeping my eyes open for a house, too." So far, he hadn't had much time to look but hoped to start searching in earnest soon.

He had already decided to stay here permanently, if things went as well as he anticipated. Being Maisie's acquaintance might become another incentive, since she was someone else who liked to make sure dogs and people were well cared for. And she was certainly worth looking at.

"Come on in," she told Kyle. The invitation wasn't really suggestive, but it still planted hints of what could go on if they both wanted… "I'll just go change," she continued, and the thought of her getting undressed also made a certain part of his body react—just a little. "Plus, I want to feed Griffin before we go. He deserves a good dinner, too." That was why they were there. Not because she was inviting him for anything, but so she could take care of her dog, and Kyle had somewhere to wait while she got ready.

Once they were inside the front entry, Maisie walked briskly down the hall and turned right, into the kitchen. Griffin remained at her side, and Kyle followed them.

"I thought about taking Griffin along to the restaurant," she said, "and we've been there before, but even if I left his vest on so they'd know he was a K-9, I think his having some time to relax on his own and rest his paw tonight would be better."

Kyle watched as she removed Griffin's leash and vest and fed him a high-quality kibble with some meaty canned food. Then, excusing herself, she headed down the hall and through a door that presumably led to her bedroom—which once more got Kyle thinking inappropriately of what they could do here, in her house...

When Maisie next showed up in the kitchen, where Kyle waited and watched Griffin finish his food, she wore a casual civilian outfit of a striped blue knit shirt over slacks. "We're done here," she said. "I'm ready to go."

"Me, too," Kyle said. "I'm hungry." He turned to go back the way they'd come without even looking her directly in the face...forcing himself to show no hint of any interest in a kiss. Or more.

The drive to the restaurant with Maisie in the passenger seat took less than ten minutes. The Joint Restaurant was located on a corner, and he found a parking spot on the street in front of the place. They walked inside and were seated immediately at a wooden booth in the middle of the row, even though the place was pretty well filled with customers whose voices filled the air. Pictures of various places in downtown Chance decorated the walls.

He'd been here a couple of times before with some other veterinarians from the downtown clinic. It was a place everyone seemed to like, in a convenient location and serving good food at fairly reasonable prices.

At the moment, he didn't see any other vets, which was probably a good thing. It wasn't as if he was out on a date exactly, but he'd undoubtedly get razzed now or later and would have to explain the situation.

The server laid a couple of menus down on the vinyl tabletop. "Can I get you anything to drink?" she asked.

Kyle had a sudden urge for a nice strong drink after what had gone on in the shelter clinic that day but didn't think that was a good idea. He did order a beer, though, and Maisie asked for iced tea.

Kyle decided on meat loaf with coleslaw after Maisie ordered barbecued chicken and a salad.

Then it was time to decide what to discuss: the difficulty with the store owner?

But, no. Not yet. First was a brief discussion of the California law regarding sale of pets in stores by rescue organizations only.

Then, at Maisie's request, Kyle gave a rundown of his own brief peace-officer career and explained he'd walked away after the death of his father. He'd been served his beer by then and took a deep swig as Maisie expressed her sweet condolences that sounded quite sincere.

She told him then about her brother and said Kyle would have to meet the town's other K-9 cop.

They next started talking about the Chance Animal Shelter. Kyle, the newbie, had a lot of questions that he undoubtedly would be able to get answered at work, but Maisie seemed glad to give him her take on the facility, though she wisely talked in generalities, in case anyone was eavesdropping.

They definitely didn't want to be the ones to even hint to the public about the true nature of the facility.

She also kept her voice low while describing anything that could give away even vaguely what was to be kept secret about the shelter. Smart woman. She'd glanced around first, anyway, as had Kyle. The tables nearest them were filled with people having loud conversations. No one was likely to be listening.

"Great stuff," Kyle said when she finished. "I'd heard some but not all of it, although I figure I'll continue to learn more the longer I work there."

"If there's anything else you'd like to hear from me, let me know—and vice versa, please. I want to keep up with what's happening there so I can continue to help out as much as possible, even if that is only to tell my superiors at the department if something needs to be dealt with…to help those poor animals being sheltered there." *And people*, she mouthed, so she couldn't be overheard.

"Deal," Kyle said, raising his beer bottle to toast her.

"Deal," she agreed, raising her glass. They clinked their drinks, and Kyle basked for a few seconds in the highly appealing smile Maisie levied on him.

They of course also talked about the two dogs that had been dropped off at the store. Kyle was as concerned as Maisie seemed to be about their future well-being. "I think I'm going to need to buy some dog food or something for the downtown clinic tomorrow—and stop in and see them to make sure they're not being displayed for sale if no other rescue organization has taken them in yet," he said.

"Funny, I had the same idea. Maybe we can go together." But they didn't come up with a mutual time then. They could work that out the next day.

They soon finished their meals since they'd both been eating as they conversed. But Kyle had enjoyed himself enough to regret that their time together was going to end.

On this nondate, he reminded himself. They had mostly shared information relevant to their working relationship, hopefully helping each other learn more about what they needed to do.

But...he definitely hoped to get to know her better.

Kyle attempted to pay the check, but Maisie objected. "At least not unless I can treat you next time."

Which made him feel good as he paid their bill. That suggested there would be a next time.

But of course there could be, as long as they kept everything cool, relating to how they each could be of assistance to that very special shelter.

Chapter 3

As Kyle drove Maisie home along the uncrowded downtown streets of Chance, they chatted more about the disagreement Kyle had had with nasty Greta at the shelter and the two poor dogs in her possession. That led into more about the origins of the Chance Animal Shelter, which they'd only been able to hint at in the restaurant, and about how they provided protective custody for people in trouble, not just the animals. That included giving them new identities, finding them new lives, giving them someplace pleasant to live. Things Kyle already had heard, of course, but now he was part of it and so, apparently, was K-9 Officer Maisie.

It was dark out now. Kyle soon pulled his car to the curb in front of Maisie's home, where wide sidewalks and streetlamps enhanced the residential development.

Maybe he should look for his new home in this area, too, once he was ready to leave his downtown apartment. Since traffic in Chance was fortunately limited, it wouldn't take long for him to get to either of the clinics where he worked.

But becoming Maisie's neighbor? That might look bad to anyone who noticed. It might also feel a bit odd to him, appearing to like her enough to attempt to get closer to her that way.

And, well…he did like her. A lot, despite having just met her. But more someday?

He stopped, parked and looked over to see her looking back at him. "Thanks for driving," she said.

"Anytime." A thought came to him. "Will you be walking Griffin now that you're home?" She might just let her K-9 out in her backyard to take care of things for the night, but just in case…

"That's what I planned. Would you like to join us?"

How did she get that idea—because he had mentioned it? He laughed internally at himself even as he said, "Sure. I wouldn't mind a little exercise before I head home."

Griffin was waiting right inside the front door. Maisie grabbed his leash, hooked it on and grabbed a bag from a nearby drawer. "Okay, boy. Walk?"

Griffin jumped a bit on three legs, holding up the bandaged one, and quietly woofed, making Kyle smile. "You and he communicate well," he said to Maisie.

"He's my partner," Maisie reminded him unnecessarily.

Kyle wondered what it would be like to have a partner in his work with whom he could become that close.

"Okay, let's go," Maisie said. She and Griffin were already outside her door on the concrete walkway, and Kyle followed without comment, closing the door behind him.

The streetlights did a good job of illuminating the sidewalk and the lawns leading up to it. Many houses also had lights on, so Kyle continued to view the pleasantness of the neighborhood.

The air was chilly but not too cold. It was a great time and place for a walk.

And it was also a good time for a conversation, one that didn't involve the animals or people at the Chance shelter.

"So how did you decide to become a K-9 cop?" he couldn't help asking Maisie. He'd wondered that from the moment he'd met her.

"I guess my brother Doug and I kept talking about what we'd be when we grew up. We were really close to our Uncle Cy, and he was a cop. We also liked watching TV shows and movies about cops, particularly since in those fictional formats, things always came to a satisfactory conclusion, and relatively fast. So growing up in Riverside, California, we just decided to head in the direction of law enforcement. Plus, we had dogs as kids, mostly German shepherds, and somehow our discussions morphed into becoming K-9 cops. And here we are." She'd been watching Griffin walk at her side, sniffing and doing what dogs do—and barely limping—

but now she looked at Kyle. "How about you? Why did you decide to become a veterinarian?"

After his question to her, Kyle had been waiting for this. "Also childhood dreams, I guess," he said. "My family always had dogs, usually mixed breeds we adopted from shelters, which I learned to really appreciate when I realized how many people were cruel to animals and were willing to let them loose or even die. I intended early to try to end that, but I was pretty naive to think I could do much, although I volunteered at a local shelter in LA when I was a teenager, a no-kill one I really liked. And when someone just left an abused dog in horrible condition at the curb one day, I thought he would die, but the veterinarian who treated him managed to save him. That vet was smart and caring and... my hero. So I eventually became a vet, too." After his aborted prior career as a cop, but they'd already discussed that a little.

"That's so wonderful." Maisie and Griffin had stopped walking. She looked up at him. Her hazel eyes sparkled in the dim lights from the streetlamps, and she looked so impressed, so happy, that—

Impulsively, Kyle bent down and kissed her, briefly, on her full and warm lips. Damn, but it felt good. And he wanted more.

But did she? And here they were in public, on the street where she lived, where neighbors could be peering out windows at them and they wouldn't even know...

That was enough.

Only...it wasn't. Maisie dropped the end of Griffin's leash and stepped on it so he couldn't move far. Then, to Kyle's amazement and delight, she reached up and pulled his face down close to hers again.

Their kiss this time was far from brief, and damn, but it turned Kyle on even more.

This K-9 cop he'd just met might drive him nuts.

Maisie realized that sharing such a hot kiss with this utterly handsome veterinarian right there, in the middle of her neighborhood, wasn't a good idea.

Even though she wasn't in her uniform right now. But some neighbors knew she was a cop. Cops weren't supposed to do such things. At least not in public, for everyone to see.

When it ended, she just gave Kyle a wink and turned around, and they quickly headed back to her house.

She liked this kind, animal advocate of a vet. A lot, partly due to his helpful treatment of Griffin. Maybe too much.

But they'd just met. Could they develop a relationship? Maybe, but certainly not this soon. They'd probably see each other often at their respective jobs, but for now, at least, there couldn't be anything between them—except, perhaps, admiration, and interest.

They reached the front door, and she dug into her pocket for the key. Only when she'd opened the door did she turn back to look at Kyle. "Thanks again for the ride, and dinner, and for joining us on this walk, and for taking care of Griffin, and—" She stopped and smiled at him again without finishing.

He undoubtedly knew what she wasn't saying. Those kisses... Well, she didn't need to thank him for them.

Hopefully he had enjoyed them as much as she had, but they were over.

"We'll need to talk tomorrow about when each of us, maybe together, will visit Greta's store. And I'll be back at the shelter at least some of the time tomorrow," he said. "Will you be visiting?"

"Sure," she said, although she generally didn't go there every day. But why not, as long as her official schedule allowed it?

And, she had to admit to herself, she would enjoy seeing Kyle again.

"Hope to see you one place or the other. Or both." Kyle appeared to hesitate, and then he drew close to her and kissed her again, in a strong, sexy, prolonged manner like the last one. "Good night," he said, and in moments he was gone.

Physically, at least. But Maisie thought about him as she got ready for bed. "What do you think, Griffin?" she asked her dog as they both settled into the bedroom and prepared to go to sleep. Assuming she could, Maisie thought.

Heck. Oh, yeah, she liked the guy.

But she'd already warned herself. She might see Kyle a lot when she visited and observed the shelter. Sure, they could be friendly, but she would have to remain professional and rein in any flirting.

And for now, he was practically a stranger. They had just met.

So instead of Kyle, she made herself think about the day she'd had and all the strange situations, especially concerning that odd Greta and her attitude about keeping shelter dogs in her store.

Maisie would be hearing more about it as time went on, she figured, as she finally dropped off to sleep.

Kyle received a call from Scott early the next morning. He was already awake and had planned to head to the downtown clinic first, but apparently one of the dogs at the shelter had fallen off a concrete ledge in one of the enclosures and injured his side. Of course Kyle agreed to head there first—especially since that dog was Spike, a retired K-9, whom he'd heard had been brought to the shelter by Maisie a few months ago.

He hoped he would be able to help Spike heal quickly, as he had with Griffin. And he also hoped he would see Maisie there, let her know what he was doing for another K-9.

He left his apartment shortly thereafter and reached the shelter quickly. One of the other managers, Nella Bresdall—Scott's pretty, dark-haired girlfriend—brought Spike to the clinic immediately after Kyle let Scott know he was there. Sure enough, there was a large, bloody gash on the German shepherd's right side. Kyle shaved the area and cleaned and bandaged the injury, and also gave the poor dog antibiotics and pain relievers.

"Will he be okay?" The expression in Nella's light brown eyes was clearly worried.

"I think so, but let's keep a close eye on him—and find him someplace to hang out that doesn't have concrete areas where he could hurt himself more."

"Will do." Looking somewhat relieved, Nella put Spike back on his leash and led him slowly from the clinic.

Kyle soon followed and also walked through the shelter, checking in all the buildings containing enclosures to make sure all the dogs, as well as the cats and smaller pets in the rear building, looked well. He also stopped to talk to a few staff members—some of those being protected here—before he finally headed downtown to his other part-time job.

Being at the shelter also reminded him of yesterday, when he had met that nasty Greta—and the two poor animals she was manipulating.

Would he be able to help them at all by visiting the store later today and seeing them again? That was, assuming Greta still had them there, maybe on display for adoption from another shelter if she'd found one that did as she wanted. It would be better, though, if she'd just left them at an appropriate rescue organization.

He finally left the shelter, ready to go to work at the other clinic. Too bad Maisie hadn't shown up while he was at the shelter, but he really hadn't expected her to. When he arrived downtown and parked to go into the clinic, he gave in to a whim while still in his car and texted her for the first time. Of course they had exchanged phone numbers. He just said hi, told her about Spike—knowing she would care a lot about that former K-9—and let her know the shepherd should be okay.

Her return text was quick and sounded grateful. You certainly know how to take care of injuries to some of my favorite K-9s. She said she and Griffin were out on

an assignment attempting to find someone who'd stolen a car from an apartment building parking lot. And she had no idea when she might be able to go to the pet store with him to check on the dogs. Would he do it on his own? Sure, he told her, though he felt a little disappointed. Maybe they wouldn't see each other later today after all. Then he went inside.

Noting that the reception room was busy, he said hello to the receptionist, Jada, and entered the clinic itself. Jada, a young African American woman who was also studying to be a vet tech, entered the hallway and asked if he could start seeing patients now, and of course he said yes.

And so began his day at the downtown clinic. When Jada popped into his small office quickly to tell him about the patient in one of the exam rooms, Kyle walked down a short hallway with multiple doors and opened one to room B. Like all of them, it had a metal table attached to the wall on one side, along with a glass-doored cabinet along another wall and a couple of chairs across from it for the patient's owners to sit as the exam was conducted.

"Okay, fella," Kyle said to Boris after the owners introduced him to the deep brown pit bull who was there for his annual exam and a Bordetella shot to avoid potential kennel cough. Kyle put the dog on the table and got started.

Boris was fine. So were the next three dogs Kyle examined, all mixed breeds of different sizes.

He checked his phone in between patients. Nothing

from Maisie. Maybe he would wind up going to the store on his own later.

In between patient visits, he ran into the two most senior vets of the five on staff there, Dr. Ernest Martin and Dr. Pedro Nerez. They were both friendly, of course, but as busy as he was, so they only exchanged greetings.

After the four patients, Kyle finally had a breather, so he returned to his office. Still nothing from Maisie on his phone. He looked up the pet store's website on his computer. It was open until seven that night. He also noted a picture of Greta with Esther Dane, her partner, who appeared a little older than Greta. There were also photos of business taking place in the shop: customers buying lots of dog and cat food and beds and toys and more, and clerks helping them, though he didn't see Beth among them. The place looked successful and welcoming. And the website did mention how they sometimes displayed pets available for adoption from shelters. For whatever reason, it sounded as if this was something Greta considered important. And if many of those pets were actually adopted out by those shelters, that was a good thing.

After lunch and a few more patients, Kyle's busy day eventually wound down somewhat. Only...

He saw when he returned to his office that he had a message on his desk phone. Probably something professional, since Maisie had his cell number.

It turned out to be, of all people, Greta. It was as if she knew somehow that he intended to pop in at her store. He called her back right away, unsure why she had contacted him and how she had gotten this number—online, maybe.

"Hey, Doc," she said, then apparently spoke to someone else. Beth, maybe? "It's our buddy the vet calling back. I just wanted to tell him that Fido and Toby still haven't been taken in by a shelter, and I'm not displaying them because I can't sell them."

"That sounds right," Kyle said.

"Yeah, it is, but I'm worried about what can be done with these dogs," she said. "I wanted to let you know I'm still working on it—so you'll feel guilty for not insisting that the Chance Animal Shelter take them in but let me show them off in my shop. Oh, and guess what? Someone dropped another pup here today." She hung up.

And he had an urge to hurry to the shop now—but he still had a couple of patients to take care of.

Some of his patients that day had been rescue dogs who'd come from various shelters, including the Chance Animal Shelter.

None appeared to have been shown off at the pet store, which was probably a good thing, he thought. But he wished he knew how many pets Greta had in fact displayed to help get them adopted. And what she was up to now.

Okay, he was obsessing over this, and her call had made it even worse. Visiting there soon might help him get this out of his system. Or not. Since those two dogs he'd met were evidently still there, how could he help them, get them out of Greta's hands? Maybe find a way to get Greta to agree to allow the Chance Animal Shelter to take them in without her displaying them?

He needed Maisie's advice, at least on the possibilities. And maybe just because talking with her might calm him down.

After he'd conducted one more regular exam for the day, he returned to his office and shut down the computer.

But before he could finally leave, he was waylaid by his fellow vet Pedro, who was rushing down the hallway where Kyle stood. "Exam needed quickly," Dr. Perez called to him. "Someone just brought in a cat with a bleeding paw."

"Need help?" Kyle asked, starting to follow Pedro.

"Never hurts."

They both hurried to the reception area, where two women, presumably mother and daughter, sat crying, with a cat lying on the older one's lap atop a blanket. "We thought Whiskers was already downstairs with us," the woman moaned. "But then…then…we heard him thud onto one step after another."

Unusual for a cat, but anyone could lose their footing, Kyle thought.

It was probably just as well Kyle hung out with Pedro who, after getting the owners and cat into an exam room, cleaned the bloody paw, then x-rayed it. Then Kyle joined the pet's owners for a minute to attempt to soothe them.

Pedro soon returned with Whiskers and gave instructions on how to help the cat at home, beginning with carrying him up and down the steps for now. Then, it was finally time for Kyle to leave, not much before the store's closing time.

One more text to Maisie as he got in his car, but still no response. And so Kyle finally headed to the store, driving the short distance from the clinic. He parked outside and looked at the front windows. Unsurprisingly, the lights were still on despite the late hour. Was the store actually open, or was Greta just waiting for him after her goading phone call? Not that he'd told her he was coming. But he'd no doubt the witch of a woman wanted him there so she could taunt him some more about what she would do with the poor, abandoned dogs—three of them now.

He left his car and walked to the front entrance. The door was unlocked, so he didn't have to knock or call Greta.

But as he entered, he didn't see her or any customers, either. He made sure the door closed behind him. After all, he didn't know if the dogs she now had custody of were loose or confined somewhere.

He didn't see her anywhere in the merchandise display, though he walked around the stacks of familiar products, so he called out, "Greta? It's Kyle Kornel."

She didn't respond, so maybe she hadn't heard him. Might she be in the back storage room? He assumed that was what was beyond the door behind the counter. He headed over there and knocked. And heard a couple of dog barks.

"Greta?"

Still no response. Had she left the dogs alone there and gone home? Not with the front door unlocked, he figured. But maybe she was in the bathroom or otherwise occupied.

He tried the knob on the door. It turned, and he pushed the door open. Hearing barking again off to the right, he knocked, then opened another door that led into an office. The dogs he'd been worried about, Fido and Toby, leaped out at him. Another dog, a little white one resembling a Maltese, stood along a wall. "Hi, there," Kyle said. "Good dogs."

He considered leaving them loose, but something didn't feel right. He closed that door again, leaving them in the office. And then he went back into the main room.

"Greta?" Kyle called out.

And stopped.

He'd found her. She was lying on the concrete floor in the middle of the room, blood around her head, and she wasn't moving. He quickly checked her pulse and found none.

He'd call 9-1-1 first, then try CPR. What had happened to her?

But as he pulled his phone from his pocket, he heard a noise behind him and pivoted. The woman whose photo he'd seen with Greta's on the website—her partner, Esther—hurried into the room, sent a curious stare toward him, then looked down.

"What did you do to her?" she screamed.

Chapter 4

The assignment Maisie and Griffin, and Doug and Hooper, his German shepherd K-9 partner, had been on that afternoon had increased in intensity.

It had started out fairly simple, with just an exercise between them and other Chance PD officers to practice working together on various tasks.

But then a real call had come in. There'd been some damage to cars in the town's main shopping area, and even a theft. Some robberies, too—face-to-face. They'd had to check that out.

And it turned into a major, time-consuming case. The area had a three-story parking structure, plus a small mall and a couple of streets lined with retail establishments and restaurants. The location had been targeted by one perpetrator at first, then others had joined him.

They knew the first suspect was a male, since the tall, bulky person had been seen, wearing a mask, breaking into the initial auto and driving it away. The vehicle was found in a lot in another neighborhood, but the situation had escalated when he managed to accost some people there and swipe purses, wallets and car keys. Plus, the same types of incidents were occurring at other places nearby at the same time. It looked like he had several accomplices.

Griffin had been given items to sniff from inside the original car, including a floor mat, and he had seemed to follow the scent until the person had seemingly entered a vehicle that was no longer there. Griffin halted at an empty space and did not attempt to follow any farther.

Maisie remained in contact with Doug, and Hooper was having the same kinds of issues. The regular officers also kept finding evidence of minor crimes being committed, such as dropped packages from inside the nearby stores, long scratches on several cars parked near one another and so on.

Eventually, Griffin did alert on someone inside one of the stores: a teenage girl carrying a bunch of bags that were full. After checking the contents and finding some items reported stolen, Maisie called on one of the investigating officers to take that kid into custody while she and Griffin looked around for other teens. This might have just started out as a prank for some young friends after school, since it was late in the day.

Time-consuming, yes. Stupid, yes. But it appeared that Griffin—and also Hooper—eventually helped the police department achieve success. Maisie didn't know what would happen to those kids now in custody, but hopefully they would receive some kind of consequences to prevent them from doing it again. And when news of their apprehension got out in the media, it might discourage other kids from trying something similar.

During the time all this was going on, Maisie had received a couple of texts from Kyle but hadn't responded yet. She'd had no idea when her assignment would be completed or she could be free to join Kyle in his foray to the pet store, if at all, that day. And interrupting Griffin, Doug, Hooper or her fellow officers on this challenging assignment had not been an option.

But it was over now, thank goodness. And Kyle might have already gone to the store. Time to text him, but not while she was still there. Only—

Heck. Before she left the station, Assistant Police Chief Kara Province called her into her office, so Maisie hurried there with Griffin. "I know you've had a full day," the assistant chief said, standing behind her desk. Her uniform was similar to Maisie's, but hers had a lot more badges and bars on the shirt. Her hair was as dark as her uniform pants, and it was short, too. She had another assignment for Maisie. "There's been an apparent homicide," she said, "and the detectives on duty thought a K-9 or two might be very helpful in determining a suspect."

Why? Well, it was weird—and coincidental.

The homicide had happened at that very pet store where Maisie had had hoped to go next.

"Do you know who the victim is?" she couldn't help asking. Possibilities raced through her mind—including Kyle, if he'd happened to get there as they'd discussed.

Surely not.

Or Greta… She was not an especially nice person, so she might have enemies. And if it was her, that didn't mean Kyle, who'd argued with her earlier, was involved…did it? Or, might Greta have killed her partner Esther? Or—

"Not certain," Kara said. "One of the partners who own the store is what I was told, but I don't know which one."

Maisie felt a pang of relief that it wasn't Kyle. Even so, she remained worried.

Whoever it was, whatever had happened, Maisie agreed to take Griffin and head there fast.

She wanted to contact Kyle—but there were a lot of reasons not to. First of all, she was on another official assignment.

And what if he was somehow involved…?

On the short drive, with Griffin fastened onto the back seat of her SUV, Maisie's mind continued to race about the possibilities. She forced herself not to draw any conclusions, of course. She'd have more information soon.

She called Doug. He hadn't returned to the station yet, but now he, too, was on the way with Hooper to this latest crime scene. And he didn't sound any more knowledgeable about what was going on than she was. In fact, he hadn't even heard that the victim was connected with the store.

"We're here, Griffin," Maisie soon told her K-9 after ending the call with her brother. She parked as close to the store as she could. Streetlights illuminated the area so it appeared nearly as bright as daylight. The street was filled with vehicles, many that were police cars, and lots of others that weren't. Media?

Some people were taking pictures as she and Griffin walked slowly toward the store. He was still limping, though not as much as before. Maisie started to square her shoulders even more than usual, then stopped. She didn't have to impress anyone.

Doug must have been closer to this location when he'd been called with the assignment. He had already arrived and now stood inside the entrance with several other uniformed cops, Hooper at his side. Maisie looked at her brother and asked, "What have you heard so far?"

"Homicide, as we were told. The body of one of the store owners, Greta Styles, is in the back room. Her partner, Esther Dane, evidently came in just before someone attempted to revive her—although, that person is also a suspect."

Judging by Doug's expression, Maisie figured who that person was. Quietly, she asked, "Kyle?" She had, of course, told her brother about meeting the vet who now ran the shelter clinic and how he had helped Griffin.

Doug nodded. "From what I gather, though, he alleges he had come in to check on a couple of dogs Greta had brought to his clinic at the Chance Animal Shelter earlier, and that Greta had called him, goading him a bit, to let him know she still had those dogs plus another one and was still looking for another shelter. His position is that he had planned to check on those dogs and that he found the body. Someone had attacked her before he arrived."

Maisie had also filled Doug in on what appeared to be happening here with some dogs and that Greta had been very pushy about getting a shelter to take the animals in on her terms. Maisie hadn't described the irritation Kyle had shown, though.

Still… Well, Maisie wasn't surprised he was a suspect. He might have been one even if Esther hadn't found him there with Greta.

Esther. She'd happened to walk in at an interesting time. Had she planned this? Had she murdered her partner with the idea she could pin it on someone else who'd argued with Greta?

Had she set Kyle up?

Maisie sucked in her lips. She realized she was already attempting to find a path to clear Kyle, and she didn't have any of the facts her fellow officers might have already found. Foolish. She hardly knew him.

Even so, she wanted—badly—to talk to him. To learn what he knew, or at least what he was willing to say. And hopefully get his reassurance…

"Do you know why we were called in?" Maisie asked Doug. She glanced around the store. It appeared as it had before, filled with a lot of pet products shelved in categories. But if theft had been a motive, the more likely scenario was that money would have been stolen rather than inventory.

Was there some evidence the investigators wanted K-9s to sniff and attempt to find the source?

"Not certain."

"Then—" Before Maisie could continue, the door at the back opened and Assistant Chief Province entered the store. She hadn't told Maisie she was coming, too.

Not really surprising, though. There weren't a lot of murders in or around Chance—fortunately.

Kara joined them. "I got a call right around when you left, Maisie. They're about to take the body to the coroner's for an autopsy. Also, two suspects are in the back room where the body was discovered, so Griffin and Hooper can sniff around and check out the murder weapon, which was apparently there, to determine if the scent of either of those suspects is on it. One of them allegedly attempted CPR while the other called 9-1-1, so your K-9s might alert on the man who tried resuscitation, because of the vic's scent on him."

Him. Kyle, probably.

With Esther and Kyle still in that room, Maisie could only hope that the K-9s would alert on Esther rather than Kyle, if they did at all.

Either way, she hated to think about it, but Kyle had been arguing with Greta. He clearly didn't like her. And Maisie gathered she had hung onto those two dogs, as well as a third, without yet finding a shelter to care for them despite the Chance Animal Shelter's offer to take them in—without their being displayed in her shop.

Kyle had definitely expressed concern. Could he have gotten so angry that he'd—

No. She didn't want to think about it.

Even so, she was a cop. She had to keep an open mind or at least as much as she could.

The guy she hoped was innocent might actually be guilty.

Okay. Professional. That was her.

She started leading Griffin toward the door, paying attention to breathing calmly, acting normally, ignoring the fact she was about to see Kyle not just as a friendly veterinarian who attracted her but as a murder suspect.

Kara directed them to enter first, and Doug and Hooper preceded Maisie and Griffin. Low voices filled the storeroom, and Maisie saw Kyle, who stood near the farthest wall holding the leashes of the two dogs that sat beside him and hugging a small white dog Maisie hadn't seen before, as he talked with Detective Vince Vanderhoff. Kyle's obvious protection and caring for the three dogs was enough to make Maisie certain he wouldn't—couldn't —have done anything bad. Right? Okay, that was mostly her hope talking.

On the other side, also near a wall, Esther stood talking with Officer Shelly Dandridge, middle-aged but a relatively new recruit whom Maisie liked a lot. The place was small enough that those in charge hadn't yet moved the persons of interest someplace else, quite possibly because they wanted to see if there were any reactions by those suspects first.

And in the center, EMTs knelt on the floor around a body. Greta's. From what Maisie could see from this distance, there was blood around her neck, but she couldn't tell how the woman had been killed.

Yet. Since Maisie had been called to come here with Griffin, she figured she was about to get up close and personal with the victim's body. Or at least Griffin was.

Sure enough, Kara moved from behind Doug and Maisie and faced them. "Come with me." She gestured for them to follow. She took the few steps to reach the side of the body. "Now, until an autopsy is performed, we won't officially know the cause of death. But all signs indicate it was the wound around the victim's throat."

The emergency medical technician who knelt at Greta's side pointed first toward her bloody neck. "Looks like it was done with the knife we found beside the body."

And yes, there was a regular chef's knife on the floor near her, wide with a point and a dark handle, and it was covered in blood.

Well, at least Griffin wouldn't have to look for the murder weapon. And maybe there were fingerprints to be found on the knife when the department forensics team checked it out. Plus, there might be more evidence around, including the scent of the murderer.

"Okay, Griffin," Maisie said. "Come." She didn't need to pull on his leash to get her still-limping K-9 to approach the body. Griffin also didn't need to be told to begin scenting the scene, although Maisie kept him from stepping in the blood.

Griffin spent a while smelling the body, the blood and the knife. Then he moved away.

Would he alert now on Esther? Kyle?

Griffin did sniff Kyle for a minute and alerted on Kyle by sitting down. But Maisie had already been told Kyle had attempted CPR on the body—or at least a male in the room had—so that could explain any scent.

Griffin then conducted a brief hunt around the room as if searching for something connected with the killing, as he was trained to do. He sniffed at a door that Maisie then opened, finding a small office inside. Griffin entered it and took a little time smelling the floor. But when they got back into the main room, he sniffed some more but didn't alert again.

And when Doug had Hooper participate similarly, his results were about the same.

Did that mean that, since Kyle had evidently touched the body for an appropriate reason, both Esther and he were innocent?

No. Maisie realized that. But at least the guilt of either one wasn't clear thanks to any scent the perpetrator may have left.

"Nothing?" Kara asked, sounding miffed.

"They must not smell anything that leads them to alert on Esther Dane, and you already told me that Dr. Kornel touched the vic to perform CPR, so that could explain the K-9s alerting on him."

"Okay, then. Oh, and it's not surprising, by the way, that your K-9s seemed interested in that office. The three dogs over there—" she gestured toward Kyle "—were apparently inside it when Dr. Kornel arrived." That explained Griffin's sniffing around it. "Thanks for coming," Kara finally said, "but you can go now."

Which allowed Maisie to take a deep breath of relief. And as she started toward the door with Griffin, Doug and Hooper behind her, she finally dared another glance toward Kyle and saw him walking in her direction, the three dogs still with him. Detective Vanderhoff was allowing him to leave. She forced herself not to smile.

Okay, his release didn't mean he wasn't a suspect, but at least they hadn't any evidence that required them to keep him in custody. And Esther, too, appeared to be heading their way.

Maisie hoped she could hear the whole story about what both of them had been asked, what they'd said, what their own suspicions were...

She hoped to get a chance to talk to Kyle soon, though not here. But how could she keep that appropriate?

She heard some loud voices as she opened the door into the shop. Several police officers were in there, evidently attempting to ensure that no one entered the business, but a few people had already.

As soon as Beth saw Maisie and Griffin, she broke away from where she'd apparently been confronted by Officer Penny Jones and headed in their direction. "Officer Maisie, what's going on? The news said…something happened to Greta. Is that right?"

"Yes, is it?" Cora, another employee whom Maisie had met before, asked.

Of course people who worked here would be upset and worried about their jobs—and maybe even mourn Greta despite her sometimes nasty disposition.

"It is. They told me so." Another employee Maisie had met, Stan, had shown up and was now behind one of the counters. Who'd told him? One of the cops inside?

One of the reporters outside?

"What happened to her?" Beth wailed.

Maisie had to hang onto Griffin's leash. Her K-9 seemed very interested in sniffing the three employees. Was he alerting on one or all of them? Maybe, but he seemed more relaxed than that. He spent the most time smelling Beth, but he had met her before and did not act as he usually did while alerting. Plus, before Maisie could stop her, Beth fed Griffin a treat that they must have carried at the store. And then so did Cora, but Maisie didn't allow anyone else to do so.

Of course Griffin was well trained enough to ignore people who weren't his scenting targets, but treats nevertheless got some attention from him. Still, he didn't actually alert on anyone. And Maisie trusted her K-9. But she also couldn't stop considering all of the nonofficial people here as being potential suspects. Too bad she couldn't have a conversation with Griffin to learn what he was thinking.

Maisie was glad to see Kara stride back into the shop

from the storeroom. "Assistant Chief," she said, "all of these people are store employees. I suspect you'll want to have them interviewed, right?"

Their expressions seemed to morph immediately from upset to scared, especially when the assistant chief said, "Right. Please come over here." She gestured toward the area behind the cash register counter.

Fortunately, Detective Vince Vanderhoff had come out of the back room, too. He'd heard what Maisie said. "Thanks for coming," he said to the employees. "Now we won't have to seek you out. I'll get our interview process started." He nodded at Maisie and Doug. "Thanks for bringing your K-9s. We'll take over here."

"Time for us to leave," Maisie responded and saw that her brother was following her. Kyle, still leading the leashed dogs and holding the small white one, stopped to talk with Esther. To make sure she wouldn't give him a hard time for hanging onto Fido and Toby and the new little pup?

Apparently she was okay with it, since Kyle and the dogs soon followed.

But Kara joined up with Kyle and Esther, and Maisie heard her say, "Dr. Kornel, you are free to go for now, but stay in town. We will most likely want to interview you again, at the station. Soon."

Kyle couldn't help grinning just a little, relieved about his freedom. Yes, he couldn't leave town, but he hadn't planned to anyway. And he wouldn't exactly look forward to additional questioning by the police.

But for now, he was finally outside on the well-lit sidewalk in front of that abominable pet store.

Okay, the store itself wasn't so bad, but the situation now connected with it...

One good thing was that Greta's blood had mostly been on the floor. Though he hadn't been gentle in his attempt at CPR, he fortunately hadn't gotten any of that blood on himself—as he probably would have done if he'd been the killer.

Now, he hugged the little Maltese he held in his arms. He hadn't grabbed a leash for her, but that was all right. He still held the leash handles of the two larger dogs, too. "Okay, Snowy," he said. Probably not her real name, but it fit her coloration. "Let's get out of here, pups." As quickly as he could, particularly considering how crowded the sidewalk and street were. Lookie-loos. Curious, noisy members of the public who were chatting loudly about what they saw.

And undoubtedly folks from all kinds of media who took pictures and probably made up their own version of what was happening.

Kyle knew Maisie was near him. In fact, as he started to move, Griffin caught up with him, sniffed noses with Fido and Toby, then stared up at the dog he held. And so he stopped.

Talking with Maisie was inevitable. He knew it. And even wanted to discuss all of this with her. But he also knew, cop that she was, she might consider him a murder suspect.

He'd watched, while talking with that Detective

Vanderhoff, when Maisie and her brother had their K-9s do their specialized investigation of Greta and her body and any evidence around her.

Rather, he'd watched the dogs, who had both sniffed him and sat down. He didn't want to look at Greta again. Not in the condition she was in.

And he hadn't done that to her.

He knew how the evidence against him looked—his being there with Greta's body and the knife that killed her, no one else in that storeroom at first while he was there... Well, it didn't look good. But they'd let him go, so it wasn't that bad, either. At least for now.

And... Okay. Of course he'd talk to Maisie. Staying away from her would only make him look worse.

And besides, he liked her. Maybe too much, after such a brief acquaintance. And he had the sense she liked him too. Or, at least, she had before.

Maybe now, she could even advise him what to do to make sure his innocence was obvious to all of those, cops and whoever else was investigating this murder.

"Hi, Kyle," said the feminine voice beside him that he'd been anticipating. "How are you doing?"

He turned to face her. He still found her one strikingly beautiful woman, but before her cop uniform hadn't fazed him.

Now... Well, okay. Unless she started accusing him of the crime or arresting him, he could let himself remain as friendly as he'd been before, right?

"I've been better," he replied. "This whole situation is..." He looked into her lovely—and intense—hazel eyes. He couldn't read what she was thinking, as much as he wanted to. "Look, I didn't do anything but talk to Greta on the phone, then…then find her that way and try to help her." He knew he was keeping his voice low so none of those around them could hear, and he doubted Maisie could hear him well, either. "Just so you know, I found these dogs in that office. Greta must have put them there before… She'd left me a message teasing about having just gotten this little one—" he held up Snowy "—dumped at the store. I need to take them to the downtown clinic to give this one an initial exam and secure all of them there tonight. I'll go back first thing in the morning and complete her exam, then take them all to the shelter. Would you—could you join me at the clinic tonight?" There would be at least one of the techs there then, but maybe they could talk in private.

The idea of being alone with her sounded really good, even if it was just for a short while, in one of the clinic's rooms. In fact, he had an urge—one he definitely wouldn't fulfill—to take her into his arms and hold her tightly against him to soothe his nerves, at least temporarily.

"No," she said, immediately smashing that stupid idea out of his mind. "Griffin and I need to go to the station now to file our report. But I'd already planned to go to the shelter tomorrow. Let's talk there, okay?"

That would be fine. They could go into his clinic and remain alone there as they discussed what was happening. That idea helped his nerves a bit, too.

"Sure," he said. "That'll work." Then, he couldn't

help it. He bent down a bit, ostensibly so Griffin and Snowy could exchange nose sniffs, but it also brought him closer to Maisie. He spoke softly into her ear. "I understand how this looks. And you know I was no fan of Greta's. But—"

"I understand," Maisie interrupted him, also speaking quietly. "I want to hear more of your side of things, but my intention is to help find out what really happened and who did this to her."

"Great," Kyle said. But her words didn't exactly reassure him. She hadn't asserted a belief in his innocence; although, neither did she accuse him of anything, and she did appear to intend to search for the truth, which wouldn't involve him.

He'd stress all that when they finally had an opportunity to talk tomorrow.

"And in the meantime," she continued, "since things seem so uncertain right now, I'd suggest you find yourself a lawyer."

A lawyer? Then she did think him guilty. His insides plummeted.

Still, what she thought didn't really matter. Although... Well, yes, to some extent it did.

And the detective who'd interviewed him had made a similar suggestion.

"As things go on," Maisie continued, "you'll have someone to talk to and get questions answered on your behalf. And be there to represent you if—"

"I get it." And he did. She was just trying to be helpful. That didn't mean she considered him guilty, then...did it?

Detective Vanderhoff's suggestion had gotten Kyle's mind whirling on that before, in addition to everything else he was thinking. And he fortunately had an idea about whom to contact.

For now, he thanked Maisie and started to say goodbye, then saw another uniformed cop edging his way through the crowd toward them.

He didn't recognize the guy, but Maisie immediately introduced them. "Kyle, this is Greta's nephew, Officer Jackson Styles. Jackson, this is veterinarian Dr. Kyle Kornel." Fortunately, she didn't mention anything else about him, like his being there with Jackson's aunt's body.

"What's happened here?" Jackson demanded of Maisie. "I heard something on my car radio. Is it my aunt?"

"Let's go inside, Jackson," she said, "and we'll talk."

Chapter 5

Even though Kara had dismissed her before, Maisie wanted to remain with Jackson for now so he would have someone to talk to under these difficult circumstances.

And as she and Griffin headed back into the store with Jackson, Maisie felt a little bad that she had suggested to Kyle that he get a lawyer. She could see how that had hurt him, as if she was sure of his guilt. Well, she wasn't. But as a law-enforcement officer, she knew that a good lawyer could help people deal with allegations against them, especially if they were innocent.

Still, she wished now she could have gone along with Kyle to talk with him more. Interview him in her way so she could convince herself there was no possibility he could have been the killer.

Well, okay. She already felt more convinced than she probably should have, but maybe she could have found more justification in her beliefs if she spoke with him further.

But tomorrow would have to do. Assuming he didn't flee because he really was guilty.

No. He wasn't, and that wouldn't happen.

And right now—well, she had to stop overthinking this just because she liked Kyle but had inadequate evidence so far to be certain either way. And more important for the moment, she had to attempt to help a colleague deal with a really difficult situation, the murder of his aunt.

She was back inside the store now behind Jackson, and Esther and the employees Maisie had seen before remained there. So did some of her other police colleagues, including Assistant Chief Kara. As far as she knew, only the EMTs and the people from the coroner's office remained in the rear room with the victim—if they hadn't moved her out the back door yet. And two people in the department forensics team were ushered past her into the back room by Kara.

But Kara turned back quickly. "Jackson," she said right away as he approached her, "I'm so sorry." She clasped his arms and looked up into his face, which Maisie thought looked nearly as pale as his white uniform shirt. He was tall, and his shoulders now looked shrunken somehow with his emotion. "Your aunt is in the back room, but the coroner's office will be taking her away soon. I'll try to answer your questions, at least as much as I can."

Good. It appeared that Kara wasn't going to allow him to see Greta as she was right now, even though he was her relative. But that would have been against procedure. And he'd only get in the way of the coroner's representative and forensics team if he did go back there.

Or could this be an act? Jackson was a cop, after all. He would know how to kill and keep anything to identify him, like fingerprints, from being part of the evidence. Maisie knew Greta was his aunt, but she had no idea what the relationship between them had been. Had they gotten along well? Was he now going to inherit her part of the store?

Maisie didn't know him well and hadn't worked any assignments with him. He seemed like a good guy, but who knew?

She realized she was attempting to leap on others as potential suspects. There were a bunch here in the store, too. She might not have seen any disagreements between Greta and her partner or employees, but that was certainly something to be investigated.

By Vince and his detective team. Not her. She was a K-9 officer, and investigating murders was not part of her job.

Not even when she wanted to prevent the vet—who'd helped Griffin—from being at the top of the list. Assuming he shouldn't wind up there.

Enough. It didn't appear that Maisie's presence was needed here any longer since she gathered that Jackson wasn't looking for her support. Assistant Chief Kara was much better equipped to deal with Jackson, and

Detective Vanderhoff, who was also in the room, could help answer Greta's nephew's questions, too.

And perhaps ask Jackson some questions as well. Had he been angry with his aunt over her treatment of dumped dogs? Maisie didn't think so, but he could have had different issues with her. Maisie couldn't rule out anyone right now as a suspect.

Not even Kyle…

Doug was still outside with Hooper, Maisie surmised. Or maybe they'd already started home.

Which was what Maisie did, too, as soon as she said her brief goodbyes. She used her phone to call her brother as she walked to her car with Griffin, maneuvering around the people who remained on the sidewalks, although the crowd seemed to be thinning.

"You have any insight into what happened?" she asked him. "Does Hooper?"

She heard a snort, and Doug said, "I figured you'd be the one with the insight since you knew the vic and also some of the potential suspects. So what do you think?"

Maisie and her K-9 had reached her vehicle, and she pushed the key fob to unlock it. "I think more information and evidence are needed."

"And the likeliness of Dr. Kornel's guilt?"

She had to be honest with her brother. "I don't think so. But because of my relationship to the shelter and the fact he visits there, too… Well, I may have more ability to investigate him than most people." And find a way to prove his innocence. She hoped.

"Got it. Be careful, though. It isn't your job to investigate this, even if you have some useful knowledge and contacts to point at Dr. Kornel—or someone else, for that matter. And even if this was your assignment, you don't have enough facts, at least not yet, to be sure how to handle it, although I'm sure your K-9 partner will do all he can to help you figure it out."

"And to provide me some therapy, too." Maisie managed to smile. Doug had a relationship going with Elissa Yorian, a nurse who also helped to train therapy dogs at the nearby Chance K-9 Ranch. She had given both Griffin and Hooper some lessons. Hooper had gotten his certification. Griffin wasn't yet certified, but Maisie hoped to follow through with that eventually to give her wonderful dog a purpose when he became too old to be a K-9. And now, because his company was so valuable to her, he did in fact somewhat act as her therapy dog.

Doug, who was younger than her, had helped Elissa get through some difficult times. He'd shared their house with Maisie before but now lived with Elissa, and that was why Maisie had the house to herself.

"Got it," Doug said. "Anyway, Hooper and I aren't far from home now. Where are you?"

"At my car, and I need to hang up to get Griffin settled in the back. Let's talk tomorrow." As she would be doing with Kyle… Or so they'd agreed.

Maisie quickly fastened Griffin in and started driving. She had to maneuver a little to get around the traffic that still tied up the streets in the area, but she soon was able to get to her nice, suburban home once shared with Doug. She walked Griffin for a few minutes, remaining on as high alert as she expected from her dog, even though this was a great, safe neighborhood. Or should be. But Maisie was now dwelling on the murder investigation, and her nerves were crackling.

After eating a salad for dinner and walking Griffin briefly again, to her surprise she did manage to get a fair night's sleep. And her morning at the station the next day wasn't eventful, although everyone was discussing the state of the investigation. A lot of it hinged now on the coroner's report, although having seen Greta's body Maisie figured the cause of death was pretty obvious.

The forensics team had already checked on the knife. The blood on it was, unsurprisingly, the vic's, and there were no prints or other blood types on it. The killer had apparently been careful. And fortunately for Kyle, he'd not had any rubber gloves in his pockets, nor had any been found in the storeroom. So things remained unclear, but Kyle's explanation of his presence still made sense. And so far, it seemed that no evidence found on-site had clearly pointed to anyone.

That day, Wednesday, she and Griffin were sent early on an assignment to patrol the area around an elementary school, and she gathered that was because teachers and parents were nervous after what had happened in their usually calm town. Maisie figured her uniformed presence, with her beautiful and smart golden retriever, helped to relieve some of the insecurities those in the area felt before heading into the school buildings even though she couldn't allow anyone to pet her K-9.

Next, she received a call from the station's dispatcher, who told her to take Griffin to the site of a convenience-store burglary downtown. A few other cops were already there when she arrived, including

Officer Glen Kreake, whom she didn't know well, but she respected the tall, dark-complected guy she always thought of as being really good at his job even without her having worked with him much before. He had a good reputation with those he worked with.

None of the other cops who'd been at the murder scene last night were present then, not even Doug, and Maisie had decided not to call her brother till sometime late in the day when neither was likely to be on duty. If he had something to report to her, he'd undoubtedly get in touch.

From what Maisie gathered, someone had snatched money from the convenience store's register, as well as some food, then rushed outside. Patrol cars were also canvasing the area searching for the perpetrator. Maisie and Griffin were directed to help in that patrol, but they hadn't been at it long when she received a call that the suspect had been captured a few blocks away.

Which meant it was time for her midday break—a nice long one today. Time to head to the Chance Animal Shelter, and once she was in her car with Griffin in the back, she called Nella to let her know she and Griffin were coming. She also managed to ask whether Kyle had arrived there yet with the two dogs who'd been at the shelter before, and the little Maltese he'd rescued last night. From what she'd understood, he was going to make sure they were all examined at the downtown clinic, and then he would take them to the shelter.

Kyle had only brought one of the rescue dogs so far, Nella told her, with the other two planned for later that day. "You were there at the pet store, weren't you?" Nella then asked. "I'll want to hear all about it."

"Of course." So what Maisie would do at the shelter that day would include not only patrolling the inside area and talking with staff members, giving lessons to the dogs they walked and making sure there were no obvious threats around, perhaps seeing the new rescue dogs, but also discussing the murder at least a bit with manager Nella—and maybe director Scott and the other managers, telling them what she could.

And talking even more, she hoped, with the on-staff veterinarian who was involved with that murder...only peripherally, she really hoped.

After she parked outside the shelter and entered the reception room, Maisie wasn't surprised when Nella popped in fairly soon. Nella brought her up to the offices in the nearby building right away, which meant Maisie and Griffin passed through the reception building's hallway, and with its door open, Maisie could see lights on inside the veterinary clinic.

Kyle was there. Which of the rescue dogs was with him?

For now, though, Maisie kept her thoughts directed at the questions the managers of the shelter asked her, once Scott and managers Telma and Camp joined them in the director's office. Other than Maisie, who remained in uniform, they all wore standard Chance Animal Shelter T-shirts with the word *Manager* on the pocket.

"We're interested in what happened for a lot of reasons," Scott said, sitting behind his desk. Everyone else sat in chairs facing him. His blue eyes looked concerned as he regarded Maisie. "Of course, we've learned what we know from the media, which might not be accurate or have the whole story as known right now. But since our new vet here seems to be involved—was at least at the store when the owner's body was found—we need to know what's going on and whether he'll be able to continue working here."

"I wish I could tell you more, but even if I knew anything, at this point it would still not be something I could discuss. And though Griffin and I were brought in for my K-9 to examine the site, we certainly didn't solve the crime." Which might indicate the perpetrator took steps to ensure that a K-9 didn't find sufficient evidence.

"I understand," Nella said. "But I'm sure you also understand our position. We're concerned about the people who live here, as well as the animals. Though we understood that Greta Styles wasn't a particularly nice person, we certainly don't want whoever harmed her to have the right to be at our shelter, just in case. And what's in the media at the moment all appears to be looking at Dr. Kornel as the person of most interest. Not sure how they got their info or why that's their direction, but it's out there now."

"I get it," Maisie said. She, too, leaned forward as Scott did and rested her hands on his desk even as she continued to hold Griffin's leash handle around her wrist—more for appearances than any need to control her K-9. "But I'm sure you don't want to falsely accuse anyone, either. Or kick out a highly qualified and skilled veterinarian without knowing if he actually commit-

---

And despite how much he'd her apparently inappropriate behavior regarding dogs, he was sorry she'd been murdered and hated the idea that some people thought he might be guilty of killing her.

Like that Detective Vince Vanderhoff, although he'd let Kyle leave after interrogating him last night. But Kyle knew Vince—who had acted somewhat friendly at first and told him to call him by his first name— wanted him to come to the station within the next day or so for further questioning. That could go on forever, or at least until they had a viable suspect to determine that wasn't him. Kyle was just hoping they wouldn't determine that viable suspect was him.

And how about Assistant Chief Kara Province? He hadn't talked to her much, but she hadn't shaken his hand and announced his innocence, either.

Then there was Officer Maisie Murran. Her suspicion hurt the worst, even though they had just met.

ted a crime, right?" Maybe she shouldn't have a
She didn't believe they could fire Kyle just for
a suspect, but they could possibly request ano
to take his place for now. But she certainly w
encourage any of it—at least as long as she c
lieve Kyle to be guilty of anything except a
to protect animals.

Although, she of course couldn't comm
erate her new acquaintance yet, either…

Nor did she want the residents to po
danger, another reason for her to help
resolved as fast as possible. And unde
cumstances, she could attempt to b
more as she kept her eye on him.

"You're right, of course, Maisi
please keep us informed as muc
And we've also appreciated you
have—and hope you'll continu
more often till this gets resolv

"I'll do what I can," Maisi
she could promise at the m
disclose much, but of course sh
the investigation into who murdered Gi
ing up with Kyle as much as she could, hopefull
him cleared. Assuming he deserved it.

Including right now.

And the idea of visiting Kyle in his vet clinic here at
the shelter, talking to him, getting his sense for what
happened yesterday?

She was definitely looking forward to it.

Probably too much.

Could he convince her of his innocence? But even
trying might make her suspect him more.

All right. He needed to change the subject in his
own mind.

He wished he had been able to bring the other tw
dogs at the downtown clinic back here to the shel
the same time as Snowy. But though he'd gotten
okay to bring them all in, he hadn't wanted
to handle all three at once in his car. The o
ger guys had become buddies, so he w
together for now. He'd drive them bo
if he could, and also place them officially within the
care of the Chance Animal Shelter.

But for now, Snowy was loose on his office floor.
He wasn't certain of her age, maybe a year. She did
appear to be housebroken, fortunately. He wondered
where she'd come from before someone dumped her
at the store.

He'd already filled in the little he knew about her
on the form, including that she'd had a complete physical examination at the downtown clinic, that she was
spayed, and that she didn't have a microchip or anything
else like an ID tag that would identify her owner. He
read the form over again just to be sure it was accurate
and had just pressed the Send button when he heard a
knock on the door, which startled him.

Snowy, too, since she let out a sharp bark and ran
to the door. He stood and picked her up under one arm
as he opened it.

And wasn't surprised to see Maisie and Griffin

standing there. She was in uniform, and she looked up at him with a totally unreadable expression on her face.

Was she glad to see him? He was glad to see her... unless, of course, she was here to arrest him.

"Hi, Maisie. Come on in. You, too, Griffin." It would be interesting to see how little Snowy got along with the smart and well-trained K-9.

Maisie smiled as she looked at Snowy and put her hand out to stroke her little white head. "So you've brought this pup here to the shelter. Will he—she?—be staying for now?"

"She. Yes, and hopefully they'll find her a new forever home soon. Toby and Fido, too, when I bring them here later." He stepped back and waved Maisie toward his desk and the chairs facing it.

"Thanks."

As she sat down, Kyle put Snowy down on the wooden floor and watched as the little dog approached the larger one again. They traded nose sniffs, and when Griffin lay down Snowy sniffed him further, then joined him. They were comrades already. That was a good thing.

But what was Maisie's mood now that she was there?

No matter what he had reasoned before, he jumped right into discussing the elephant in the room. And let himself smile briefly as he momentarily wondered if he would ever have the opportunity to treat an elephant while he practiced veterinary medicine.

"So, K-9 Officer Murran, what's the status of the investigation into Greta's death?" He looked her straight in her lovely hazel eyes, hoping to read in her expression anything she didn't tell him.

"I don't know. I'm not working directly on that case now, and most likely won't be again unless there's more need for a K-9's assistance in obtaining evidence." Her face remained impassive, and he wondered what she really was thinking.

Well, damn it, it didn't hurt to ask. "Got it. But what's your opinion. Who do you think murdered her?" *Me?* But of course he didn't ask that.

"I'm keeping an open mind right now." But her expression had changed into something that appeared highly charged, as if she wanted to demand that he confess to her. She must have tensed up, too, since Griffin, who'd lain down on the floor beside her, sat up, which also caused Snowy to rise and start trotting around the desk.

Kyle hated the unspoken tension between them. He hadn't had a good opportunity to talk with Maisie since he'd found Greta's body. Of course, a cop wasn't likely to dismiss him as a suspect under those circumstances. And he hated the hurt feeling that pulsed through him.

He liked Maisie. A lot. He'd thought she liked him. How could he convince her of his innocence?

By telling her? Maybe that wouldn't help, but he had to try.

He stood and walked around to the other side of the desk near her, stooping to pat Snowy on the back, which caused the little dog to sit. Kyle then sat on top of the desk on the other side of Maisie from Griffin and looked down at her.

Her expression now seemed quizzical, as if she was attempting to read his thoughts.

"Okay, Maisie," he finally said. "I know how things appeared last night. I understand why I'm considered a suspect in Greta's murder. I know what cops look for: motive, means and opportunity. I recognize that it looks like I had all three."

He was relieved that she seemed to lighten up at least a little, even sending him a brief grin. "So tell me what they were."

"What? And have you use them against me?"

She laughed, then stopped and rose to face him. "Look, Kyle. My job is to help enforce the law, with Griffin's help." At his name the dog moved again, this time rubbing his back against Kyle's nearest leg. Kyle was standing now, facing Maisie. Closely. He had an urge to get even closer…but stayed still.

"I understand," he said. "And I figure you're entitled to your opinions about things, but those opinions may be swayed by what other officers or your superiors think. I know I look bad, after my argument with Greta and my obvious anger with her, and being found with her the way I was. Not that I had a knife like that, so there goes means. And even though I argued with her, I didn't wish her dead, so there goes motive. And opportunity? She was already gone when I got there. And please keep in mind what I do for a living. I try hard to save and heal wounded or ill beings. Animals and not people, sure. And I certainly do all I can to prevent other people from harming animals—as Greta was doing, in her way. But I'd never—"

"Kill a human being, even a horrible one who was hurting dogs?" Maisie looked him straight in the eye. "I hope that's true, Kyle. But it may take a lot of effort to convince those who are investigating the homicide that it wasn't you, especially the way you were found with her. I just hope we can determine who it was and find enough evidence to arrest and convict them."

"We?" Kyle repeated the word, stressing it. "You're on my side, then?"

"I haven't seen anything to convince me you're guilty, Kyle," she said softly. "Please convince me you're innocent."

It wasn't what she had requested, he was sure, but he took a step closer to Maisie and pulled her into his arms.

Their kiss was tentative at first, but as he tasted her mouth, felt her warm, curvaceous body against him— never mind that it was in a police uniform—he wanted more.

The kiss deepened, and he was gratified to realize Maisie wasn't pulling away but seemed as invested in it as he was. He gently put one hand at the back of her head, touching her smooth and short hair, stroking it, wanting to stroke more of her.

But not here, in his office where shelter managers could walk in at any time. And not now, in the middle of their respective workdays—and maybe not ever. They certainly hadn't known each other long.

Attempting not to let his growing attraction—and lust—for this woman get in the way, he forced himself to pull away.

And look back down into those alluring eyes once

more as his hands still grasped her upper arms. Was she also as hot and filled with desire as he was? She appeared to be...but that could just be hope on his part.

"Okay, Maisie," he said. "I know that's not the way to convince you of my innocence...although it possibly will convince you of my interest." And yes, he was interested in her. In many ways, including having a desire to have hot sex with her, especially after that kiss. But that was unlikely to occur ever, and certainly not while he remained a murder suspect. "But just know I'll do anything I can to prove to you that, no matter what it might have looked like, no matter what my opinion of Greta Styles, I didn't do anything to hurt her."

"I appreciate that, Kyle," she said softly, taking yet another step away from him and bending down to pat Griffin's head. The dog was upright now and appeared almost to be attempting to understand what the humans around him were saying. And Snowy was now at the larger dog's side. "And just know that, although I won't do anything to violate my obligations as an officer of the law, I will do what I can to help you clear yourself... unless I ever see or hear anything that makes me doubt your innocence."

Kyle couldn't help it. He pulled her back into his arms.

This time the kiss was quicker and less heated. She pulled away first and looked at him. "That's only because I don't really believe you're guilty. Not now, at least. But I just don't know where the investigation will go, and—"

"I get it. I'm not guilty, and I intend to convince you of that." And when he took another step toward her, he looked into her eyes again. "Believe me."

Chapter 6

Wow. What kind of cop was she, Maisie wondered, allowing a murder suspect to kiss her that way? And not only had she allowed it, she had wanted it, had thrown herself into it.

It had, of course, been entirely consensual. Oh, yeah. And she wouldn't have done it if she'd actually believed him guilty.

But she couldn't yet prove his innocence, either.

Well, sure, they'd kissed previously. And not just in a simply friendly way. But that was before the murder. And this kiss was even more…well, stimulating.

Heck. That had to stop. She was a cop, not a starry-eyed teenager with a crush. She would remain detached…pretty much. And she certainly wouldn't allow any sexual attraction she might inappropriately feel for Kyle stop her from attempting to find the truth.

What if he was trying to seduce her in order to convince her of his innocence?

That wouldn't happen.

A thought came to her, and not for the first time since she'd become involved with this murder case, although she had made up her mind not to focus on it. It wasn't relevant.

But she would keep it in mind to make sure it wasn't.

There had been a situation she'd learned of while she was a rookie in which a young cop had been fired from a department near Sacramento, she believed. A female cop. She had allegedly been seduced by a suspect in a local murder case, and the story that later was made public indicated the guy had actually committed the crime—and attempted to get the cop's assistance in clearing himself by trying to make her fall in love with him.

Evidently he'd succeeded—or at least that rookie had been fired, rightly or wrongly, and disciplined, and the suspect was brought to trial and convicted of the murder.

Now, what had made Maisie remember this? She laughed at herself. Good thing she had thought of it. Maybe. But the recollection would make her even more wary of getting involved with Kyle.

Still, she'd told Kyle she would attempt to help get him cleared, and the kiss hadn't had anything to do with that—not much, at least. It might even have made her more cautious. And she'd only help if he deserved to be cleared, of course. She had indicated the same thing before, but now she felt even more committed.

Assuming clearing him was justified. And in case it wasn't, and what loomed over her was a similar situation to what had gone on with that rookie cop... She would be damned careful.

And now that kiss was over—well, she watched as Kyle returned to the other side of his desk and sat down again. "Interested in joining me in the interior walking area?" he asked. "I'll have to head to the downtown clinic soon, but in the very long time I've been working here—" he smiled at her, and she knew, of course, that it had been less than a week "—I've gotten into the habit of walking around the shelter and taking a look at our animal inhabitants to make sure they don't have any obvious medical problems. And of course if any did, or if some staff member or manager believed they did, I'd bring them in here to the clinic to check them out. While I'm at it, I take a look at the staff members, too, in case anyone appears upset or scared or otherwise in need of protection, but I haven't seen anything like that. Not yet, at least."

"Got it," Maisie said. "And I'd love to walk with you. Visiting is what Griffin and I do most of the time when we come here, but mostly to check on staff members. I work with them and help show them doggy commands that they can then use to work with the resident dogs."

"I know," Kyle said. "I've heard about that. Before I head back there, though, I need to quickly send the application I was filling out for Snowy to become one of the resident pups. Just give me a minute."

And almost immediately after he finished, his cell phone rang. He grabbed it from his pocket and looked at the caller ID. "It's Scott," he said.

Rather than attempt to eavesdrop, Maisie sat down on the floor with Griffin and Snowy and played with them a little, patting them and pushing them slightly away so they came closer to wait for her to push again as part of the game. She wondered if Snowy would make a good therapy dog, with the potential of cheering up sad people. Maisie always figured Griffin would be a wonderful therapy dog if he wasn't a K-9.

After a minute, Kyle said, "Hey, Maisie. Come with me. I'm taking Snowy into the center area, too, rather than leaving her here in an enclosure. Even though I haven't finished her application, Scott's looked at what I've already done online and said it was good enough— especially since Snowy has passed the health tests— and now she can stay here and this shelter will help her find her forever home."

"That's great!" Maisie exclaimed, reaching for the little dog and pulling her onto her lap. "Did you hear that, Snowy? Things are certainly going to change for the better for you." Snowy licked Maisie's fingers as if thanking her, and Maisie laughed.

Kyle put a collar and leash on Snowy, and the four of them soon left the clinic and headed down the hall to the interior of the shelter, passing the other dogs who were in the enclosure at the end that day. "You might get to hang out there someday," Kyle, who was walking Snowy, told the little dog, who pulled a bit on her leash as if interested in meeting the others now.

Maisie laughed, and Griffin also regarded the dogs there with apparent interest, as he often did when they walked through this area.

Kyle used his keycard to open the door from the entry hall to the outside area. It was time to walk there, too. It was November in Chance, and the Southern California rainy season had begun, although it hadn't been raining much lately. The temperature was rather cool, since they were up in the mountains. She might need to start wearing her uniform jacket soon. For now, though, Maisie and Griffin followed Kyle into the yard.

Maisie had gotten to know the central area well. The reception building had a couple of other buildings beside it, one containing the shelter's dining location downstairs and staff members' apartments upstairs. The other held the managers' offices. The main area was a long, grassy central lawn surrounded by a rectangular concrete walkway with several buildings around it used to house the shelter animals. There were four staff members out there now, each with a dog.

Before they headed that direction, Kyle said, "I'll want to pop into the building where the enclosures for the smaller dogs are once we're done with our walk."

"That doesn't surprise me," Maisie said. The farthest building on the left contained enclosures for cats and, in the back, smaller pets, and the one just before it housed some of the smallest dogs at the shelter. That was where Snowy would end up when they were through walking her, along with water and a good meal, Maisie was certain. She was sure that the pup's caring handler would see to it.

For now, though, she and Griffin led Kyle and Snowy down the lawn that was the center area till they caught up with the staffers who were there. Unsurprisingly, they included Bibi, a very friendly and outspoken staff member who seemed to be everywhere within the shelter. Today she wore a red shirt with the Chance Animal Shelter logo in the middle, the same kind of shirt all staff wore. She was walking Jack, the Jack Russell terrier.

"So glad you two are here." She looked from Maisie to Kyle, smiling so that the gap between her front teeth showed. "We've got some great news. A brand new staffer has joined us today, and you should meet her. She loves dogs."

"Then, I'd love to meet her." Glancing around, Maisie saw a young woman standing near where staff member Denise stood with Mocha, a small terrier mix, and another staffer, Leonard, stood with Bruno, a Doberman. The stranger was walking Fräulein, a dachshund.

"Great. Come on over. We're just showing her around the inside shelter area now. Her name is Chessie and— well, we're probably not supposed to talk about it, but what we heard is that her ex-husband tried to kill her, and no one can find him now, not the police or anyone. I'll bet you've heard that story around here before, right? We all have."

"Yes," Maisie agreed, "it does sound familiar." In fact, as she recalled, Bibi's reason for being here had involved an abusive ex, too.

Maisie looked toward Kyle, who nodded. She didn't know how much he was aware of staffers' backgrounds.

"Come with me," Bibi said. "I'll introduce you. I'm sure she'll be happy to meet our wonderful new veterinarian and our favorite K-9 officer, too. First, though—" she looked down at where Snowy sat near Kyle's feet "—who's that little white dog?"

"This is Snowy," Kyle responded, bending to pat her head. Snowy's tail began to wag energetically. "She's just been approved to become one of this shelter's residents."

"That's great!" Bibi got close, encouraging Jack to heel then sit while she petted the top of Snowy's head, too. "Welcome, cutie…er, Snowy."

They then moved to where the others stood. Maisie said hello and introduced Kyle, who might already have met some of them.

Denise—midtwenties, moderately deep-toned skin, long, black hair pulled back into a clip—and Leonard—a youngish guy—also said hi, but Chessie hung back. She appeared nervous, not surprising for a new member of staff.

"Hey, Chessie." Maisie moved around the crowd a bit to approach the blonde woman who was also clad in a Chance Animal Shelter T-shirt. Hers was blue. "I'd love to take a walk with you and Fräulein so you can get to know my police K-9, Griffin, better. And Dr. Kornel—Kyle—this shelter's new veterinarian can join us with Snowy, okay?"

"Sure, go for it," Bibi said, turning to get closer to Chessie, too. "They're good people, like the staff, You'll see, after you get to know them a bit." She was grinning as usual.

"Well…" Chessie's hesitation appeared painful, judging by the way her light brows drew closer together. But then she said, "Well, sure. Will we stay inside the shelter?"

"Of course," Maisie said. Maybe this wasn't a great idea, but she hoped it would ultimately help Chessie feel more comfortable. And give Kyle more insight into how this shelter worked—for people.

There were times Kyle wanted to read his patients' minds to learn what they were thinking—although often dogs and cats communicated well by just looking at people.

But here was a person he wanted to know more about. A new staff member who'd just moved in. Why was she in this particular shelter? She'd evidently been accepted because of a really bad relationship with her ex. Was the danger continuing despite her being in protective custody? He assumed so, if her ex was missing as Bibi had said.

Kyle realized he didn't know the backgrounds of many of the human residents, and he wanted to.

And he wanted to work more with the managers and help with the security, as Maisie did.

"I gather you just moved here," Kyle said to Chessie. "I'm new to this shelter, too. What I do is a bit different from what you do, but maybe we can compare notes." He leveled a big smile at the woman, then turned it on Maisie for a moment before returning it to Chessie. But for that brief time, he felt a strange surge of pleasure jam through him. Maisie was also smiling at him encouragingly and—well, he might be reading too much into it, but that smile also appeared somehow appreciative and even caring. And definitely sexy. Especially after that kiss.

Did she really believe in his innocence?

And the extra good thing was that Chessie smiled back, kind of. Plus, she did appear to relax, at least a little.

"Okay," she said. "Let's do that."

The three of them, holding leashes of the dogs they were walking, began strolling along the paved path that circled the lawn, in the opposite direction from where the staff members they'd just been visiting with went, toward the front of the shelter rather than the far end.

"You know," Maisie said to Chessie, "I give lessons on dog training here sometimes. I'd be glad to show you some commands, if you'd like. But before we do that—"

"Before we do that," Kyle interrupted. He wanted to continue what he'd started first. "I'd like to ask you some questions to help me learn more. I recognize they might make you uncomfortable, though..."

"You want to know why I'm here, right?" Chessie didn't stop walking, though she lowered her head and seemed to stare more at the pavement than at Fräulein. "I get it."

"That's right," Kyle said quietly, even though, thanks to Bibi, he thought he knew the answer. "I've been here helping the pets who need examinations and veterinary care, but I have a background of helping people, too. In fact, I used to wear a uniform similar to Maisie's." He gently elbowed her as Chessie turned enough to look inquisitively toward him.

Maisie was watching him, too. Wondering if he was a murderer, maybe. Chessie might also be aware of the suspicions against him thanks to the media, since she was new here. Certainly none of the other staff members here knew—although all the managers probably did. He wouldn't be surprised if Maisie had even discussed the situation with Scott and the rest.

Not a good time to think about that.

"So tell us a little about when you were a cop," Maisie said to Kyle. Why now? Maybe she figured that hearing a little more history of one of her questioners might make it easier for Chessie to describe her own. Or maybe Maisie just wanted to hear more about it from him. They'd discussed it a bit before, but why not talk about it some more? And if he stressed his cop background, maybe she'd be more inclined to believe in his innocence.

He began talking about how he'd decided to become a cop to follow in his father's footsteps. "He liked the idea, encouraged me, even took me to his police station in LA to introduce me around before I joined up and began the process of becoming a police officer. I could tell he was well-liked, especially when some of his fellow cops told me how much the bad guys didn't like him."

Surprisingly—or not—Maisie laughed at that, but she stopped at his answer to Chessie's next question.

"So why aren't you a cop now?"

Kyle hesitated before responding, then said, "Well, I

always really liked animals, even more than I liked arresting bad guys. And when my dad was killed in the line of duty—"

"Oh, I'm so sorry," Chessie said, and he heard Maisie draw in her breath, though she already knew that. In sympathy? He figured so.

Kyle wasn't about to delve into more details of that story. Instead, he said, "Sure, it was hard. But I think I'm better cut out to be a veterinarian, anyway." He bent to pat Snowy on the head before they continued walking. When he rose again, he turned toward the newest resident. "Your turn now. I know how special this shelter is for people taken into protective custody. Why are you here?"

Chessie slowed down, rubbing her hand against the side of her light blue jeans, then squatting down to pet Fräulein a little. She bent her head forward so her light colored hair covered the sides of her face. Kyle had noticed, of course, how good-looking the young lady was, with smooth skin, prominent cheekbones, green eyes, and a cool expression. Now, her expression turned icy as her face reddened.

"My husband. My ex-husband, whenever I can work that out. He…he was abusive."

And then she stopped talking and started walking rapidly. Both Maisie and Kyle matched her pace, as did the dogs, and Kyle said, "Sorry to hear that. I gather it was pretty bad for you to wind up here." That's what he'd come to understand when he talked to Scott and the managers about all aspects of this place, including how important it was for them to bring in people with nowhere else to go, to protect them, to give them new identities and new lives eventually.

"Can you tell us about it?" Maisie asked from Chessie's other side. "You don't have to, of course, but you know everyone around here cares, including us. And sometimes it helps to talk about a terrible situation. To vent, and not keep the issues inside. What do you think?"

"I feel more comfortable telling *you*," Chessie said, facing Maisie.

Which made Kyle sad, but he certainly understood. "I get it," he said. "I'll give you some space."

That must have been the right answer to gain her trust a bit. As he stood, Chessie said, "Wait. It's okay. I'll tell you, too."

Wow, Maisie thought. She liked Kyle's attitude. No pushiness. He'd been prepared to go, no questions asked, when Chessie indicated she wanted him to.

He really did seem to care.

Which, possibly stupidly, made her care about him more, too. Even though he was a murder suspect... And she had to keep reminding herself about that. A lot, so she would stay away from him more—figuratively, at least.

The loss of his father. She knew that. But how he'd become a veterinarian...she hadn't heard much about it before. And now—how could she help but feel sorry for him? Care for him?

No. Only on a professional level, and only if he was innocent. And not trying to use her.

She wasn't about to tell Chessie about the current murder situation and Kyle's involvement with it—innocent or not. It was better that the staffer believe everyone else here was nice and caring and wanting to keep her safe.

Which Maisie believed Kyle was. Surely, he hadn't killed Greta.

For now, she said, "Are you ready to tell us about it?"

"Could we go somewhere other staff members won't be able to watch us?" Chessie asked.

Maisie said, "Sure. Let's go into one of the buildings where the animals are secured. We can always move if there are other people around."

They headed to the building where Snowy soon would be housed. Inside, Maisie watched Kyle look around, and she assumed he was trying to figure out which of the fenced enclosures might be available to put his new little protégée. Of course that would be determined by Scott and the managers. Only a few dogs were in there now, but she knew there were more being given attention by the staff members.

No other people were there at the moment, though, so Maisie, Griffin at her side, led them all to a nice, plastered wall at the far end of the inside walkway, where they and the dogs they had with them stopped.

No further requests were needed to get Chessie to talk. The nervous, pretty woman described the horror that had been her life before she'd learned about the Chance Animal Shelter and been accepted here in protective custody and given the name Chessie. Appropriately, she didn't mention what her real name was.

But she leaned her back against the wall, sometimes stooping to pat Fräulein or the other dogs, other times standing straight except for bending her head.

The story she told was ugly and made Maisie want to work with Griffin to go after Chessie's husband. But the cops who knew the situation apparently couldn't find him now. He was on the loose.

Which made things even harder for this poor woman.

Her husband had wanted kids, as did she. But for the past year or so of their marriage, he had beaten her every month when it became obvious she hadn't gotten pregnant.

The guy had abused her, raped her when she hadn't wanted sex, to impregnate her, but it hadn't worked.

Maisie had to ask. "Did he ever undergo any kind of testing to determine if he was fertile or not?"

Tears streamed down Chessie's cheeks. "No, never," she said, shaking her head. "He was certain it had to be my fault, and I was going to pay for it."

"I'm so sorry," Maisie said.

"Me, too," said Kyle. "I'm just glad you're here under our protection—well, the shelter's protection—and I'll do everything I can, too, to ensure you stay safe."

"But…but he's gotten away from the police," Chessie wailed softly.

"I'll look into it further," Maisie said, "and see if there's anything else my colleagues or I can do."

"She's a damn good cop," Kyle added. "We can't promise anything, of course, except that this shelter will do all it can to protect you. Everyone here cares."

Maisie liked his compliment. She liked his attitude. Too much.

She said, "Thanks so much for trusting us and talking to us, Chessie. Both of us. And now, are you okay with going back out to walk Fräulein again? I suspect a little more exercise will do us all a lot of good."

"Yes," Chessie said. "I like that idea. Let's go."

Chapter 7

Kyle was surprisingly happy, walking with the dogs and these two women—a resident under protection at this shelter and a cop in uniform who had her K-9 with her. A lovely cop. A caring cop.

A sexy cop.

One he shouldn't hang around so much, particularly since he was a murder suspect. Was that why she now stayed near him—to investigate him, watch to see if he made any missteps?

He didn't want to think that was why she'd given into that latest kiss, but—

Too bad, in a way, that he wasn't still a cop. Maybe he should conduct his own investigation of the murder, but how could he do it without appearing guilty?

Kyle figured he should leave these two, find one of

the shelter's managers and hand over Snowy, then go back to work at his downtown clinic. And stay away from Maisie.

But it felt good to be hiking slowly in this flat and limited area with such good company—at least on the surface—so he hung out with them for now. Stared ahead at some of the others also walking dogs and taking them aside to teach them commands and tricks.

He felt at home not just in his clinic here at the shelter, but in the central, vital part of this place.

And traded glances with Maisie quite a bit.

He was glad Chessie had let him hear her story. He really wanted to do something to help her.

Sure, he'd known what this shelter was all about, but now that he'd heard one of its residents describe her reason for being here—and that reason was one that made him want to do all he could to find her miserable cad of a husband—he intended to do even more to help not just the animals but the people here.

But he first had to find a way to help himself.

"So, K-9 cop," he called now to Maisie, wanting to do something to help the mood of all three of them. "How about Griffin and you demonstrating some special dog commands? You can invite some of the other staff members over, too."

"I'd like that." Maisie stopped, and so did Griffin at her side. "What do you think, Chessie?"

"Sounds good to me," she said. "Maybe not so much to Fräulein." Chessie gestured at the energetic dachshund at her side who was tugging on the leash, as if she wanted to join other dogs playing fetch at the end of the grassy area with some humans.

It didn't take long for Maisie to get Griffin set up to hear and obey commands. Maisie told Griffin to heel—which he did, as she began walking in circles, then turned and went the other direction.

Did Snowy know any commands? Kyle had no idea, but he told the little Maltese to heel, and though she tried pulling away at first, she soon actually began obeying him.

Fräulein didn't seem especially excited about obeying Chessie, but she did so part of the time. And the other staffers who were out there—Bibi, Denise and Leonard—must have seen what they were doing and quickly joined the three of them with the dogs they'd brought out to work with.

Soon, all the humans had dogs listening to them and mostly obeying their commands. Kyle knew that all the dogs sheltered here were trained as part of the plan to make them eligible for rehoming and also part of the plan to keep the residents busy and focused on something they hopefully enjoyed, helping the animals.

"Sit," Kyle told Snowy, and the little dog actually did. Kyle watched as Bibi first got Jack quieted down a bit, then encouraged him to sit and stay after Maisie demonstrated those commands with Griffin. Easy ones, maybe, but it was good that the dogs here knew them. Snowy would learn. So would Fräulein. And clearly Mocha and Bruno had already mastered them, too.

And here were three people who'd also had horrors built into their prior lives like Chessie but now spent time under protection and helped these animals learn enough to hopefully find new forever homes with loving families soon—as well as a K-9 cop who clearly gave a damn about all of them.

And maybe about him, too.

Or not.

In any case, as much as he would have loved to stay here all day, he had work to do. Other animals to help. People? Not so much, although he made a silent vow to himself to come into this area and work with the staff as often as he could when he was on duty.

Especially if Maisie, too, was present.

But for now, he needed to find Scott and officially turn little Snowy over to this shelter.

Happily, Scott, Telma and Camp came toward them now from the building housing their offices. Great timing.

Soon, Telma was holding Snowy's leash, and Kyle let the others know he was heading downtown but would be back tomorrow. At the moment, none of them was aware of any animal who needed veterinary attention.

And as Kyle said goodbye, so did Maisie. "I need to get back to the station now," she said, "and find out what my next assignment is with Griffin. But we'll be back too, maybe tomorrow."

That allowed Kyle to walk toward reception with the K-9 cop and her dog. They exited and said their goodbyes at the lot behind the shelter where their cars were parked.

Kyle felt somewhat at a loss for words. How could he say his farewell appropriately? He wanted to see Maisie again soon, of course. But he remained concerned about how she felt toward him. Professional, yes. But in a dedicated, arrest-mode cop way, or as someone else who liked to help animals...and people? Including him?

Her goodbye felt highly appropriate. "Good job today helping Chessie and Snowy," she said, sending him a smile that lit her lovely face with no apparent hesitation or underlying message. "You're doing great around here. And that other situation?" She hesitated but not long enough for him to comment. "Let's just hope it gets resolved soon in the manner it should."

"Right," he said as she unlocked her SUV and secured Griffin in the back seat. "See you again soon, I hope." Which he did hope, even though he recognized her words were far from indicating she felt certain of his innocence.

Nor was he able to give her a kiss goodbye, not even just a friendly one, since she was now in her car.

Okay. It was better that way.

Kyle got into his own car and started back down the mountain toward town and the main veterinary clinic.

What would be awaiting him there—just ordinary exams and vaccinations of healthy pets, or more serious vet concerns? He'd find out soon.

Only, as he reached the first traffic light, a few blocks from the clinic, his phone rang. He didn't recognize the number. He answered it on the car's Bluetooth. "Hello?"

"Hello, Dr. Kornel," said the female voice on the other end. "This is Assistant Chief Kara Province of the Chance Police Department."

He knew who she was and where she worked, of course. But why was she calling?

This couldn't be good.

He was right.

"We have some more questions for you in the matter of the homicide of Greta Styles. Would you please come to the station right now?"

His heart rate sped up. He couldn't say no—could he?

"I'm on my way to the veterinary clinic to help care for a dog in trouble," he partially lied, "and—"

"I think you had better let your fellow veterinarians deal with that. We'll expect you here within the next half hour."

After leaving the shelter, Maisie and Griffin had been sent on an assignment that had fortunately gone well.

Maisie couldn't help grinning as she drove Griffin back to the station with her. She wished he was sitting on the seat beside her so she could pet him, though that wasn't nearly as safe as his being secured in the back seat. But her wonderful K-9 had done his job this afternoon and done it well.

"You're so great, Griffin," she said, glancing into the rearview mirror toward her K-9 partner, who was sitting up looking out the window. He turned toward her and panted slightly as if he was smiling.

Smiling back, she turned the corner onto the street behind the department, surrounded by a bunch of other buildings of differing heights. She'd soon park in the lot there and strut inside to what she figured would be a lot of kudos from her fellow officers regarding what she'd accomplished after leaving the shelter and reporting here a while ago. Doug and Hooper hadn't been on this assignment with them, so only she and Griffin would get the well-deserved applause.

The station had received a 9-1-1 call from a preschool that morning, just after she'd arrived. A four-year-old had wandered off after an outdoor play period, and the teachers hadn't noticed at first.

They could suffer a whole lot of criticism and maybe even lose their license as a preschool if word got out about this. That was their problem.

The most important part was that no one had been able to find the little boy—at first.

The school was on the edge of town, across the street from a park that had a small, wooded area at the back. Fortunately this kind of disaster hadn't happened before. Or if some kid had wandered off, they'd been able to find him or her fast.

Not this time. And the logical thing had been to call in a K-9 who sometimes did search-and-rescue assignments.

Which Griffin had. Successfully. He'd sniffed some crayons the teachers said the boy had been using and had shown Maisie the logical direction little Joey had gone, despite no one seeing him there in the park so far.

Of course the kid had been there, sitting on the ground in a ditch surrounded by underbrush, crying. Griffin had located him quickly. Maisie slid down the small hill, greeted him gently, explained she was a police officer in case her uniform didn't give that away to the youngster and introduced him to Griffin. The sweet golden retriever's gentle sniffs and nuzzles had calmed the boy, Maisie had called in that she'd found him and soon other officers joined her at the school as she brought the boy in.

Mission accomplished. And she and Griffin got lots of thanks from everyone at the school, including little Joey and his mother, who'd shown up when notified about what had happened.

Maisie pulled her car into one of the empty spaces behind the station. She grinned, got Griffin out and let him walk around on his leash a little in the alley.

"Hey, boy," she said. "You're our hero of the day, and everyone here will know it. And if they don't, I'll certainly let them know."

She let him lead her to the station's rear door, which she opened. Then, she had Griffin walk at her heel down the hallway to the reception area.

Only, before she got there, when they'd nearly passed one of the closed doors where interviews were conducted of victims and suspects and anyone else not brought into the offices of those in charge, she stopped.

A voice from inside sounded familiar. Too familiar.

"No way," it said loudly. *He* said loudly.

Kyle.

What was he doing here? Considering where he was in the station, Maisie could guess. He was undergoing additional interrogation. But why?

Had further evidence been unearthed that indicated his guilt in the murder of Greta Styles?

Or had no evidence been unearthed, making her fellow officers start pushing everyone who could be considered a person of interest to talk more about the case and their feelings about Greta—and their last contacts with her?

Maisie had been aware when that had happened in a few other investigations. It wouldn't be surprising if it was happening again.

Even if she hated to see it happen with Kyle. Unless there was actual evidence beyond what she'd heard about that linked him to the murder.

But there wasn't anything she could do. Was there?

Taking a deep breath to calm herself, she continued with Griffin down the hall into the large reception area, which she had to pass through to reach the stairs to the office that she and Doug shared.

Officer Penny Jones sat at the reception desk. The young cop had been here long enough to be sent out on assignments, but mostly she remained the station's part-time receptionist. "Hello, Officer Murran," she said formally, not surprising since there were a few civilians sitting in the waiting area. "We heard you had a very successful afternoon—you and Griffin. It even got into the media, online and on TV, I think." Penny rose and came around the desk, bent down and gave the K-9 a hug. Her brown eyes were gleaming as she rose again and looked Maisie in the face. She was slightly taller and slightly heavier than Maisie. "Good thing you're back, though. Detective Vanderhoff wants you to join him in room 6, where he's questioning a suspect that he says you've had contact with."

Maisie felt her own eyes widen, and she drew in her breath, looking away so Penny couldn't see the sad scowl she now felt on her face. Yes, it had been Kyle she'd heard as she passed the room. And Vince was aware she knew Kyle and wanted her to join in his interrogation. Did she want to? Heck, no. She might want to believe in Kyle's innocence, but it wasn't up to her to prove—or disprove—it, or to question him officially.

Only, it was, apparently, up to her to join in the investigation and to be there when Kyle was questioned, at least this time.

"Got it," she said, turning back to Penny. "But, er... is it Dr. Kyle Kornel we're talking about?"

"I think so." Penny resumed her seat behind the desk.

"Do you know why he's being questioned again?"

Penny shook her head so her shoulder-length brown hair brushed her shoulders. "Sorry, no."

"Okay. Well, I'll go join them." As much as she was reluctant to do so.

She'd walked Griffin a little before entering the station, so she couldn't really use him as a valid excuse for delaying. And in fact, she was curious enough that she didn't necessarily want to procrastinate.

She would simply listen, at least at first. She had nothing to contribute to an interrogation anyway, other than to confirm she had met Kyle and seen him work with animals. And, today, she had also seen him work well with at least one person in protective custody at the Chance Animal Shelter.

Unless she was asked again if she had ever seen Kyle arguing with the murder victim, but that was nothing new.

It took only moments for Griffin and her to go down the hallway. She passed other colleagues in uniform on their way into the reception area and said hello but arrived too quickly at room 6, which still had its door closed. Hesitating only a moment, she knocked on the wooden door and braced herself to be greeted by Vince as he opened it from the inside.

Instead she heard his voice. "Come in, Officer Murran."

So he knew who was here. Because she was the only one he'd asked to have join them—or because Penny had called to let him know she was on her way? She suspected the latter.

She entered, Griffin, as always, at her side.

"Hello, Officer Murran. I believe you know Dr. Kornel." This time, Detective Vince Vanderhoff was standing at the far side of the room, the chair he'd probably just vacated behind his suit-clad body. Other chairs formed two semi-circles from his, each ending at the door.

The closest one to him, to his left, must have been occupied by Kyle, who was now standing, too. So was a man she didn't know, another guy in a suit. That had to be Kyle's lawyer, and he'd been smart enough both to follow her suggestion and to get his legal counsel to join him this time.

"Yes," Maisie acknowledged, her gaze meeting Kyle's, "we've met. In fact we spent some time together today at the Chance Animal Shelter, and previously while checking into the health of various dogs."

Kyle's expression was hard and angry, but he didn't say anything, either to confirm or deny the innocuous things she'd said. She didn't believe he was angry with her—not yet, at least. And she'd heard his voice before, here at the station as she'd walked by, and he hadn't sounded happy. She assumed the interrogation wasn't going well for him. Or at least, unsurprisingly it was troubling him.

Her assumption was soon validated. "Hello, Officer Murran," said the man in the suit. "I'm Attorney Mark Brown, and I'm here to represent Dr. Kornel."

"Hello," she said and shook his hand. She could only hope he did a good job of representing Kyle.

"Well, here's the reason I've asked you to join us," Vince said. "I want you to tell me in front of Dr. Kornel whether you heard him threatening Ms. Styles. You indicated before that you had and why. Tell us again."

Taking a seat, Maisie hesitated, glancing first at the lawyer and then at Kyle, who had also both sat down. She still had to tell the truth, of course, and not edit it to help Kyle. And so she said slowly, "Yes, I saw them together in the small veterinary clinic at the shelter. And yes, I recognized that Dr. Kornel was unhappy with Ms. Styles's attempts to find a shelter that would take in the dogs she had and let her display them for adoption the way she wanted."

"Okay. But the threats…?"

"The only things I could consider to be threats were his indications of doing what was necessary to ensure she allowed a shelter to take in the dogs in compliance with California law or suffer the legal consequences."

Maisie had been looking into Vince's brown eyes. Vince's hairline of brown hair was receding, and he had a narrow, currently intense, face. "But that was the only kind of threat?" he asked.

"That's all I heard," Maisie responded, and she hadn't said otherwise before because it was true—mostly. Kyle had told Greta to comply with the law. He hadn't been threatening, but he had been insistent. And if she didn't, and he learned about it? Well, his loud insistence was one of the things that troubled Maisie. She then shot a quick glance toward Kyle's face. He wasn't smiling, of course, but the anger she'd seen there before had been replaced by something a lot easier to look at. Gratitude? His attorney's expression seemed nice and calm.

"I see," Vince said. "That's not entirely what I heard from others who might have been with you."

That surprised Maisie—not necessarily that anyone had said something contradictory, but what was Vince trying to accomplish here? Was he trying to intimidate Kyle because he allegedly had other witnesses who could testify against him?

It seemed she wasn't going to find out just yet.

Although... Vince would undoubtedly get upset if she asked him during this session, because she might allegedly put those others in danger if Kyle truly was homicidal. But who'd been with them? Beth? Scott? Had anyone else been present during the argument she'd heard? She didn't think so.

Maybe she should check with them about what they'd said—or not. But she could ask Vince more later, when Kyle wasn't around, including if there was anyone else he was referring to.

As she recalled, even she had wanted to discuss the

Greta situation with her colleagues to try to find a way to get her to obey the law. But she had never gotten that chance.

"Well," Maisie now said to Vince, "that's all I can tell you. Griffin and I need to get back to work. I'd better go."

"And I'm assuming I'm not under arrest," Kyle said, standing. "So I'm leaving, too." He didn't wait a moment for Vince's okay, but he strode through the room toward where Maisie and Griffin now stood. And as he reached them and passed by, Maisie heard him say softly, "Thanks. Let's talk."

And then he walked through the door, followed by his lawyer.

Chapter 8

Kyle half expected Vince to yell after him to stop or come back or, as his lawyer would, to least advise him not to leave town, and he walked quickly down the hall, past the cops and civilians in the reception area, out of the station.

But fortunately, he heard nothing from Vince.

"Okay," Mark said as they both stopped on the sidewalk in front of the station.

Kyle had met Mark Brown at the downtown animal clinic. Mark's borzoi, Roscoe, had become Kyle's patient when he developed a skin condition, fortunately now on the mend. Kyle hadn't thought he would need to associate with Mark as his attorney—but he had been glad he knew him and his criminal-law background. He'd also been glad that Mark agreed to represent him after they'd met and discussed the situation—and of course the lawyer was aware of the murder thanks to media coverage in this town.

"That wasn't good," the lawyer continued, "but it could have been worse. Just let me know if you hear from them again, and I'm glad you informed me about this meeting."

"Me, too." A thought came to Kyle. "And look. I'm kind of friends with K-9 Officer Maisie Murran as we both have a relationship with the Chance Animal Shelter. I'm sure I'll still be talking to her some of the time, and I won't call you in on those conversations."

Mark's expression grew stern. "I understand, but I hope you'll back off and get in touch with me if at any time they turn accusatory or if she tries to get you to admit anything."

"I will, of course," Kyle said. He then thanked his lawyer, who'd definitely been helpful.

But Kyle hoped he'd never need to call him in again.

Mark took off in the direction of most of the town's major office buildings, while Kyle headed a block away to his car.

He felt relieved. He was still free. At least for now.

Had Detective Vanderhoff finally conceded, after their discussion, that Kyle wasn't really a viable suspect? Kyle doubted it, considering the questions he'd been asked—some more than once. Did he hate Greta? Did he threaten her? What had he really intended to do to get her to finally hand those dogs over to a rescue organization in accordance with law? And more.

So what if he hadn't given the answers Vince undoubtedly hoped for out of a suspect, not before or now? He was still on their list, at least as a person of interest—but maybe not at the very top of it.

Who knew?

And Kyle realized that, if nothing else, that interview, with his counsel present, had made him even more uneasy than he'd been before.

Other people walked by him as he slowed on the sidewalk looking for Maisie and Griffin. Which was also foolish. If they even were around, they were probably somewhere within the station. That was where Maisie worked. She was a cop. She had answered questions about him honestly, yes, but without asserting his innocence. So why did he want to spend any time with her, when he remained on the cops' radar as a possible killer?

Maybe because he had the sense he still wasn't on her radar that way. Or was she just a skilled manipulator, pretending she would try to help clear him but instead get him to confess?

It was somewhat warm outside for November—or was the heat radiating from inside him, from his anger at not being believed, as well as his deep discomfort at still apparently being considered a major murder suspect, perhaps by Maisie as well as by Detective Vanderhoff?

He had whispered to Maisie he wanted to talk to her, which was true. Even though he wasn't sure what he could and would say to her if they had an opportunity to talk.

She clearly was aware he'd been the object of the detective's inquiry even before she'd joined them.

But all Vanderhoff had asked Maisie was whether she'd heard Kyle threatening anyone. And she had told the truth. She definitely hadn't heard Kyle threatening Greta physically, of course, but with the possibility of doing something—yes, turning her over to authorities would work—for violating the California law that didn't permit pet stores to sell dogs, only to display some available for adoption from shelters or rescues.

Which Greta had seemed to be obeying, with something else in mind. Had she been working on ways to skirt that law? Had she been doing something with her supposedly discounted products to derive profits in an inappropriate way?

Even if she had, that wouldn't make Kyle want to kill her, just stop her and help the dogs.

He'd reached his car. Time to hurry to the clinic and get to work saving animals' lives.

But would he be a good veterinarian today? His hands were shaking, if only a little, but depending on the circumstances that could be deadly for a patient.

He had an idea, though—assuming there were no emergencies awaiting him at the clinic.

And if he followed through with it, he just might wind up seeing Maisie again today and couldn't convince himself that was a bad idea, even without knowing for certain what was on her mind as far as his being a possible killer.

He got into his car and began driving slowly and carefully. He was a good driver anyway, and his shaking had mostly stopped now that he'd left the police station behind, but this was certainly no time to get into an accident and hurt someone…and what, if anything, was left of his reputation as a good citizen.

The clinic wasn't far from the civic center, where the police station was located. But he didn't head there yet.

He waited as patiently as he could behind a small line of cars till the light ahead changed to green, then turned a corner and drove until he passed the Best Chance Pet Store.

It appeared open despite part of it being a crime scene. At least, he saw lights on inside through the display windows in the front.

So who was inside? Just cops, or were there any customers—curious ones, wanting to know more about the murder that had occurred in the back room? Or genuine ones seeking food, treats, toys or other things for their pets?

If so, who was waiting on them? Esther, Kyle assumed. And the store's employees, including Beth, who'd been interested in the shelter, and the other two he'd met briefly, Cora and Stan. Some or all of them?

Kyle would love the opportunity to talk to them, get the opinions of each about who had had it in for their boss Greta. Would they point fingers at one another?

Was one of them the murderer? Or could it be someone else altogether who'd been in Greta's life that Kyle didn't know about?

Kyle hated not being able to act on ideas, especially one as important as this. But he couldn't exactly dash out of the car and confront one or more of the people in the store.

With a sigh, he headed toward the clinic. And when he arrived, he was glad to learn that things were fairly quiet.

At receptionist Jada's request, he planted himself in one of the exam rooms and gave a large Great Dane named Big Boy a checkup and some shots, then examined a couple of sibling cats who had both been fixed a week ago and the owner wanted to make sure they were healing well. Fortunately, they were.

But there were only a few more appointments scheduled that afternoon that hadn't yet been assigned to one of the vets, nor had any emergencies come in.

That meant Kyle could probably leave now and let the remaining doctors take on those appointments. He could therefore take the other two dogs, Fido and Toby, back to the shelter, since they'd both been found healthy and neutered and Scott had agreed to their return.

Just in case it was a problem, he asked Dr. Martin and Dr. Nerez if he could go. They were both fine with Kyle's leaving early for the happy purpose of letting the shelter help to find new homes for those poor dogs.

Pedro sounded as if he knew some of what else was going on in Kyle's life, though, and before Kyle could leave his office, Pedro stood, hands thrust into the pockets of his white lab jacket, and regarded Kyle with troubled brown eyes. "You okay?" He walked over to face Kyle as he stood near the door. "And...well, will you stay out of trouble so we can count on your being here when we need you?"

"You can be sure I'll do everything I can to remain out of jail."

"It is that bad, then? I wasn't sure."

"Yes, it is," Kyle said. He told Pedro he was considered a potential suspect in the death of the pet-store owner because he'd been arguing with her about breaking the law regarding what dogs could be sold in her shop.

"But I didn't do it," he finished. "And I'm not under arrest, just under suspicion. Hopefully they'll find the guilty person soon."

"Yeah, I certainly hope so—for your sake and for ours." Pedro's deep-toned Hispanic features modified into a sort of smile, and Kyle, sticking out his hand to shake his boss's, attempted to smile back.

As Kyle then headed into the back area where animals were held pending their being well enough to go home, he called Scott and confirmed that bringing the dogs in question to the shelter now was fine with him.

Kyle then took Fido and Toby out of their enclosures one at a time and conducted a brief follow-up exam, checking their hearts, ears, teeth and standard body parts that sometimes indicated when a dog wasn't well. All still seemed fine, fortunately.

Then, for the heck of it, Kyle called Maisie to see if she'd be able to help by driving one of the dogs back to the shelter. It wasn't necessary, since they got along fine together in his back seat, but it gave him an excuse to be in touch with the K-9 cop.

He'd already told her he wanted to talk with her, after all.

"I'm just finishing a couple of reports," she told him. "I can be at your clinic to help in about forty-five minutes, if that will work."

"Definitely." That allowed Kyle to tell Jada that, notwithstanding what he'd said earlier, he could take on one or two of those remaining scheduled patients with only short exams pending that day.

He saw one of those patients, a rottweiler mix who was there for a general checkup. Kyle conducted a normal exam and gave the dog a couple of vaccinations that were due. All seemed fine.

But when Kyle returned to the reception area to confirm with Jada that he was ready for his next patient, she had an odd, distant expression on her face. "Dr. Nerez wants to see you in his office right now," she said.

"Sure." But what was that about? Of course, he would find out.

He walked down the hall where the offices were located and knocked on the door of the last one on the right.

He immediately heard "Come in."

Kyle entered and closed the door behind him, figuring that whatever they talked about, it wouldn't be good for anyone to overhear.

The senior vet was standing behind his wide metal desk, hands again thrust into the pockets of his lab jacket, and regarding Kyle with troubled brown eyes. Pedro's dark eyes suggested he was anything but happy. "Sit down, Kyle," he said.

His tone and appearance suggested to Kyle that he might be ready to fire him. But they'd already discussed the fact that Kyle was a murder suspect. Surely, that wasn't an issue now.

Kyle made himself smile as he did as Pedro directed and planted himself in one of the chairs facing this boss's desk. He hoped he appeared happier than Pedro. "It's been a busy day," he said to start what he hoped would just be a pleasant conversation but suspected would not be the case. Pedro clearly had something on his mind.

"Yes," Pedro said, "it has. And—well, I'd better get right to the point. I understand what you said before, that you weren't responsible for the death of Greta. Yes, I knew that pet-store owner, but not well. And I've no reason to believe you're anything but innocent." His expression seemed to harden, and Kyle immediately wondered if something had happened to cause Pedro to doubt that was true.

And it had.

"The thing is," Pedro continued, "we've been receiving communications from several media sources saying they'd like to interview Ernest and me about your continuing to work here as a veterinarian."

So the other senior vet, Ernest Martin, was involved, too? Why wasn't he here? But Kyle was just as glad Ernest wasn't with them. He felt certain it would be hard enough to hold this discussion with Pedro.

"I assume you told them no interviews," Kyle responded, hoping that was the case.

"Of course. But, of course media, online and otherwise, want to report on stories they consider nice and juicy, and a murder certainly can fit into that category.

We're mostly just trying to ignore them, but a couple said that some of their readers or watchers or whatever have been urging them to learn more and report it, since you appear to be a person of interest. And, supposedly, at least one person bugging the media said they are owners of patients of ours and are very concerned about what might happen next if you're allowed to continue working here."

"Why, they think I'll murder a dog or cat next?" Kyle attempted to sound sarcastic, but his insides were churning. "Did those media folks tell you which owners they're referring to? Maybe we could talk to them. I could reassure them."

Pedro leaned over his desk closer to Kyle, his arms crossed and his eyebrows pressed toward each other. "I did inquire a bit, but no names were given—unsurprisingly. The reporters undoubtedly figured we'd contact whoever they were and give them a hard time—potentially a really hard time."

Kyle closed his eyes in pain. "They thought I'd go murder those sources, too."

"Maybe, maybe not, but they clearly weren't taking any chances."

Kyle thought he knew what was coming next and jumped right on it, despite how hard it was. "Would you like me to take a hiatus, not come to the clinic for a little while?" Or was Pedro about to fire him altogether?

If so, he could still work in the shelter's clinic, right?

Or had Scott also been contacted by the media?

"Well, yeah, I'd like that. Ernest would, too. We discussed it."

Kyle clenched his fists in his lap but refused to allow any emotions to show. "All right, then—"

"Let me finish," Pedro interrupted. "Sure, we'd like it, under the circumstances. But we'd also hate it. You've been here long enough for us to like and respect you as a skilled vet. And from the little we've learned from the media, and from you, we just can't believe you actually did it. If you want to continue working here, acting as your usual self and living your life as if you weren't a murder suspect, then that's what we'll do. Unless you want to leave."

"Leave? No. Oh, no." Kyle stood. "I love what I'm doing here and want to stay. And I certainly don't want to appear guilty by changing anything in my life I don't have to." He leaned over and held out his hand to Pedro. "Thank you so much. And thank Ernest, too, when you see him. I certainly will." They shook hands, and this time Kyle's grin was genuine. "Guess my day is over for now, but I will definitely see you tomorrow." He turned to leave, then pivoted back. "And let me repeat what I said before. I might not have liked that pet-store owner, but I definitely didn't kill her."

He left the office then as quickly as he could, concerned on some level that Pedro would change his mind. He looked at his watch.

It was five o'clock, about the time Maisie had said she could be there. Kyle hurried to his office and changed out of his scrubs. Sure enough, when he walked into the waiting room, there she was with Griffin.

He had to turn his mind in a different direction from

where it had been. Maisie was there for a reason, one he had requested that she participate in.

He had to act normal around her, as if the conversation with Pedro had never happened at all, as if his job here hadn't been in jeopardy. Wasn't still in jeopardy if things turned in the wrong direction.

"Hi," he said immediately, forcing brightness into his tone. "Are you and Griffin prepared to take one of the healthy rescue dogs to the shelter for eventual rehoming?"

Maisie stood and cocked her head so her short blond hair moved a little. "Will Esther want to bring them back to display in the store for potential adoption, the way Greta wanted?"

"She hasn't said anything about it, so I'm hoping not." And he certainly didn't want to deal with that kind of situation again. Not if he could help it.

He had enough to deal with.

"Great. Let's do it! Although, are you feeling okay?" Maisie looked concerned, even though he had tried hard not to allow his difficult mood to show. "I know it's got to be hard to be considered a murder suspect, and you seem upset. Should you be dealing with the dogs right now?"

"Absolutely," he said in a brusque tone he immediately regretted. "Now, let's go."

Maisie had Toby the Australian shepherd with Griffin in the back seat of her police SUV as they drove up the hill to the shelter. It was probably just as well that Kyle and she drove separately, she thought. Otherwise, she might be lobbing all kinds of questions at him about what he was thinking. What his mood was really about.

Whether he actually was guilty and having a hard time keeping quiet about it.

Maybe his mood was a result of his latest interview by Vince. She knew Vince still considered Kyle a prime suspect in Greta's murder, since no one else had been taken into custody. But why did he call Kyle in today and ask Maisie questions, too?

Kyle wouldn't know the answer as Vince would hardly have enlightened him. But Maisie might be able to figure out Vince's motive if she had an opportunity to quiz Kyle about what the detective had asked him when she wasn't there, in what order and with what intensity.

Or maybe, at some point, she could find a tactful way to quiz Vince more about it, although he probably wouldn't reveal much.

In any case, her assumption was that this was just part of the investigation and interrogation process.

Or had someone else come forward with evidence, or at least allegations, against the veterinarian who'd wanted things done on the up-and-up at the store regarding displaying shelter dogs there for adoption—or not?

Or had Vince tossed away the possibility of any of the others he'd questioned as being Greta's likely killer? Had no one been obvious? Had anyone seemed at all likely?

Was the list now narrowing down to only one possibility, Kyle?

If so, the investigation hadn't gone well so far. There

had to be others out there who weren't obvious if Vince had eliminated all the other likely candidates.

Or... Well, she was just speculating on the rationale for Vince's focus today on Kyle.

And whatever it was, she still wasn't ready to assume Kyle was guilty.

She wondered, though, if there was some other reason besides his interrogation by Vince that had made Kyle seem so gruff and difficult today since they'd been together. Of course, being accused of murder would hardly put someone in a good mood. But that same difficult mood would make it hard for her to ask Kyle if there was anything else bothering him. She would just have to act as if everything was normal.

She'd try, at least.

The narrow road was almost empty except for Kyle's car and hers. They reached the parking area for the shelter fairly quickly. Maisie parked beside Kyle and got the leashed dogs out of her back seat, as he did the same with Fido.

Then all of them entered the reception room at the shelter.

"Do any of the managers know we're here?" Maisie asked Kyle as they sat on a couple of chairs and got the dogs to sit on the floor near them.

"Scott knew I was coming. I'll call him now and let him know we've arrived."

Which he did, and they waited there with the dogs even though Maisie knew Kyle had a keycard. It was Nella who showed up at the entry room a few minutes later. "Two new residents!" she exclaimed as Maisie and Kyle—and the dogs, too—rose to greet her. "Ones who've had excellent health screenings, I understand, thanks to you, Kyle." She of course wore one of the Chance shelter T-shirts, a green one this time, with *Manager* by the logo.

Maisie liked her—especially her attitude not only toward the staff members in protective custody but also toward the animals awaiting their new forever homes.

"Well, they've both passed health checks, they've been neutered, and they don't have microchips. So, yes, they've been screened." Kyle, somehow appearing less stressed than previously, smiled at the shelter manager, who nodded as she smiled back and reached for one of the leashes—Fido's.

"Okay," Nella said. "Let's go upstairs to the main office, and I'll get their info into the computer. Then we can take them to the back and start introducing them to their new home and the others—people and pups—who live here, although I gather they've already met Snowy."

"That's right," Kyle said.

Maisie was glad the process didn't take long, even though she and Kyle wound up sitting across the desk from Nella for a few minutes as she asked questions and entered data into her computer. Of course Griffin remained quietly at her feet, along with the two other dogs. From his downtown clinic, Kyle had already emailed some of the new information Nella said they needed, but she also wanted a few more items about what, if anything, was known about the dogs' backgrounds, and how long they'd been in the veterinary clinic's care.

Their backgrounds? Kyle didn't waffle about that. "Like Snowy, they were dumped at different times at the Best Chance Pet Store, as far as I know. I think you're aware that Greta, the recently deceased half-owner, encouraged those kinds of drop-offs and tried to develop relationships with shelters so she could display the dogs at her shop to draw customers in but have the shelters adopt out the dogs, all in compliance with California law."

"I heard about that." Nella paused, then said, "And I also heard you argued with her about how she was doing things."

"And I was so mad I killed her—or so I assume you heard, too, even though that's absolutely wrong. I didn't like her, but I definitely didn't hurt her."

Maisie felt herself tense up at Kyle's apparent confession that he immediately retracted. She felt somehow that she had to stick up for Kyle, explain what he said or meant. "I did hear Kyle and Greta disagreeing on what she was doing," she said. "But even though I gathered Kyle was rather perturbed, he made suggestions to her about how the store could comply with the law and treat the dogs kindly by finding them appropriate shelters and leaving them there."

She believed she saw a hint of gratitude in Kyle's expression. And more? Well, she wasn't going to dwell on her possibly absurd ideas.

"So did you reach any agreement?" Nella asked.

"Not really," Kyle said. "And it wasn't up to me to enforce anything." He glanced at Maisie as if that had been her duty.

Which it wasn't. But if she'd become aware Greta was somehow breaking the law, she would have dealt with it as a law-enforcement officer should, at least reporting it to her superiors.

Their discussion was soon finished. They walked back down the office building's steps to the ground floor, each holding a dog leash. She, of course, had Griffin's, Nella had Fido's, and Kyle Toby's.

Soon, they were in the outside area where some residents were already walking dogs, but a few dashed over to say hello. Nella introduced them to the new canine residents.

Bibi, of course, seemed thrilled. "Can I walk one of them now? Are they trained the way you do it?" She was looking at Maisie.

"I'm fine with your walking one," Maisie said. "And, no, I haven't had a chance to work with either of them, although you staff members know enough to start training them. Most of you are quite good at it."

Bibi grinned her usual gap-toothed smile as she got Fido's leash. The basset hound looked a little confused, but he immediately started walking at Bibi's side as she told him heel and started off in the direction of the far side of the outside area.

By then, a couple of others had joined them. Chessie got Toby's leash, trading the one she'd been holding with Kathy, who then had Spike at her side. Maisie was glad that, despite her slight figure, the senior staff member was clearly able to handle the German shepherd, who now seemed to be walking normally.

Maisie bent down to hug Spike gently, staying away

from the wound on his side. "You're okay, boy. I'm so glad." Griffin watched her but didn't react. He was one good dog—and well trained, of course. She was glad he was hardly limping now.

A few more staff members came over to meet the newcomers. Maisie was pleased to see how Kyle reacted, talking to each of them as well as asking about the dogs they walked. His mood had definitely changed from when she'd worried about it before. He clearly gave a damn about both staffers and dogs. He cared.

Did that mean he was incapable of killing someone who mistreated animals? Incapable, no. But his attitude convinced Maisie even more of his innocence.

Or was it just her desire that convinced her...both kinds of desire? She wanted him to be innocent.

Although, she hadn't really followed through on her idea of trying to find the actual perpetrator.

"Okay," she said, looking at Nella. "Looks as if you've got a lot of people who'll help get the three newcomers—including Snowy—ready for rehoming. That's the kind of diversion that works out well around here."

"That's for certain," Nella said. "And I hope you—" she looked then at Kyle "—both of you will come visit a lot and see how things are going, work with our staff members and these pups—and the rest."

"You know Griffin and I will continue to visit," Maisie said.

"And you also know I'll be here pretty much every day to care for your nonhuman residents' health," Kyle said. Maisie wondered at the vehemence of his tone.

Was there any question about his running the clinic here? She met his eye. He nodded and smiled slightly and added, "A cop and a vet at this kind of shelter? Good deal, isn't it?"

"I certainly think so," Nella said.

"Absolutely," Maisie agreed. Okay, it was time to go. To get away from this man whose attitude about nearly everything triggered her interest much too much, especially under these difficult circumstances.

It was getting a bit late, but Maisie nevertheless hoped to get a chance to talk to Vince at the station before she and Griffin headed home.

Then Kyle asked her to stop by the shelter's clinic for a minute. Why not? After saying goodbye to Nella—not any of the staff members since they were all walking their new or prior charges—Maisie headed in the direction of the shelter's reception building with the veterinarian.

"Nothing special for me to do in here," he said. "I just didn't feel right leaving without popping in. I like this place. But fortunately, I don't have any patients I needed to look in on."

"Great," Maisie said. "I like it, too." But she wondered why Kyle had said that, as if there might be some doubt.

For now, she looked around the small clinic, too, impressed as always with how efficient it appeared even without any patients present.

Kyle didn't stay long, and they soon walked out of the hall and into the reception room, which also was empty.

"Well," Maisie said, "maybe I'll see you tomorrow."

But why? Because he'd be in custody at the station? Hopefully, they'd just run into each other here.

But she couldn't help smiling at the vet's next words. "I'd like to talk to you more tonight. Will you join me for dinner?"

She only hesitated for an instant. "Sure," she said.

"Then, let's go to my apartment. I've got some food I can prepare pretty easily there."

Chapter 9

Was that a good idea? Probably not, Kyle thought. But though he wanted Maisie's company, at the moment he didn't particularly care to be out in public, especially not with a cop. Not that he was well known, but anyone who knew who he was, and the situation now surrounding him, might assume he was being brought in to be interrogated yet again, not just going for what hopefully would be an enjoyable dinner. And talking.

And if he got his way they'd discuss what he could do to help clear himself, assuming she'd make suggestions—which wouldn't be something he'd want eavesdroppers to hear, either.

Would he mention the threat to his job? Probably not. Pedro had already said he could stay on.

For now, at least.

But would Maisie have any ideas about how to deal with the media that had contacted the clinic and therefore endangered his position there? He'd have to ponder whether to ask her.

"I need to make a quick stop at the station first," Maisie said. "Just let me know where to go, and I'll call you when Griffin and I are on our way."

"Sure." He lived at an apartment complex in town, and he gave her the address and the unit's number.

For now, they went their separate ways. Kyle made a quick stop at the downtown clinic on his way home. It was getting late, around seven o'clock, and there wouldn't be any more appointments scheduled for that day. Even so, Kyle wanted to drop in there—partly to demonstrate to himself that he could.

He parked and went inside the waiting area, which remained open. The receptionist had gone home, so he used his key to get inside the clinic, where he greeted the couple of techs remaining on duty that night. Plus, he looked into the holding area to quickly check on the few animals secured in enclosures there for observation—a Weimaraner mix, a Chihuahua and a couple of cats.

Fortunately, things seemed quiet, with no emergencies pending. He wasn't the vet on call for that night anyway, though hopefully he would be again soon. But no need for him to remain this evening.

"See you tomorrow." He waved to a tech, Lena, as he walked back down the hall and went out to his car.

Good. He hadn't wanted any reason to call off his dinner with Maisie, but his patients—and job—came first.

Or maybe he had actually been looking for an excuse to cancel their get-together that night. Why? To avoid talking about that elephant—or cadaver—in the room, and who they each considered to be potential murder suspects…and why?

No. He needed to do that, especially now that he'd been interrogated again by Vince Vanderhoff. And his job had almost been jeopardized.

Now, since he was running a little later than anticipated, rather than play games with the frozen meals and other food he kept at his place, he stopped at a take-out restaurant and picked up a roast chicken with side dishes. Hopefully, Maisie would like that meal, and as long as they were careful with bones they could also give Griffin a chicken snack.

He soon parked in his usual spot. He had just entered his second-floor unit when his phone rang. As he hoped, it was Maisie.

"We're on our way," she said. "We should be there in about five minutes."

Then they really were on their way. Soon, Kyle, feeling more pleased than he should, walked downstairs to the parking lot to meet them and accompanied Maisie and Griffin up to his place.

He was amused to see she wasn't wearing her uniform—one of the few times he had seen her without it. She looked cute and relaxed and even more curvy than he was used to seeing her, in an outfit that included jeans and a familiar-looking Chance Animal Shelter T-shirt, a blue one. He'd already acquired a couple, too, but had decided not to change into one that night, continuing to wear his brown plaid button-down shirt.

She had brought a bottle of wine, a merlot. "Hope this is okay," she said. "I don't know what we're eating."

"I picked up a chicken dinner," he said. "I'm not a wine purist anyway, but I think a merlot will go fine with it."

He walked into his small but well-equipped kitchen, where he'd put the bag containing their dinner into the stainless-steel refrigerator. He took it out and placed it on the serving counter in the middle of the room, then washed his hands well, something that was his constant habit as a vet. Bringing out plates and flatware, he cut the chicken into pieces and placed spoons into the sides of salad, broccoli and mashed potatoes. They each served themselves and placed their plates, without salad yet, into his microwave oven.

Maisie's K-9 sat at her side, and the golden's nose was in the air, clearly aware that dinner was about to be served.

As things warmed, Kyle pulled his highly unfancy corkscrew from a drawer beside the sink, and when Maisie stuck out her hand he passed it to her. Then he got out some wine glasses and watched as she effortlessly removed the cork.

Soon, they were seated at his table across from one another, their warmed meals, salads and filled wineglasses in front of them.

"So," Maisie said after swallowing a bite, "what did you want to talk to me about?" The corners of her mouth turned up just a little, and her hazel eyes sparkled before she looked at her glass as she picked it up and took a sip.

What a lovely and engaging woman, Kyle thought. And teasing, of course.

"Oh, since you're a cop, I thought we could talk tonight about how I can commit my next murder in the slyest way possible."

Her expression hardened a little. Surely she didn't think he was serious.

"Sounds like an arresting idea." She took another sip of wine, which made him also take a sip. "First thing, though, I'd like all the details about your first murder. Assuming it was your first."

Her eyes gazed into his, and her hardened appearance suggested she was serious.

Which worried him. A lot.

"Okay, enough of this teasing," he said. "I didn't kill Greta Styles, or anyone else for that matter. And I believe you know I wouldn't have harmed that shop owner, even though she clearly wasn't my favorite person in the world. You surely wouldn't have joined me for dinner if you thought I was a murderer."

Maisie leaned over the table toward him, just a little. "Okay, Kyle." Her expression was somber. "I want to believe you and probably do." She cocked her head just a little, causing her short blond hair to bob a bit, and frowned as she looked into his eyes. "Would you like to hear about the discussion with Detective Vince Vanderhoff I had just before Griffin and I headed here?"

Conversing about it would be fine. As Maisie, sitting across from Vince in his office, had finished chatting with him before about his earlier interrogation of

Kyle, she had asked the detective if it was okay to discuss this with the suspect and be forthright about it. Let him know that she'd talked with Vince, and that anything he did or didn't admit to her would be relayed to the detective.

A good way to conduct an investigation?

"Maybe not," Vince had said, "but I know you're buddies with the guy." He'd looked at her then through his glasses in an inquisitive way. "More? Don't answer that. I probably won't believe you anyway." His smile showed his teeth and then vanished. "And yeah, you can talk to him about this."

Vince had told her that he had questioned Kyle this time as if it was the first, partly because he'd had long sessions by then also with the victim's business partner and their employees.

None had admitted any major issues with Greta, though they'd worried a bit about Greta's encouraging people to dump strays at their store so she could find a shelter to take them in, as well as the sales discount she was giving to people who adopted rescue animals that they had first been introduced to at the store. It had been sizable, but she had also insisted the adopters commit to buying a minimum amount of merchandise for their new pet as part of the adoption. Her partner and employees had been concerned. Was this backdoor way of making money legal? Some had even argued with her about it—and other things. But kill her for it? Of course not. And did any of them suspect someone else who worked there? Also no way.

Who, then, did they believe did it?

Surprise! It had been Kyle for all of them.

Maisie wasn't sure whether she'd relate that to the vet now. But she would ask him a few questions herself, probably duplicating what the detective had done at least once. She pondered them all as she'd hurried home to change clothes.

The meal Kyle had bought was tasty. It tasted even better, under the circumstances of their current discussion, with the wine she'd bought.

And Maisie kept looking down at the wonderful K-9 on the floor beside her when she didn't want to meet Kyle's gaze.

But she did, in fact, ask the questions that had been on her mind, getting the answers she anticipated and had sometimes heard before—and wanting very much to believe them.

"So did the games Greta was playing before she was killed irritate you? Like taking in poor Snowy while the disagreement was going on?"

"Of course they did." Kyle didn't seem upset by the question. He took a bite of chicken. "And I felt that irritation when I went to see Greta and whatever new dog had been dumped at her store. But…" He looked at Maisie, and his expression had changed into one filled with pain. "When I got there, she was already dead." He shook his head. "At least I was able to help Snowy and the other dogs."

"Yes," Maisie agreed, "you were." She liked his attitude. And hoped his answers were true.

Was this entirely professional on her part? Most

likely not. But she'd already told a superior on the force what she was up to, and he hadn't discouraged her.

And she probably wouldn't have anything useful to report to Vince when she was through here. This was just a conversation, after all. She wasn't really interrogating Kyle, just talking with him about something on both their minds.

Had it been a real interrogation, she'd have had to suggest he bring his attorney in. But she wasn't authorized to subject him to a genuine interrogation, anyway.

She continued by asking Kyle questions regarding what he knew about animals, primarily dogs, who were sold in stores elsewhere in the country. She was well aware that many were purebreds but were bred in puppy mills that didn't give a damn about their health.

She asked what he thought about the California law. He liked it, since now the only dogs available in stores were adopted out by shelters, which did give a damn about their health and backgrounds.

Then she got to the important stuff again. Watching his good-looking, if sad, face, she got Kyle to give a narrative of how he'd first met Greta, learned of her underhandedness, faced her down and even threatened her—though, not with anything physical.

Stuff she'd heard before. No inconsistencies on his part. She believed he was telling the truth as he knew it—or was doing a damned good job of fooling her.

"So here we are," she said when he had finished. "I assume you still don't admit to killing her."

His glare seemed to slice right through her, but though she flinched, she also appreciated it.

He definitely seemed sincere.

"I don't admit to it because I didn't do it," he said through gritted teeth.

"Got it." She grinned at him. "I can't completely clear you because you told me you're innocent, but I can convey the crux of our conversation to appropriate people in my police department. And I can also let them know that nothing you said or did causes me to disbelieve you."

"Really?" His tone was both bright and relieved. "I'm glad to hear that." He reached his hand across the table toward her. His palm was anything but smooth, but of course the man was a veterinarian and had to help animals by using his hands as well as his intelligence and medical equipment.

Hands that helped animals...

Hands that she suddenly—or not so suddenly— wanted to feel on herself.

She stood then, as did he.

In moments, they were in each other's arms. Kissing. His mouth on hers was hot, very hot. And searching. His body pressed against her was hard, muscular, more sexy than any other man she had ever been with. Especially when she felt his erection against her middle, large and rigid and really, really enticing.

What was she doing?

"Would you like to see my bedroom?" Kyle whispered against her lips.

Yes was the answer that shouted inside her.

But she knew better. This was all wrong. She cared

for Kyle. Was attracted to him. Wanted to have sex with him.

But she was a cop. Despite her wanting to believe—believing—in his innocence, he was still a major suspect in a murder. And until he was officially cleared, she simply couldn't go that far with him.

See him, yes. Talk with him, yes. Because while they were together, he could theoretically say something that would lead to his conviction, if he was guilty.

That could remain her justification for being in Kyle's presence for now.

But going that far? There could be no justification for it.

Not now.

Time to put an end to this before there was no turning back.

"I assume, since you seem to be thinking so much about it, the answer is no," Kyle said.

"I… You're right," she finally conceded. "I wish—"

"I wish, too," Kyle whispered as he again pulled her into his arms. His body was clearly ready to take her to bed. She felt his hardness, and it made it all the more difficult for her to maintain this correct decision. Still… it was the appropriate one.

She felt Kyle's lips on her ear as he said, "Maybe you're the one who'll kill me." And then he let her go.

Chapter 10

Okay, Kyle thought as he released Maisie and walked back to his place at the table. He sat down, grabbed his glass and took a deep sip of wine. He understood what she said.

But he wanted more.

Somehow, he had to convince this sexy but dedicated cop that he really was innocent. And of course she wasn't the only one he had to convince, but she was the one who mattered most.

She sat back down across from him. "That wasn't the reason you invited me here for dinner," she said, looking beautiful as she cocked her head and regarded him closely, then took another sip of wine, too. "Right?"

"Of course not," he said. "It was just—well, it could have been a fun benefit of getting together tonight."

He watched as Griffin came over to Maisie's side of the table and stuck his head on her lap. "Down, Griffin," she said. "You'll get a treat later." Of course the impressive K-9 immediately obeyed. Maisie looked back at Kyle, her chin up, her expression appearing bemused as she stared at him with her lovely hazel eyes. "So why did you invite me here?"

He laughed. "To talk to you. To get your advice. And why did you come?"

"To get you talking to see if you said anything at all that suggested you could be guilty and therefore change my mind about you. And if I was wrong, to catch you with your guard down...although an attempt at seduction by you had crossed my mind."

"My attempt at seduction? Well, for a few moments there it seemed mutual." He paused as she laughed. Good. She might have backed off, but she hadn't backed away completely.

For now, she lifted her glass again. It was empty. He wasn't surprised when she said, "I'd love another glass of wine."

"Sounds good to me, too."

He stood and picked the bottle up from the table, then went behind Maisie to pour more into her glass—placing his hand gently on her shoulder as he leaned over to do so. He felt her tense up, then relax.

Maybe he shouldn't touch her at all. Did it freak her out?

He removed his hand and walked quickly away, then went to his pantry where he extracted a healthy dog treat for Griffin. He was a veterinarian, after all, and kept some supplies like that in his home. Besides, he had planned, once he'd settled down in his two jobs, to adopt a shelter dog of his own. But he had put that idea on hold for now.

"So," he said as he returned to his seat and placed his glass back on the table. Time to talk—again. "Look, I'm not guilty—and I'm not just saying that to get you into bed now or ever, although I still like the thought..."

"I understand," she said, "but—"

"You need to tell me more about how I can convince you. I have my own point of view as a former cop but need your advice. How do I get the others in your department to work harder at finding who really did do it, since it wasn't me? That way, maybe you'll be convinced, too."

"I can't really advise you on that. Even if I knew what to tell you to say, and who to have you tell it to, I might jeopardize my job if I did so. And actually, convincing someone there to dig deeper like that is my responsibility, not yours. Or, I could just work harder. I'm not officially on your case, but I'd like to look more into other possible suspects, like store employees, Greta's ex-husbands, and maybe someone at the shelter where she used to bring strays. And if you have any more ideas, please let me know. Although, with my actual job, it will take me a while to get more into this."

"Of course." But even if she found the time, he might be arrested before she got anywhere.

Still, Kyle appreciated how frustrated Maisie looked. Good. Of course it might be a little sexual frustration— he hoped—but most likely professional, he figured. And she was right, at least to some extent. She was the cop, not him—not anymore. If he acted too nosy with her fellow cops, maybe the higher-ranking officers would assume he was trying to pin the murder that he committed—ha!—on someone innocent.

Even so...

"Thanks," he told Maisie, "but I can't let you do it all."

And could he trust her to do it, anyway? Well, he thought so. But...

"But I'm the cop here," she said, as if reminding him yet again. "And I think what I'm going to do first is try to get to know some of the other likely suspects better, the people at Greta's shop."

"I can do that, too. Since I'm a veterinarian, it won't be out of line for me to pop in there and buy more supplies—food and treats and whatever. And chat with them while I'm there. Express my sympathy for their loss and all."

Maisie took a sip of her wine, appearing somewhat pensive. "We'll need to be careful, probably not go there together. At least, not often. But it wouldn't hurt for you to check and see if they're still accepting dropped-off dogs even without Greta, in her memory. Then if they are, you can take those dogs in for exams and support the people who're doing the right, legal thing and seeking a shelter to take them in. I can do that, too, of course, but I'll also be able to go there to buy supplies for Griffin, as I have before, and maybe ask questions about how they're all doing...and oh, by the way, have they had any further thoughts on who killed Greta? After all, I'm a cop, so it won't be surprising if I appear to be attempting to solve the crime. They won't necessarily know that the crime committed there isn't a focus of my job—especially since Griffin and I were called in for that K-9 check at the scene."

Kyle couldn't help grinning. "We'll each conduct our own separate little investigation."

"As long as you're not too obvious, and you're careful. Then, as long as it doesn't feel inappropriate to me professionally, we can potentially discuss what we've found when we're both at the shelter or meet each other elsewhere." Her gaze landed on the doorway to the rest of his apartment, but she drew it quickly away.

Kyle felt his body react but tamped it back down. "Sounds good," he agreed. But he had been thinking all along about his other problem: the possibility of losing his job. There wasn't anything Maisie could do about that, although it would go away once he was cleared. That meant timing was important, too. And so he took a deep breath and said, "By the way, there's something else that's bothering me. A lot. And it's related to the suspicions against me."

"What's that?" Maisie asked. She held her glass but leaned slightly forward across the table toward him.

"I might lose my job because of this situation." He related to her his conversation with Pedro, whom he described as one of the lead vets at his clinic and had the power to fire him. "He didn't fire me, not yet, at least. But what he was told by several different media sources might lead to it. Apparently they were contacted by the owners of some of our patients who expressed concern about having a murder suspect as their vet. Not surpris-

ing, although even if I killed a person—which I didn't—
I still could take good care of their pets." Kyle didn't
mention that he hadn't yet updated his lawyer Mark,
which he wouldn't, unless he did get fired.

"The murder's been reported in various media
sources already, of course," Maisie said. "I haven't seen
anything against your skills as a veterinarian, though I
have seen allegations that you're the killer."

"My bosses may have been concerned that just having me named as a suspect might have meant the loss
of some of our clientele, and they're especially worried now after being contacted by the media like that."

Maisie was frowning. "Did they tell you which
media, at least?"

"No, but I gather they did attempt to learn from those
reporters the names of people who had been in contact
with them, so they could get in touch and alleviate their
concerns. But the media folks, whoever they were, refused to name their sources. To protect them from me
was the implication."

"I see." Maisie appeared thoughtful. "I can ask the
officers in my department who handle media contacts
to look into it, but of course I can't promise anything."

"I understand. But I'd appreciate your trying. And
for now…well, I hate the idea that there'll possibly be a
lot more reporting against me, especially where everyone can see it and judge me despite no evidence." Kyle
smiled slightly at that, and Maisie raised her blond eyebrows in amusement.

"I get it. And I hope we can find the real killer soon

and alleviate all of this as soon as possible. Assuming, of course—"

"Assuming, of course," Kyle interrupted, "that I'm innocent. Which I am." He stared at her as if his eyes could bore the truth into her.

But she didn't say anything in response.

Maisie felt sorry about this additional issue of Kyle's. But it certainly wasn't as significant as his being a murder suspect.

They were related, of course. If he was cleared of the homicide, he wouldn't have to worry about his job. At least, not for that reason.

But she wasn't going to get involved with trying to get the media to leave him alone. And she really doubted those connected with the Chance PD who dealt with the media would take this on, either.

So the best she could do in regards to this job issue was to help determine who the real killer was.

If it did turn out to be Kyle, he'd lose his vet job anyway, the least of his problems.

She would have loved to have stayed at Kyle's longer that evening. But the temptation to join him in bed hadn't gone away, even though she had acted appropriately.

She simply couldn't hang out here.

Besides, if someone saw Griffin and her here for a limited time, that could easily be explained as sharing a meal. But the longer she stayed, even though she could claim they'd had a lot to talk about at dinner, the

"Ditto. It's certainly a lot more interesting than most law-enforcement stuff that's been going on in town recently."

"Right," Maisie said, rolling her eyes. That was a good thing. Chance, California, had had its share of difficult situations in the past year or so, but even though Doug and Hooper, and Doug's girlfriend Elissa, plus her golden retriever therapy dog Peace, had had some involvement with one in particular, she and Griffin hadn't had much beyond her usual K-9 cop duties, although they had spent a lot of time patrolling the shelter's neighborhood when there'd been some issues regarding Scott and Nella a few months ago. But she certainly hadn't wished for this additional situation.

Sure, she was happy keeping an eye on the Chance Animal Shelter and its very special residents to ensure they remained safe. But her handling only appropriate situations for K-9 officers was certainly best for the town—and for Griffin and her.

An unsolved homicide? Not her favorite project to get involved in. But she certainly was involved, despite it not being her assignment.

She and Doug hung up, and Maisie walked Griffin around the yard before they entered the house. Later, she watched TV and saw a talent show and a newsmagazine show that featured the kidnapping of a child who was ultimately found alive and physically unharmed.

She regretted watching the latter. Not quite what she was involved with, but it would have been better to continue viewing completely upbeat shows.

She had no trouble falling asleep, although lying

alone in her own bed caused her to recall what she'd been tempted to do earlier.

When she awoke the next morning, that was also the first thing on her mind. She forced it away. Nothing had happened. But thinking of Kyle, as she did much too often, reminded her of at least one thing she wanted to accomplish that day.

Before she headed to the shelter that afternoon, if all went well.

First, though, she went into the small den she used as an office and booted up her computer. Maisie wasn't addicted to computers the way some of her colleagues were when they weren't on duty. Even so, she wanted to look up a few things relating to Greta's murder, including what the media had said about it since the last time she had looked, the day after the murder, when it appeared to be the primary feature in many sources and speculation was rampant.

Now, a number of those sources and others mentioned—or even featured—Kyle as the main suspect. Nothing seemed to indicate, though, that the owners of any of his veterinary patients had expressed concern about the care of their animals.

But maybe that was to come, given what Kyle had learned from his bosses at the vet clinic. She would try to keep up with that.

She printed a few pages that discussed the murder in a way that didn't seem as lurid as the rest. She also printed others that focused on Greta and her background.

Then it was time to go to work.

She and Griffin were given a couple of assignments when they arrived at the station early, one just hanging around that school again during the time kids arrived and during recess, since the faculty remained a bit concerned about nasty emails the facility had previously received.

Then there was a brief stint at a clothing store that had suffered a theft this time, and Griffin smelled the cash register the thief had touched and easily found the guy down the street at a gas station. Dumb guy; smart dog.

Then they were through for the morning. Kind of.

Maisie knew where to go before having lunch. Back to the station, briefly. She wanted to touch base with her fellow cop who was the murder vic's nephew, Jackson Styles. He hadn't been there when she'd gotten to the station that morning or before she'd left on her assignments. She wanted to talk with him but hoped for it to look spontaneous, not planned, so she'd see if he was there now.

And though he of course had known his aunt, he wasn't a true suspect, but Maisie kept him on her mental list, anyway.

She drove there quickly, parked, and she and Griffin went inside.

No Jackson in the reception area, although a few cops hung out there, a couple talking with citizens who'd come to the station for whatever reason.

Next stop was upstairs in the main room where officers often hung out while at the station between assignments. They all had offices like she and Doug did, although some were larger and contained a bunch of desks. But her fellow officers tended to like to hang out with each other here and grab some coffee and conversation, both serious and often joking to lighten the stress of being a cop.

Sure enough, Officer Jackson Styles just happened to be there, coffee cup in his hand, as he stood on the periphery of a group of his fellow officers, both male and female. He seemed to be listening, and Maisie didn't see him jump into the discussion. She didn't know what was going on in his mind, especially without talking with him, but he appeared to be there maybe to avoid being alone...

Okay, she was making assumptions. But she hopefully could find out his mindset easily enough.

Griffin at her side, she approached Jackson. "Hi," she said softly, looking up into his face, which didn't show any emotions. "Have a minute? I'd like to speak with you."

"Sure."

Maisie didn't catch any enthusiasm in his response, but at least it had been positive. Plus, he followed Griffin and her past the crowd out the door.

She found a spot down the wide, empty hallway near a closed office door. Was someone inside? She didn't know, but she wouldn't speak loudly.

"What's up?" Jackson asked, again not sounding particularly enthused.

"I just wanted to touch base with you about your aunt. I know the situation is difficult for you, especially—"

"Especially because there've been no arrests yet,"

Get ready to relax and indulge with your FREE BOOKS and more!

**Claim up to FOUR NEW BOOKS & TWO MYSTERY GIFTS –
absolutely FREE!**

Dear Reader,

We both know life can be difficult at times. That's why it's important to treat yourself so you can relax and recharge once in a while.

And I'd like to help you do this by sending you this amazing offer of up to FOUR brand new full length FREE BOOKS that WE pay for.

This is everything I have ready to send to you right now:

Try **Harlequin® Romantic Suspense** books featuring heart-racing page-turners with unexpected plot twists and irresistible chemistry that will keep you guessing to the very end.

Try **Harlequin Intrigue® Larger-Print** books featuring action-packed stories that will keep you on the edge of your seat. Solve the crime and deliver justice at all costs.

Or **TRY BOTH!**

All we ask in return is that you answer 4 simple questions on the attached Treat Yourself survey. You'll get **Two Free Books** and **Two Mystery Gifts** from each series you try, *altogether worth over $20!* Who could pass up a deal like that?

Sincerely,

Pam Powers

Harlequin Reader Service

Treat Yourself to Free Books and Free Gifts.

Answer 4 fun questions and get rewarded.

▲ DETACH AND MAIL CARD TODAY!

	YES	NO
1. I LOVE reading a good book.		
2. I indulge and "treat" myself often.		
3. I love getting FREE things.		
4. Reading is one of my favorite activities.		

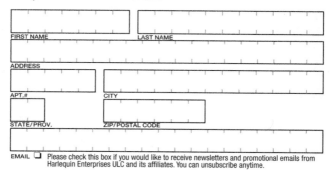

TREAT YOURSELF • Pick your 2 Free Books...

Yes! Please send me my Free Books from each series I select and Free Mystery Gifts. I understand that I am under no obligation to buy anything, as explained on the back of this card.

Which do you prefer?

❏ **Harlequin® Romantic Suspense** 240/340 HDL GRCZ

❏ **Harlequin Intrigue® Larger-Print** 199/399 HDL GRCZ

❏ **Try Both** 240/340 & 199/399 HDL GRDD

FIRST NAME   LAST NAME

ADDRESS

APT.#   CITY

STATE/PROV.   ZIP/POSTAL CODE

EMAIL ❏ Please check this box if you would like to receive newsletters and promotional emails from Harlequin Enterprises ULC and its affiliates. You can unsubscribe anytime.

© 2022 HARLEQUIN ENTERPRISES ULC
™ and ® are trademarks owned by Harlequin Enterprises ULC. Printed in the U.S.A.

HI/HRS-520-TY22

he finished, his face now looking a bit ironic. "And I know that the vet who was with her at the back of the store is still a suspect but there's not enough evidence to bring him or anyone else in."

Maisie felt her brows rise. "That's my understanding, too. Do you get a sense yet about whether he's guilty or someone else is?" *Including you*, she thought. Not that she had any reason to think nephew had offed aunt, but at the moment it could have been anyone.

The tall guy with short, dark hair bent down a little more. "Look, Maisie. I know you know that Kornel guy from the Chance Animal Shelter. And because I'm related to the vic here, I'm not authorized to conduct any investigation on my own. I have my own suspicions, especially related to the arguments my dear Aunt Greta generated about her store with the vet and everyone, including me. But everyone investigating the homicide is aware of all that, too. Do I think it's the vet? I'd rather it be him than anyone else I'm aware of who had it in for Greta, but, well, just know, in case you didn't already, that I'm innocent. I think you're innocent even though you apparently were present during at least one disagreement. The vet? Partner Esther? Employees? One of her wonderful exes? Someone we haven't even thought of?" He shook his head. "Wish I knew."

"Me, too," Maisie said. "But if you happen to hear anything, figure it out, or—"

"If I can, I'll let you know," he told her.

Which was the best she could hope for, especially since he really had no reason to keep her informed. This investigation wasn't part of her job.

She accompanied Jackson, Griffin still at her side, back inside the meeting room and got her own cup of coffee. Then she headed down the hall to attempt to do what little she could to help Kyle with his job situation, hoping it was appropriate.

Maisie hadn't dealt much before with Shay Camber, the department's information officer who handled media relations, but fortunately the senior, highly experienced expert was in her office and available to talk.

Although Officer Camber petted a tail-wagging Griffin, she wasn't much help.

"This probably isn't appropriate for us to deal with," Maisie began, "but on the other hand it might lead to some additional information or even evidence to prove the guilt or innocence of Dr. Kyle Kornel, the suspect in the Greta Styles murder."

"Yeah, I've been dealing with a lot of inquiries here from various media sources about that," Shay said after taking a seat behind her desk and waving at a chair for Maisie to occupy. "What's your interest?"

Maisie explained she knew the suspect from her patrols at the Chance Animal Shelter. "He's a veterinarian at the clinic there and at another downtown."

She told Shay about why he was a murder suspect. She explained she was involved because she knew him and kept asking him questions to hopefully lead to something useful either to convict or exonerate him. Then she described what Kyle had just told her about his employers at the downtown clinic being contacted by media sources, as yet unidentified, because they wanted more information. That was because some owners of pets who were patients had asked them to check into Dr. Kornel. They'd said they didn't want someone in his situation to take care of their pets.

"Sounds screwy to me," Maisie said to Shay. "Could you maybe ask your media contacts if that's been happening to them, and who's been making those inquiries?" As she asked, Maisie realized how inappropriate it sounded. Even if she was successful in learning who'd contacted the media, she wouldn't want to get in touch with either the media or the civilians who'd been calling them. Those civilians had the right to express whatever concerns they had. So did the media.

Even if the situation wound up with Kyle ultimately getting fired.

"I understand Dr. Kornel's concern," Shay said, frowning at Maisie so her already lined face became even more wrinkled. "But even if the interest expressed by those civilians to whatever media sources they contacted is a bit much, I don't see anything illegal about it, and it doesn't directly involve us. Sorry. I can't get involved."

"Thanks, anyway," Maisie said. At least she could tell Kyle she tried. But she could understand why he would be worried about more media looking into his situation—and annoying his veterinary employers to the extent they felt they had to do something. She said her goodbyes and led Griffin into the hall, shutting the door behind her. Then, bending down, she asked the sweet dog at her side, "You ready to leave?"

Griffin might not have understood what she asked—

or maybe he did. He'd sat down beside her, but now he rose and looked at her face.

"Good dog," Maisie said, smiling at him, and they headed toward the door; however, it took a few minutes this time to get there since Griffin garnered a lot of hellos from the cops they passed.

Maisie led her K-9 partner to her car and got him into the back seat.

Where were they going?

To the Best Chance Pet Store. Time to do some more digging.

Chapter 11

Who would be at the store now? Maisie would only know once they'd arrived, so she hurriedly drove Griffin and herself there and parked along the street. And watched the place through her car window for a few minutes despite Griffin's restlessness in the back.

Surprisingly, the former crime scene was already open for business. The store seemed to have a lot of people inside, a few of them accompanied by dogs, there to presumably buy—what else?—pet supplies.

Well, that's why she would be there, too, ostensibly. After all, she had her dog with her, and she certainly liked to keep her partner well fed and happy and ready to take on special K-9 assignments.

What was Kyle doing now? Surely he wouldn't be here, too, at this moment, even though he'd also discussed a visit. That would be too awkward, while she was again unofficially observing potential murder suspects.

Just in case, before getting out of the car, Maisie gave him a call.

"Hi," he answered immediately. "Can't talk long now because I'm checking over a potential new doggy resident at the shelter. A rescue organization from a nearby town that we've got a relationship with just brought her in, and she looks okay, though I'll take her to the downtown clinic later if everything on the surface looks all right. Hey, but it's good to hear from you." A silence for a second. "Everything okay?"

"Yep." She told him where she was and what she was about to do. "Just wanted to make sure you weren't here, too."

"Since it's open, I might stop by later after I visit the downtown clinic with this dog. But be sure to let me know if you learn anything you can share—or think of something I should check on as a civilian interested in animals. Okay?"

"Okay." She got ready to say goodbye and hang up.

Before she did, though, Kyle said softly, "Be careful, Maisie. And will I see you later today?"

"Depends on how long you're at the shelter clinic," she said, feeling happy and hopeful of at least getting to connect again in person. While he was still a free man. But she had to stop thinking that way and help find out who really did it. "I'll be around there later, for a while, at least."

"Let's touch base when you're on your way," he said.

Then Maisie said goodbye, hung up and got Griffin out of the back seat. And prepared for her own sort-of investigation. She'd been here after the murder, spoken with the employees, but now she would seriously observe them each as potential suspects.

"Okay, boy, what do we need at home for you that we can use as an excuse for being here?" Her smart K-9 looked up as if attempting to understand what she said, so she decided to help him. "Food? Treats? Toys?" He knew all those words, so Griffin started prancing on the sidewalk, pulling at his leash, and Maisie smiled. "Aha! You can be a big help to me here. Just let everyone know what you're up to."

She looked up and down the sidewalk as they approached the front of the store. No one else was near them. But inside were shoppers of all ages, some of whom had dogs leashed beside them: a Chihuahua, a mixed breed whose background Maisie couldn't guess, but it was a fairly small brown long-nosed mutt, and another mix that seemed to have some shepherd in him. They all appeared highly interested in the place with many shelves and products, since a lot of sniffing with noses in the air was going on, including Griffin's.

Stan was behind the cash register across the room. The young clerk wore a bright green T-shirt that said *"Feed me," says the dog.* He appeared very involved with talking to the customer now paying for whatever he was buying, and Maisie figured Stan would continue concentrating so she'd have to wait to speak with him.

So who else was here? The other salesclerk she saw was near a group of high shelves filled with rows of dog-food cans. That was Cora, who, head cocked enough to let her short hair dangle, watched a woman through her glasses as she attempted to calm a squirmy terrier in her arms. Cora looked highly earnest as they talked, presumably about what to feed the dog.

Interrupting either of them didn't seem like a good idea, so for now Maisie walked through the store's aisles, looking for the others she'd met, Esther and Beth. She saw neither, and though she stopped near the door that led to the storeroom—and murder scene— she didn't go inside. That didn't seem like a good idea, either.

Instead, she and Griffin maneuvered among customers back to the entry, and she grabbed a plastic basket that would make her appear to be shopping. And, in a way, she was.

She returned to the area where she'd seen Cora, who was now talking with the same customer but closer to the aisle containing rows of kibble. Maisie put four cans of the healthy wet food she fed Griffin into the basket as he observed with great interest, then got into the checkout line so she could at least make contact with one of the employees.

She reached Stan in just a couple of minutes, which indicated he was an efficient cashier. "Hi," she said as she stepped up to the counter, and Griffin, standing on his hind legs, rested his muzzle on it. "We need a little dog food—and information. Is Esther here?"

"No, she and Beth went up to that shelter just a few minutes ago."

Interesting, Maisie thought. Maybe she'd see them

there later. And question them then. But their going to the shelter made Maisie ask, "Did someone drop a dog off here today?"

Stan blinked his wary-looking brown eyes. "Yeah. That's the reason they went there. We think we know what to do with new dogs now, but after—well, you know."

Maisie did know. And she was glad the topic had come up this way. She kept her voice low. "It's very wise to take the dog to a shelter like that, although another shelter would be preferable. And best yet would be—"

"Not to accept any dogs at all." Stan's expression grew grim. "We know that, and we talked about it before they left. But the person who brought the little French bull didn't want to take him back and just ran out of here so—"

"You did what you could," Maisie acknowledged. Maybe. This store's reputation apparently hadn't changed. Well, she'd find out more about that dog later. "I'm going to see if I can ask Cora a few questions, then I'll want to talk with you. She hopefully can take over here—" Maisie gestured toward the register "—for you then."

"Yeah. Sure." Which didn't leave Maisie feeling totally confident she'd get to question Stan, but she'd certainly try.

For now, she paid for the dog food and stuck the receipt in the basket. She wouldn't need a bag since her car was close and she hadn't bought much. She and Griffin headed down the aisle where she had last seen

Cora. Sure enough, the clerk was still there but no longer with a customer. Good.

"Hi," Maisie said. "Do you have a minute? I'd like to talk to you about the store and the food you sell here, like the stuff I just bought." She gestured toward the basket. Food was the last thing she wanted to discuss, but she hoped putting things that way would make Cora more amenable to speaking with her.

"Sure," the clerk said. "Come on over here where it's a little quieter."

Perfect, Maisie thought as the young woman, wearing a white T-shirt decorated in front with a dog that had its huge tongue out, led her to the end of the aisle where they were standing. There were shelves containing bags of kibble on one side and canned food on the other. When Cora stopped, she crossed her arms and looked toward Maisie and Griffin, regarding them through her thick glasses and smiling. "Now, what can I help you with? Kibble? I see you've already bought that canned food, right?"

"Right," Maisie said. "And I actually would rather talk about...well, how you're doing now at this store."

The smile on Cora's face melted, and her dark brows furrowed. "What do you mean?"

"I mean it's got to be hard working here after what happened to one of your bosses, right?" Maisie made sure the expression on her face looked sympathetic.

"Well, yes, but...we're handling it. Esther's handling it."

"That's good." Maisie wanted to come right out and demand that the clerk tell her who she thought had killed Greta, but she needed to be a bit more subtle. Initially, at least. "And I'm sure you know that if you ever worry about yourself or anyone else here, you should let the Chance PD know. I figure the detective who questioned you told you that, and to also make any suggestions about people you think could be suspects." *Like you*. Or not.

"What about that veterinarian, Dr. Kornel?" Cora asked. "Isn't he the one?"

"He's certainly still under suspicion," Maisie said, taking another step toward Cora. "There are possibilities I don't want to get into, but the matter is definitely still under investigation. And if you have any additional recollections or thoughts about it—"

"I'll let you know," Cora said. "Or I'll tell Detective Vanderhoff. He's the one who talked to me before."

"That's good," Maisie said. Her next thought might not be totally appropriate to convey, but she nevertheless said, "And I hope you'll let him or someone else from the department know if you ever feel uncomfortable working with or for anyone who's still associated with this store." She gestured around them.

"Like, do I think Esther, or any of the others who work with me, could be guilty?" Cora didn't sound shocked but sad.

"Well, if you do think so…" Maisie let her voice trail off, not pushing it. But she'd like to know this clerk's thoughts, especially if she said something to direct suspicion to someone other than the suspect Maisie hoped was innocent.

"I don't know. But yes, I've considered it. In fact

we've all talked about it, and it can't have been any of us. No way." She stuck out her lower lip, then looked around Maisie. "Come here, Stan. This police officer wants to know if I feel uncomfortable working with any of you because I think someone might be guilty of what happened to Greta. I like working here and trust all of you." But her wavering tone seemed to belie what she said. "It had to be that vet, Dr. Kornel, right? It wasn't any of us."

"That's right." Stan walked to stand beside Cora and briefly put his arm around her shoulders as he scowled at Maisie.

Well, they seemed to be standing up for one another, and even if they suspected one of their coworkers they weren't admitting it.

Still, that didn't relieve Maisie's suspicions.

"Got it," she said. "But since no one has been arrested yet, the cops charged with investigating this apparently haven't found enough evidence to apprehend the murderer. If you happen to think of anyone else who could be guilty—"

"We'll of course let the cops know," Stan said.

"I already told Detective Vanderhoff my suspicions," Cora said, which pricked Maisie's interest.

She looked encouragingly at the clerk. "I can learn them from him, of course, but—"

"Well, Greta used to talk about her past sometimes. She'd been married and divorced twice while running the shop. I'm wondering if it was one of her exes who killed her."

"I see," Maisie said, nodding encouragingly at the clerk. "Glad you passed that along."

Not that it was anything new, but evidently the people who worked here were aware of it.

Maisie needed to find out where things stood officially in investigating those exes. She wasn't sure she could easily identify and question them, and if she did and her superiors found out—which was likely—she might look bad. If the exes were being officially questioned, though, that should take some pressure off Kyle. Or not, since as far as she knew, nothing had happened yet. And who else was the official investigation focusing on?

Well, okay. She might mention this conversation to Vince and get his take on Greta's exes as suspects. He probably wouldn't tell her, but she had to try.

Unless he ordered her to stand down, and even then, she'd continue being nosy, asking questions when she could. Try to talk at least a little with the others who worked here—Esther and Beth.

She checked her watch. She didn't have to report back to the station for another couple of hours.

She still had time to go to the shelter. Great!

And maybe she'd get a chance to hold a similar conversation with Esther and Beth, if they were still there.

In any case, she and Griffin needed a little shelter time—with the dogs being cared for there, as well as the staff members who tended to be glad to see a cop helping to protect them. Which Maisie loved to do.

And it wouldn't hurt that she hopefully would, in addition, get to talk to Kyle a little about where things stood…and maybe more.

* * *

Scott, wearing one of his T-shirts that labeled him as a manager, had been the first person at the shelter to talk to Esther and Beth, who'd just brought in Morry, a little French bull mix, and convinced him to allow the dog to stay as long as he passed an initial check by Kyle.

Kyle knew that because he'd been called into the reception area by Scott, who told him to conduct an exam and let him know if Morry appeared to be appropriate to be taken in as a rescue.

"But," Scott had said to Esther in particular, "you know our position. Yes, we're a shelter, but we don't usually take just any animals in. We're fairly selective, although of course we'll bring in animals in trouble as well as those we think we can rehome. So, okay, today. But you know—"

"We know what you told poor Greta," Esther said, "and we understand." Like Kyle, she sat on one of the reception room's chairs. Her round face looked highly concerned as she held the orphaned dog.

Beth sat beside her, wearing another shirt applauding dogs that said *Dogs are lovable*. As seemed to be her usual style, her bright golden hair was secured in a clip. Scott sat beside Kyle.

"We talked about it on the way over," Beth said. "We'd like to bring this cutie back to the shop to display for adoption after he's checked out and found healthy and all, but we understand if you want to keep him here, though we'd be interested in taking in other dogs who've been here for a while to show off at our shop."

Interesting, Kyle thought. Beth wasn't an owner,

Esther was. But she appeared to be taking over this conversation for her employer. Was Esther grooming her to be...well, not her partner as Greta had been, but her top assistant?

Or was Beth just hoping she would?

But who would take charge if it turned out Esther was the one who'd killed her partner? Esther had probably had more to gain from it than anyone else. Kyle had an urge to come right out and ask her...but held it inside. This didn't seem the right time to try.

And now, in regards to Morry, that was Scott's call, and his boss agreed to those terms.

"We'll have to determine later if and when we'll let you have Morry back to display," Scott said.

"Got it," Esther replied. "And if you have any other dogs you've had here for a while and are cute enough to allow us to show in our shop, could we meet them?"

"Sure," Scott said. "Good idea. One or two of our canine residents might be a better match that way. Come on into the clinic waiting room. If anyone has time to bring them out, I'll have a couple for you to consider. We can talk about bringing them to you later if they interest you. Meantime, Kyle, would you please start Morry's exam?"

"Of course," he replied, taking charge of the little French bull. Interesting that Scott seemed inclined to encourage a relationship with the shop that way—and therefore keep communicating with the people there despite how secure and secret this shelter needed to remain. Although this way, it might look more like a regular shelter.

"Would you let us know how your exam goes?" Esther asked as she turned the pup over to Kyle. "I'd like to hear your initial response. I think…well, I hope we can continue to work with you. I think this shelter is special."

"Of course it is," Kyle said. "And I'll definitely let you know how it goes." Once again, he forbore from asking a question that filled his mind. This time, since he and Maisie seemed to be doing more to figure out what had happened to Greta, he wanted to know what had happened with the other shelter they'd had an arrangement with. But again, this didn't seem the right time to ask.

Now, he used his keycard to open the door that led to the reception building's hallway. The two store people and Scott followed him to the clinic's waiting room through the first door on the left. Scott didn't stay, and Kyle left the two women there while he took Morry inside for his exam.

His initial check indicated the dog had been neutered and seemed in good health, although Kyle would provide him with a more extensive examination in the downtown clinic tomorrow where there were vet techs available to help plus more equipment, although potential animal residents were generally examined here first. Morry didn't have a microchip, though, so there was no indication where he'd come from.

Kyle brought Morry with him when he returned to the clinic reception room so the two store people could say goodbye to the dog before Kyle ushered them out the front of the building. A couple of staff members were in his reception area, too, and they'd each brought in a dog who was a shelter resident: Cheesecake, a poodle, and Sheba, the old English sheepdog. The staff members there were newcomer Chessie and longer-term resident Bibi. It was surprising that they were out here and not in the much-better-protected inside areas.

"These are the dogs Scott thought you should see," Chessie said to the store people. "He was talking to Nella, one of the other managers, but she's busy right now so Bibi and I decided to bring them out."

Interesting that Scott had chosen possible dogs to let the store display so quickly. But having them brought here this way was a bad idea, Kyle thought. It went against the shelter's rules for its protected staff members. Well, these two visitors might not know what the shelter was really about. He'd get them to leave soon— and tell Scott about Chessie and Bibi.

"We need to go back inside," Bibi said to Chessie. The long timer seemed to be advising the newcomer.

But Chessie didn't pay any attention. "Scott's not ready to show them off yet," she continued, addressing the store people, "but he said if Nella got a chance she could bring them out here to say hello. Since she said she didn't have time and left, I decided to."

Chessie patted Cheesecake on the back as Beth bent and did the same thing, then stood again and looked directly at Chessie. "They're both so cute," she said. "I hope we can take them to display at the store. Right, Esther?" She looked toward her boss, who was likewise stroking Sheba.

"Sounds good to me," Esther said. "Can we talk to

Scott about it? I know he said he doesn't want us to take them now, but it would be great if we could."

"I'll check," Kyle said, still holding Morry in his arms, "but I believe he's busy. Why don't you spend some time with the dogs while I find him?" And he would encourage Bibi and Chessie to go back inside with him.

"Fine with me." Esther looked at Beth, who nodded too. Interesting that the woman in charge kept seeking her new employee's opinion. "And I hope we can also come back for you later, too, little guy," she added, walking toward Kyle and petting Morry. "But for now, I'll be eager to hear what Scott says about those guys." She gestured toward Cheesecake and Sheba.

Kyle was both amused and concerned about this new wrinkle. Well, Scott had made the suggestion, if Chessie had described it right, although this undoubtedly wasn't the follow-through Scott expected. Where was Nella now?

In any case, Scott might actually be willing to work this out on his own terms with the pet store.

For now, Kyle unlocked the door that led to the reception hallway and showed them into one of the rooms where potential adopters were allowed to spend time with the dogs they were interested in. Chessie followed them, and Bibi didn't leave her.

Discussing which dogs could be shown off at the store was another good reason for Kyle to find Scott right away. He quickly took Morry back into his clinic and put him in one of the enclosures. Since Scott hadn't answered his phone, Kyle decided to look for him and make sure the door at the end of the hallway into the shelter was locked, to keep the store folks out. But did the staffers have a key to get back in? Most likely, since they'd gotten out here in the first place. But that seemed a bit odd to Kyle.

He hoped he'd see Scott quickly, or another of the managers, to let them know what was going on with the staffers and about the presence of the store folks.

The store folks. In a way, Kyle felt somewhat sorry for them on their loss of Greta—assuming they were innocent. But he wished he'd been able to talk to them more individually.

He knew Maisie was going to try to get more information from the pet-shop employees to see if any suspected that one of the others might have done Greta in. He'd be interested in hearing the results of her visit to the store today. Without these two there.

Almost as if she'd heard him, he received a call from Maisie. "Hi, Kyle," she said. "I won't have long to stay today, but I'm almost at the shelter. I don't have much to tell you, but—"

"No matter what," he said, "I'll be glad to hear it."

And to see her, he thought.

Chapter 12

After parking, Maisie walked into the shelter reception area with Griffin, as usual. She most often called Nella to let her inside, but today, since Kyle was expecting her, she called him instead, then waited for a few minutes in the empty room. And then a little longer.

Finally, the door opened, and Kyle stuck his head into the room. "Come on in," he said. "We need to talk, but not now. I'm still looking for Scott."

Maisie did as he said and hurried through the door with her K-9 and watched Kyle walk quickly away from her. He pointed toward a closed door down the hall from his clinic. "In here," he called and then exited into the main shelter area, closing the door behind him.

What was that all about? Maisie didn't know, but she didn't like it. She agreed with him—they needed to talk. But she disagreed with its not being now. Not that she could do anything about that.

She continued down the hall toward the door he'd pointed at, just beyond his clinic. She heard voices emanating from there.

Esther and Beth? Just in case, she headed inside and found the two women in the room playing with a couple of shelter dogs. Staff members Bibi and Chessie stood near the door watching them. What were they doing here, outside the secure area of the shelter?

"Hi, Maisie," Beth said. "See these two dogs? They're shelter dogs from here, and these nice ladies brought them out here to meet us. They said that Scott might let us take them to the shop soon to show them off. Isn't that great?" She looked really excited by the idea.

Interesting, Maisie thought. Was this for real? Was this why Kyle was trying so hard to find Scott? And where could the director be, if he was inside this highly enclosed shelter somewhere but Kyle couldn't locate him?

Maisie recognized the dogs. Cheesecake and Sheba hadn't been here very long, so even if this was Scott's idea or it was okay with him, the reason couldn't be that the shelter had been unsuccessful rehoming them from here. Besides, from what Maisie understood, animals accepted into this shelter could stay here forever if they weren't taken home by adopters.

If this was Scott's idea, maybe he now felt sorry for the remaining people at the store and wanted to help

them bring more customers in to see adoptable dogs—
and buy things. She'd have to talk to him about that.

Or maybe get the information from Kyle.

Anyway, Maisie had known the store people were
here and was glad to see them. She wanted to question them now about their suspicions about who had
killed Greta.

But not with Bibi and Chessie in the room. What
were those staff members even doing out here? she wondered again.

"Hey, Esther and Beth," Maisie said. "You can probably spend a little more time with those dogs later, but
I'd really like to talk to you. You know I just visited
the store and talked with Cora and Stan, don't you?"

She had no idea if the other employees had called
about her visit, but maybe talking about it would make
the women curious enough to step into the hallway with
her and discuss it.

Would they only be okay talking when they were together? Or could she separate them? Maisie's attempt
at the store to converse with only one of the clerks at a
time hadn't completely worked out. But why not give
it a try here?

Would they both point fingers at Kyle? That might
be a reason to bring him in to listen, since they were
less likely to accuse him if he was with them, right?

On the other hand, they might not point fingers at
one another this way, even if they had reason to. Or
maybe not at Stan or Cora, either. Greta's exes? Someone else?

She would just have to see…

"This would be a good time for us to go back inside the shelter," Bibi said, looking at Chessie. "While Officer Murran and Griffin are here." She wasn't smiling now, so Maisie couldn't see the gap between her teeth. In fact, the frown on her round face looked a bit angry, unusual for this sweet and gregarious staff member.

Her concern seemed reasonable to Maisie. To her knowledge, the staffers might be okay coming into this area briefly, depending on circumstances, but mostly they were to stay inside the shelter.

"But isn't this part of what we're supposed to do—introduce visitors to the animals who need a new home to see if they'll adopt them, or find someone else who can?" Chessie's face appeared confused. She'd only been here for a few days. Maybe she still didn't quite get what this shelter was about—even though she'd told Maisie what had brought her here.

"Yes," Bibi said, "but we usually only come out here when we have a manager near us and the people have contacted the shelter about a specific animal or two from the website." She was standing now. "I'm going back in. You should come too, Chessie. You'll see. The managers—Scott, too—won't be happy if we don't hurry back inside."

She opened the door and stepped into the hallway. Maisie told Griffin to stay, and she followed Bibi. She closed the door behind her and asked, "What's really going on? Does Scott want those two dogs to be shown at the pet store?"

Bibi's chin lowered toward her chest as she said, "I don't know. I heard him talk about the possibility with

Nella, too—but I know he didn't want us staffers to bring them out here now. I tried to explain to Chessie, but she's still not used to this shelter's rules and regulations. I thought I could help her, but I think she'll need a reminder from Scott or another manager before she gets it."

"I get it," said Chessie. She had followed them into the hall and closed the door again. "I'm not sorry we did this, though. Scott was the one to mention these two dogs, and since those women were here I thought he'd want us to introduce them. They seem so excited about the idea. But I'll go back inside now with you, Bibi."

Relieved, Maisie watched the two staff members hurry down the hall. They'd be safer that way, in the enclosed and secure grounds of the shelter. Bibi must have had a keycard to let them in, for in a few seconds they'd disappeared through the door.

Good. Bibi's card had probably been how they'd gotten out here in the first place.

Time for Maisie to speak with those pet-store people—and keep an eye on those shelter dogs.

Back in the meeting room, she took a seat across from them and also told Griffin to sit beside her, which the obedient pup did—for a few seconds. Then he went to trade more nose sniffs with the other dogs.

"Those two are cute and should hopefully be easy to find adopters for if you wind up being able to take them to display," Maisie began to get the conversation going, "but tell me about the dog you just brought in."

"He's Morry," Beth said, a huge smile on her face.

The young woman brushed her shining hair with her fingertips. "He's at least part French bulldog, and—"

The smile melted a bit as her gaze scanned Maisie, perhaps taking in her uniform, which she'd seen many times. But Maisie figured it was a reminder of her job upholding the law and what her position would be about another dog being dumped at the store, even without Greta there. Or at least, Maisie assumed that was where Beth's mind was going.

Sure enough, the clerk glanced briefly at her boss beside her, then said, "I guess it's not a surprise that dogs are still being left at the shop. But we brought Morry here, and the shelter people seemed okay with it. Which is fine with us. We like this shelter and want to work out a relationship for that kind of situation as well as helping to get these two and Morry rehomed, and hopefully others. And do what we can to help this shelter, too. Right, Esther?"

The older woman rolled her eyes a bit. "Well, we do know that the people in charge weren't thrilled with the idea of helping us with dogs to display in the store before, when Greta was here acting the way she did, so things have maybe changed. Which could be a good thing." She looked then at Beth as if seeking her concurrence, and the other woman nodded.

Interesting that the longtime part-owner of the store kept looking for confirmation from her new employee. It did make Maisie wonder how the workers would figure things out over time, as they got used to Greta no longer being there.

"Well," Maisie said, "that's certainly not up to me,

but yes, I gather the people in charge here are trying to work things out with you—including maybe helping you when you do get a drop-off, although it still would be better if you didn't accept any." She'd been wondering for a while and now had to ask. "Why is it that the shelter Greta already had a relationship with stopped accepting dogs from your store or letting you display any for adoption, do you know?"

"No," Esther said slowly. "I got the impression there was a fight over what they'd do and whether they'd encourage adopters to buy supplies at our store, even at a discount… I never got involved or heard any of it, but you were with Greta for some of that, weren't you, Beth?"

Beth glanced down at her sneakers. "Well…yes, but they were the ones who were arguing, and I didn't completely get it."

Too bad, Maisie thought. It would be good for those in charge at this shelter to know what Greta had been attempting to do at that one and how bad it might have been. Had she somehow come up with a way to manipulate them that would cost them money? Quite possibly.

Maisie knew Scott and others in charge here well enough to know they'd never agree to something that harmed this shelter in any way, financially or otherwise. And though more cooperation appeared possible, it wouldn't necessarily mean the Best Chance Pet Store would get dumped dogs back for their display after this shelter accepted them. Or other shelter dogs from here, either, even if they did this time. Maybe this was a test. Or a mistake.

Would Esther argue over that the same way her former partner had? Maisie didn't think so, but that remained to be seen.

For now, it would be interesting to see how things went with the dog they'd just brought in that day. And these two.

In the meantime, she wanted to see if she could get these women talking, the way she had tried with the others at the store.

"If you happen to think of anything particularly helpful about that shelter, please let Scott or one of the managers know," Maisie said. "And, as I said, Griffin and I visited your store a little while ago." She turned back to Esther. "Cora and Stan may tell you I was asking them again about...what happened to Greta, and who they each think might have had something to do with it."

"Oh." Esther didn't sound thrilled about the idea. "Did they tell you anything?"

"Accuse anybody?" Beth piped in. Her gaze landed on Esther.

Was that who she thought had killed Greta?

"They did give me some ideas that I'll be checking with the detectives in charge about," Maisie said, purposely vague. "But now that I have you here, I'd like to hear from both of you who you think it might be... besides Dr. Kornel. He's already being investigated, and since he hasn't been arrested, there must not be adequate evidence to indicate he did it." She added the last to prevent them from pointing fingers at Kyle, at least for now.

"I've been really worried about it," Beth told her.

"But if it's not Dr. Kornel… Well, I'm sure you heard Greta had been married before. And I don't think it was Esther or anyone else at the store." She stopped and stood and put her hands on her hips as she looked at Maisie. "That's your job, isn't it? Finding out who killed Greta? You and your fellow cops."

"Like I said, it's under investigation," Maisie responded. Both officially and by her. "As you probably know. I'd imagine you've each been questioned by one of the detectives already, right?"

"Yes," Esther said. "That wasn't any fun."

"It sure wasn't," Beth agreed.

That was when Scott entered the room. Maisie was curious about where he'd been, but it no longer mattered. He was here. "Hi, ladies," he said. He included Maisie, as well as the other women, in his glance. "And you dogs, too." He petted Griffin on the head, then the others.

Kyle followed him. He must have found Scott during his search and asked him whatever questions he wanted to regarding the relationship with the pet store, since he seemed calm. Though he said nothing at first, his smile toward Maisie sent a wave of warmth through her, and she smiled back, swallowing her curiosity about what was going on.

"So," Scott continued, facing Esther and Beth where they sat on their chairs, "I'm glad you've had the opportunity to meet Cheesecake and Sheba, although this wasn't exactly the way I intended to introduce you. I'd wanted a manager here to bring them to meet you and discuss possibilities."

Not the staff members, as Maisie had surmised.

"We really like them," Beth enthused. "Could we take them with us to the store now and put them in our display? It would be so cool for us to bring them this afternoon and start trying to find them the perfect people to adopt them from you." She opened her brown eyes wide and seemed almost to bat them. Did she think flirting with the shelter's director would make a difference? She was youngish and pretty and enthusiastic, wearing an abundance of makeup that emphasized her smooth face, dark brows and eyelashes, but Maisie knew Scott well enough to recognize he was unlikely to change his opinion based on that.

"I'm sure it would. But I want you to think about it for a few days, and then we can talk again."

Beth's sweet expression turned sour quickly. Maybe even stormy, but only for a second before becoming sad.

Esther was the one to respond, though. "We understand. And you know we want to develop a really good relationship with you and this shelter. So we'll leave now." The older woman glanced at Beth, clearly giving an order. "But we'll look forward to coming back for these two. And hopefully Morry, too, so we can show them all off at our store." She stood and gestured for her employee to follow her.

For now, at least, Beth wasn't in charge, and that appeared to Maisie to be a good thing.

Soon, Scott walked out of the room holding the two dogs' leashes and following Esther and Beth. Maisie followed with Kyle. The two store women joined Scott at the reception end of the hall, then they patted Cheesecake and Sheba and said goodbye before entering the reception room, from which they would leave.

"See you soon," Beth said.

"Thanks for taking in Morry," Esther added as they left.

When the door closed, Scott looked at Maisie and Kyle. "They're rather pushy," he said, "though not as bad as Greta was. Maybe it's not a good idea for this shelter to try to help them, even though I feel sorry for them for the loss of one of their owners so I thought I'd help this time. Let's see how things go with these three dogs, then decide what will happen."

"Sounds good to me," Kyle said.

"Me, too," Maisie agreed. Then, turning to Kyle, she said, "Could I stop in and see Morry before I leave?"

"Of course," he said with a nod and a grin that shouldn't have looked sexy but did.

"Okay, I'm going back inside," Scott said. "And, believe me, I will be talking to Bibi and Chessie about bringing the dogs out here without my okay—and out of the area that's secure for staff. But I'll want to see Morry later, too." He strode down the hall as Maisie turned to follow Kyle into the vet clinic, with Griffin at her heels.

Kyle watched Maisie make over little Morry after he took the pup out of his temporary enclosure. He liked how this cop acted with animals.

He liked how she acted in general.

When she stood, she said to Kyle, "I still don't get why Scott was so nice to those pet-store people, almost encouraging them to display some of the shelter dogs at the shop."

He picked Morry up and walked into his office, making sure Maisie and Griffin followed. There, he sat behind his desk with the dog on his lap and gestured for Maisie to sit down across from him. "He's a good guy. Like he said, he undoubtedly feels sorry for them— maybe even blames himself somehow for what happened to Greta, although until we know who did it and why, we don't know who to blame for what."

"Exactly," Maisie agreed.

And then Kyle couldn't help it. "So do you know who that was yet? You did talk to all the people remaining at the store, didn't you?"

He had talked to Scott about the pet shop and gotten the impression the shelter director remained willing to work with them, take in strays they found and allow them to display adoptable pets despite all the tension in the relationship, starting with Greta.

Maisie nodded, and he didn't know why that should appear sexy, although everything about her was. She somehow even looked sexy in her black and white uniform.

"No one confessed," she said. "So it must have been you." She kept her expression fierce for a few seconds, then it melted into another smile. "Or not."

"Or not," he repeated. "So what's going on in the investigation at the moment?"

"I don't really know, although when I go to the station next I'll talk to Vince about what I was up to today. I'd feel better about doing that if I'd come up with any helpful answers, but to do my job right I need to be forthcoming with the main investigator on the case." She reached down to pat Griffin on the head. "And maybe my letting him know what I've been doing, and that I was attempting to help him in a way—well, maybe he'll let me know what's happening, what progress has been made. If any."

Kyle wanted to hug her. He knew that one of her main reasons for getting involved this way, since she hadn't been assigned this case except for having Griffin sniff out the victim's body at first, was to help him— or at least she might be more interested in it because of him.

Of course, she did patronize the pet store anyway, so maybe it didn't have as much to do with him as he thought…or hoped.

"Well, please let me know if there's anything I should be aware of." As her mouth opened for her to comment, he raised his hand and continued. "At least, anything you can tell me."

"Of course," she said. "Will you be at the downtown clinic later?"

"For a while. I want to bring in Morry and that other new dog, Basker, the little Chihuahua mix we just got from the Help Me Shelter in San Luis Obispo. It's a good shelter, and they gave us paperwork indicating the exams provided to Basker, but it never hurts to double-check."

"Got it," Maisie said. She rose. "Well, I'm heading to the station soon. Maybe I'll see you downtown later."

"Sounds good to me," Kyle said. "Dinner again,

maybe? And you can tell me then…anything you can tell me then."

She laughed, and almost as if they were programmed to do it, both walked toward each other, and Kyle felt inflamed and impassioned as they engaged in one sexy kiss.

Chapter 13

Even though she should have, Maisie didn't head straight to the station. Since she couldn't yet point to someone else Greta had known and say that person was a much more credible suspect than Kyle, she had a couple of stops to make to continue with her unauthorized investigation.

They might not lead anywhere, either, and therefore leave Kyle at the top of the list—rightly or wrongly—but at least she'd have tried a different direction.

Greta's exes.

Fortunately, they both lived and worked in Chance, from what she had found online when she had also been checking what the media had to say about Greta's murder. Both had jobs downtown. Or professions, in the case of one of them—Winston Emerly, an attorney. The other, Kirby Grazio, was the manager at the local Open Now, a popular convenience store.

Talking to them wasn't really her business or part of her job, but she would be careful how she dealt with them and continue reporting all to Vince. Hopefully, he had spoken with them already, or had one of the investigators on the case do so.

After driving to town from the shelter, she stopped first at the Open Now, which fortunately wasn't the store that had been burglarized a few days ago. It was located on a busy block of shops that included some clothing stores, not far from the center of town. She could always use some extra fruit, which would be her initial excuse for stopping there, even though she figured she could get better produce at one of the major grocery stores.

On the other hand, did she really need an excuse? She was in uniform, and she would have Griffin with her in his vest. Kirby Grazio wouldn't know that she wasn't there officially to question him.

But if she acted official, would he agree to speak with her, or find an excuse for distancing himself from her—assuming he was even there just then? She would have to see.

As she parked in the lot in front of the convenience store, she wondered briefly what Kyle would think about her being there. It was for his sake, sure. But would she learn anything useful?

Maisie didn't know what reason either of Greta's exes might have had for getting rid of her, assuming both divorces were final and there had been some agreement for division of their assets at the time. She hadn't heard of Greta having any children, either.

She got Griffin out of the back of her car, and they headed to the glass front door. The place didn't appear particularly busy inside, but she assumed they would get a steady, though possibly small, influx of business all day in this kind of shop.

As they walked in, she was greeted by a curious smile from the person behind the counter facing the entry, a young woman who was probably in her twenties. She undoubtedly wondered what a cop and K-9 were doing there.

On the other hand, Vince or another detective had probably been here before—but detectives in their department generally wore suits, not uniforms.

Maisie approached the counter, Griffin with his nose in the air, undoubtedly sniffing the store's products. Did they carry dog food?

Was some kind of competition with the pet store a reason why Greta and Kirby had broken up?

That was a reach, she realized. But at the moment she wasn't ruling anything out.

"Hi," she said to the clerk, who was still watching her. "I'm here to pick up some fruit—but is Mr. Grazio available?" She didn't say why she was asking.

"He's in the back. I'll go get him." The clerk pivoted and hurried through the door behind her.

A moment later, a man came through, probably in his forties, somewhat short but good-looking, with a well-trimmed beard that was the same color as his medium brown hair. He wore a nice button-down shirt over dark jeans.

He approached Maisie right away. "Hello, Officer," he said. He looked down at Griffin. "And hello, K-9." He glanced around them. A couple of customers had formed a line near the checkout counter. "I'm Kirby Grazio. I was told you were looking for me and some fruit. Why don't we head over there?" He gestured toward an open counter to his right where sections held various fruits.

"Fine," Maisie said and headed where he indicated. Now, how should she start this? By being right up-front, she decided. "Mr. Grazio," she said in a low voice, "I'm conducting part of an investigation into—"

"My ex's death, I assume," he interrupted, although he also spoke quietly, staring right into Maisie's face with his clearly angry brown eyes. "I've already been questioned by a detective—Vanderhoff, isn't it? I told him I had nothing to do with...what happened to Greta." He glanced around, apparently not wanting to express what had happened to her, which was a good idea considering there were a few more customers—a mother with two kids—now close to them also looking at the fruit. Kirby gestured, and Maisie followed to a nearby row of tall shelves, where no one else was around.

"I appreciate that," Maisie said to him. "I just want to make sure I understand the facts." She didn't even know many facts concerning this ex-husband, let alone understand them, but she wasn't going to mention that. "Please just give me a rundown of when you were married and when you got divorced."

Kirby shot her a curious look. "I told all that to Detective Vanderhoff."

"Of course. It's the basic information. I'm just confirming what we know."

The store manager didn't look pleased, but he did give Maisie a description of his background with Greta. They had met nearly eight years before, when he was just an employee at the store and Greta was visiting Chance, working at a pet store elsewhere. She liked the town, and she must have liked him. They were married soon after, and she started the pet store with her friend Esther. What Maisie learned did seem to indicate this guy's innocence. He was Greta's first husband, they had stopped caring for each other but had divorced on relatively amicable terms maybe six years ago and agreed on how to split their assets, and he'd barely seen her after that, except when she came in here to buy groceries now and then. He didn't have a pet, so he never ventured into her store. "I had no reason to kill her," he said, "and I didn't."

Which was the response Maisie anticipated, but at the moment, at least, she had no reason to doubt it.

She thanked him and finished by buying a good sampling of fruit and a small box of biscuits for Griffin for, yes, this convenience store did carry a few pet supplies. Nothing as healthy maybe as the cans of food she had bought earlier, but not bad.

When she and Griffin were back in her car, an impulse to call Kyle to report on this visit flashed through her mind, but she stifled it. He didn't really need to hear any of this, at least not now.

Especially since it didn't point to someone else who was likely to have committed the crime in which he was a suspect.

"Okay, Griffin," she called into the back seat. "I wonder if it will be as easy to see Greta's other ex. He's a lawyer, for one thing, and I don't have an appointment."

But she drove toward that part of town, the area not far from the Chance civic center that contained office buildings where personnel in charge of various companies were located. So were a number of law firms, including, she believed, the one where Kyle's attorney Mark Brown worked; she had looked him up. It was an area that Maisie didn't see much while on duty since she and Griffin were more likely to have K-9 assignments on the ground, in stores, in parks, and not, generally, offices.

But she had been here occasionally conducting interviews of people who'd been involved in various situations to get their take on what had happened. This also allowed Griffin to explore their scents to determine if there was any reason for him to alert on any of them and therefore indicate their connection with whatever crime the cops were looking into. That didn't happen often, though.

For now, she found a spot in the parking structure that served the two matching charcoal-gray buildings peppered with rows of windows and containing a number of law firms, including the one where Winston Emerly worked. Then, she helped Griffin exit from the car and walked across the driveway to the nearest of the buildings.

She already had the suite number for Emerly's law firm but confirmed it at the directory on the wall near the elevator. Maisie's research had indicated he was one of the name partners, and in fact his was the first name in the list of three: Emerly, Langton and Schmidt.

As she'd anticipated for a building containing law firms, the lobby was nicely decorated, with places for people to sit. One area was occupied by three men who sat there and appeared to be talking animatedly.

There was also a long counter against a wall nearest the elevator, and a couple of people wearing suits, presumably building staff, stood there. "Can we help you, Officer?" called a woman whose silvery hair was pulled into a bun at the nape of her neck.

"I'm fine, thanks." Fortunately, she didn't need to let them know which office she was heading to and receive approval to get on the elevator. She pushed the button, and when the car arrived she was glad it was empty. She hustled Griffin onto it.

When the door next opened, they were on the third floor. The Emerly firm was the first office on the left.

Should she have called ahead to make an appointment with the attorney? But she figured that seeing him unannounced was preferable—assuming he would have time to see her, or at least wouldn't claim he didn't.

Once again, she considered the reason she was here, as if it was ever far from her mind. Would she eventually tell Kyle about her visit not only to the convenience store but also the law firm?

She would just have to see if it felt appropriate. Either way, she'd decided she would have to let Vince know, since he had already interviewed Grazio and had undoubtedly also interviewed Emerly. So far, she had nothing new to impart to him from the angle of exes to help solve the case.

Well, maybe she would learn something here.

She opened the door and walked in, Griffin following behind her. A few feet inside was a gleaming wooden reception desk, staffed by a woman in a lacy blouse who perked up at their entry. Maisie immediately got the sense that this receptionist was a law student or hoped to become one. She approached the desk.

"Hello," the receptionist said, looking down from Maisie's face toward Griffin and back again. "How can I help you?"

"I would like to see Attorney Winston Emerly," Maisie responded. "Is he available?"

"Well, yes, he is," said a male voice from behind her as Griffin stirred at her feet. Without her knowing it, a man had entered through the same door they had. "What's on your mind, Officer? As if I can't guess."

Maisie had turned to look at him. The man was tall and somewhat hefty, large featured, and staring at her curiously from behind thick, black-rimmed glasses. He wore a white button-down shirt and a blue necktie.

"Is there someplace private we can talk?" she asked him without looking at the receptionist.

He did, though, and nodded at her. Maisie presumed that was telling the young woman it was okay and not to interrupt him for the time being. Or at least, she hoped she interpreted that correctly.

"Please follow me," he said and led her through a door behind the reception desk.

Maisie felt her phone vibrate in her pocket. She was glad she had remembered to turn the sound off—as she usually did when she was on duty. Even so, in case it was Vince or Doug or someone at the station, she pulled it out and glanced at it quickly as she and Griffin followed Emerly.

Kyle. What was he texting about?

And why did she want so badly to take the time to read that text?

Not now, though. She was busy.

In a minute, Emerly led her through a door into what she figured was his office. There had been about five other doors. She already knew, from looking up the firm and Emerly, that it wasn't a large firm. She gathered they specialized in commercial litigation, unlike the criminal-law specialist who was helping Kyle.

As she anticipated, the senior partner's office was good-sized and well decorated, with a large desk that resembled the one in the reception area, paintings on the wall that she figured were expensive, genuine artwork and several file cabinets.

Instead of sitting down and requesting that she do the same, Emerly took a few steps toward her, and Griffin reacted, placing himself between the two humans. Emerly looked down at him and smiled. "Looks as if you have a protector with you," he said.

"Exactly. You evidently already figured out my reason for being here."

"I've already talked with another cop about it. And no, I didn't kill my ex, Greta." With that, he did turn his back on her and took his seat in the tall leather chair behind his desk. "So are we done here?"

"Not quite," she said. "I want to confirm some of what happened between you." Maisie took a seat facing him.

Fortunately, the guy cooperated. His expression grew grim as he quickly described a marriage that had started out fine. "Yes, we met before Greta's prior divorce but... well, that marriage was pretty much over, anyway." He'd been pleased about her entrepreneurial bent and her partnership in the pet store. But things started to go wrong. He didn't go into detail, but Maisie had a sense that he was the one to start seeing someone else. "We decided to get a divorce," he finished. "The grounds were irreconcilable differences. We agreed on our division of assets. We'd kept a lot of our stuff as separate property anyway. She—well, she wasn't happy. If either of us would have killed the other, she would have killed me, given the opportunity."

Maybe, Maisie thought. But in any case, she hadn't heard anything worth pursuing. Not yet, at least. Still, she'd mull this over as she would the earlier meeting with Greta's other husband.

And when she and Griffin left a few minutes later, she felt bad. She wouldn't have anything new and exciting to cheer Kyle up.

Not that she'd have told him a lot, anyway. She was

a cop. A professional. And she couldn't tell a suspect much of anything that she learned in her unauthorized investigation.

When she and Griffin reached her car, though, she finally felt she had time to look at Kyle's text.

In between patients now and was thinking about something I'm concerned about. We can talk about it at dinner.

After fastening Griffin into the rear seat, Maisie thought about calling Kyle in response. Or even just texting him back.

But she started driving off first.

Dinner. Yes, they had talked about it. And she had come to really enjoy Kyle's company—a lot more than she should have.

She wondered what he was concerned about.

And whether she should call off getting together that evening. She had been seeing him often. Probably too often.

Okay. Since she was pondering it that much, she'd already made her decision.

Yes, she wanted to see him again. Find out what he was thinking about. But right now, she realized she needed an evening to herself.

She didn't text Kyle back, though. Not then. And once she reached the station she decided to wait till she got into her office, in case she changed her mind.

She learned right away from Officer Penny Jones,

again acting as receptionist, that Vince was out on an assignment, probably for the rest of the day.

It was already late afternoon. Maisie brought Griffin to her office. She already knew that Doug and Hooper were also out on an assignment, so she had the place to herself.

She got right onto the computer to check on what had been going on that day at the department and if there was anything she should know about—but before concentrating on anything she pulled her phone out of her pocket.

It was late afternoon. Kyle had just started a checkup on another patient, a return visit of a cat whose stomach issues he had treated last week, when he felt his phone vibrate in his pocket. A quick vibration, so he figured it was a text. From Maisie in response to the one he had sent to her?

And what had he intended to talk to her about at dinner? His gratitude, certainly. He had expressed it before. Of course he remained concerned about whether she was jeopardizing her job, or even her life or Griffin's, by asking too many questions. But she was a cop. She knew what she was doing. And he hoped for an update regarding her investigation, whether or not it was appropriate.

Damn. He'd been examining the orange tabby cat, kneading her stomach gently to see her reaction but not concentrating as he should. He immediately and purposefully cast all thoughts of Maisie and the murder and texts from his mind and focused on the recently ill cat.

Fortunately, according to her owner, her stomach had been reacting better to food, and she didn't appear to be in any discomfort now, probably because of the change of food and the medication Kyle had prescribed. Kyle was able to release her with no further checkups planned unless anything changed.

When the cat and owner had left the exam room, Kyle removed his phone from his pocket and prepared to look at the text, still anticipating it had come from Maisie.

He was right. But it didn't say what he'd hoped.

Sorry, but I can't make it to dinner tonight.

Nothing else.

Okay, fine. He'd see her again. Eventually.

He stewed about it somewhat as he finished his appointments for the rest of the day. By the time he left, he was calm. Maybe even pleased.

He needed some time off, just to relax and not even think about his problems. And when he was in Maisie's presence, no matter how much he liked her, he couldn't help recalling the accusations against him.

Driving back to his apartment, he took a different route so he wouldn't even think of passing the Joint, the restaurant where he'd eaten with Maisie. He did stop at a fast-food place on the way, though, so he wouldn't have to think about cooking. A burger and fries? Not healthy maybe, but he intended to supplement them with a salad he already had in his refrigerator.

As he entered his unit a few minutes later and headed

for the kitchen, a pang hit him. He was alone. Maybe he really should get on with adopting a rescue dog. One he could take to the clinic, too, so it wouldn't be left by itself all day.

He put the bag of food down on his kitchen table and headed toward the fridge. Ah, he had some beer in there, too. That would be a good complement to his dinner.

He got his salad together and was about to open a beer bottle when his phone vibrated. Another text message.

Had Maisie changed her mind? Too bad. He was finally settling down for the night. He pulled the phone out and looked at the message.

But it wasn't from Maisie. He didn't know who it was from.

Ready to kill someone else? Why not someone you care about? Won't happen if you confess. But it will happen immediately if you tell anyone about this message.

He put his phone on the table and stared at the message as he finally opened the beer and sat down, taking a swig. And then another. And fought the urge to hurl the bottle at the wall.

It was a threat from an unknown phone number—and not against him, not directly. It had to come from the actual killer, right? He had no way of tracing where it came from, and if he asked Maisie to have the source checked…well, the text was likely referring to Maisie. Who else did he care much about around here—even now, when she'd stood him up for the evening? And it wouldn't make sense for this to involve his remaining family in LA. He had friends here and elsewhere, of course. And coworkers. One of them?

But why did whoever it was send this? And why now? Because Maisie was somehow getting close to identifying the killer? This was further confirmation that Kyle's concern about her was valid.

Damn, but he wished he was with her now after all. But it was fortunate he wasn't. He couldn't even talk about this with her. If whoever it was believed he'd told her, her life would definitely be in danger.

Most likely, it already was.

Sure, she was a cop. But that didn't make her invincible.

He decided to call her. Since she didn't want to see him that night, would she even answer?

She did. "Hi, Kyle," she said. "Sorry about tonight, but I had some things to take care of at home. Maybe we can plan on dinner sometime soon."

"Fine," he said. An urge to tell her about the message shot through him, but he couldn't bring himself to. He couldn't endanger her more. He just said, "This is working out well for me, too. I also had some things I wanted to get done. But I assume you're still looking into the murder, right?"

A pause. "Well, yes. But—"

"It might be better if you stopped. I appreciate your efforts even if you think I might be guilty. Of course, you'll never find anything that proves it's me, because it isn't." That certainly wasn't a confession, but could he do that? Not now, at least. "Anyway, I'm becoming even more concerned that you might be putting yourself in danger. If you stopped looking right now, that would be fine with me. And in any case, please be careful. Okay?"

Another pause. "I'm always careful," she finally said. "But is there something wrong? You sound different."

"Just be careful," he repeated. "And we'll talk again soon."

Or at least he hoped so as they said goodbye and hung up.

He hoped she really would be careful.

He wished he could tell her about the text, but what if the sender found out?

He wished he could tell Detective Vince Vanderhoff, even bring him the phone to have a tech expert at the station figure out who sent it, although it probably came from a burner phone and its owner wouldn't be known. And what if that sender was at the station and would then find out he had told someone about the message? One of Greta's relatives was a cop, after all.

But now...should he confess?

Chapter 14

Strange, Maisie thought. What had gotten Kyle so concerned about her all of a sudden?

Had he learned anything helpful in his defense? If so, surely he would pass it along to Vince, if not her.

Well, maybe she would make it a point to see Kyle again tomorrow. She'd already been thinking about it, after all...

And at this point she wasn't sure how wise she'd been to decide not to get together with him that evening.

She didn't relax right away that night but watched a late show on television to occupy her mind for a while. After she turned it off, she fortunately fell asleep and recalled nothing further until her alarm went off in the morning.

After taking care of Griffin and grabbing her own

breakfast, Maisie put on her uniform and began driving them to the station, forcing herself to concentrate on what she and her K-9 might be officially involved with that day. But on the way, she got a call from Doug. Her brother told her that he had just gotten a call, and the two of them, plus K-9s, were now on assignment. She and Griffin were to meet Hooper and him downtown near a park, where there'd been a traffic stop gone bad. A civilian and an officer had been injured by a suspected DUI driver, who had then run away.

The K-9s would find him, or at least that was the mission. Doug felt certain their dogs would do what was necessary, and of course Maisie agreed.

After hanging up, she called in to confirm with the dispatcher where she was going, then headed to the park, using her blinking, colored lights but not her siren to edge around drivers on the city streets that were busy at that hour.

The vehicle at fault, a big, blue SUV, was obvious in the parking lot, since it had a bashed-in front. It had hit a couple of other vehicles, a police sedan and a compact car. The injured had already been taken to the hospital, but the officers who were there described what they believed had happened and opened the driver's door to let the K-9s get the scent of the person who'd caused the problem.

Maisie and Doug often split up at crime scenes, depending on where their dogs led them. That happened this time, too, as they each headed down separate trails through the tree-filled park.

But they soon joined up again and hurried across the

street at the end of the park toward a nearby grocery store, led by their still-sniffing K-9s. The drunk driver had fled there? Looked that way.

It took another fifteen minutes to find him because he had gotten out through the rear storage area. But dear Griffin and Hooper did locate him.

The young, skinny guy in frayed jeans and T-shirt screamed as the dogs got near, maybe expecting them to attack. But that wasn't what K-9s were about—unless they were given that kind of command. Which Maisie didn't, of course, and neither did Doug.

Soon, the guy was in the custody of officers who would take him to the station and book him. Maisie and Doug would need to go there, too, to file their reports, but that was fine.

It was late morning by then. They'd been successful. Maisie was delighted, but not surprised.

Later, after grabbing lunch, she and Doug worked on their reports together at the station. Before they finished, Vince showed up in the K-9 officers' office. Good. She had planned to speak with him as soon as possible that day.

"I heard you were here, Officer Murran," he said. "Got some news for you about a possible suspect in the homicide investigation." The senior detective's eyes sparkled behind his glasses. He clearly recognized that Maisie would be interested in what he had to say. He was encouraging her interest in the investigation, not shutting her out. She was happy about that, even though she herself had opted for a break, at least for one night.

And Vince was possibly keeping her informed? That was even better.

Surely the suspect Vince was about to discuss with her wasn't Kyle…was it? Or was this person of interest the reason Kyle hadn't yet been arrested?

"Go ahead, sis," Doug said. "I'll finish our report. Tell me later what's new and where it goes."

Maisie loved working with her brother, who thought a lot like her and even looked a bit like her. Now, he undoubtedly knew she was antsy to leave with the detective and learn what he had to say. "Great," she said. "Thanks, bro."

She stayed beside Vince as the detective, in his dark suit, strode through the station toward his first-floor office. Griffin, of course, remained at her side. Not many other officers wandered around, but a bunch of civilians stood in the entry area. Maisie wondered who they were waiting to see.

They stopped at the break room on their way, and they both got coffee. Soon, she and Vince were seated on opposite sides of his wide desk, with Griffin lying on the wooden floor by her feet. The office was larger than the one Maisie and Doug shared, even though there was only one of him and he didn't have a K-9 to share it with, either. But he was one of the top detectives, so he had earned status and this nice office.

His desk was attractive, too: plain, dark wood, but polished nicely, with quite a few drawers and glass on top. They both put their cups of coffee on it.

Despite her pleasure that he was keeping her in the loop, she wondered if his real reason for asking her to come was for her to give him a recap of her own unofficial investigation that she wasn't supposed to be conducting. But Vince and she got along reasonably well, and he undoubtedly knew that her continuing interest would keep her involved. And she'd intended to fill him in, anyway.

Sure enough, he first started talking about the official investigation, in generalities. "Not that we wouldn't have done so anyway, but we've been keeping our minds officially open to all possibilities, mostly because it's the right thing to do but also because you're one of us, and we trust you. We know you doubt Dr. Kornel's guilt in this murder, no matter what it looks like—because you like dogs and that veterinarian takes care of them, or because you've gotten to know him well enough to believe in his innocence, or whatever."

He grinned at her, and Maisie felt herself glow inside. She'd been a cop at the Chance PD for a while now, loved the job and felt she was well respected, but this made her feel even better.

"I've been keeping an open mind," she said. "Yes, I like Dr. Kornel and what he does at the shelter and the vet clinic downtown to help animals, but if I'd seen anything that indicated he'd done more than argue with Greta Styles for doing things to potentially harm dogs and challenge the law, I'd have been right on it, giving you whatever evidence I found, of course, so you could throw the book at him. And I'm glad you're keeping an open mind, too, despite the appearances at the crime scene."

"Great attitude, and just what I figured," Vince said.

Then he asked if she happened to still be checking into persons of interest in the murder herself—part of her job or not. She decided to be honest, of course.

"Now and then," she told him. "For one thing, I've conducted informal interviews of the people connected with the Best Chance Pet Store when I happened to be shopping there or otherwise ran into them. I saw two of them yesterday morning in the store, then the other two when I went to the Chance Animal Shelter. I'll tell you about our discussions, but guess what? None of them admitted to me that they'd killed Greta. What a surprise."

Maisie had lifted her brows to underscore the fact she was just being sarcastic, as if Vince couldn't tell that for himself. She wasn't surprised that this senior detective also lifted his brown brows behind his glasses, as if intending to remain in sync with her despite the fact her brows came a lot closer to her hairline than his did. "Yeah," he said, "what a surprise. And I gather they also gave you other things to think about, like maybe it was one of Greta's exes. We've been checking into that, of course."

"Well, you're not alone in that."

Vince blinked at her, then smiled wryly as she described the two additional locations she had visited, and who she had spoken with. She'd half expected him to at least frown, maybe even scold her, for going in this additional direction they hadn't discussed, but fortunately he seemed more interested than angry.

"My opinion," she finished, "is that I did not believe her first husband, Kirby Grazio, was a likely suspect.

Her second husband, Winston Emerly, was maybe a little more likely because of the timing of their breakup and its reason—a possible affair. But I gathered he was the one who had been guilty of that, so maybe she would have been more likely to do away with him. And, as in her first divorce, they'd divided assets in a way that Emerly indicated neither of them was displeased. Assuming, of course, that both men told me the truth. But back to the pet store. I'm more likely to believe someone there is the best suspect."

"Why is that?" Vince asked.

Maisie told him in more detail about her discussions, although she couldn't exactly point at any of them as the killer, either. "But I gather the partnership between Greta and Esther had its issues. And I'm not sure yet how they chose their employees, but I gather Greta wielded the greater sword about who they hired. Enough to point at Esther as the killer? Not really. Also, Stan and Cora seem to be buddies, so could they have killed her together? Maybe, though I didn't gather they hated Greta. Beth, either."

Vince nodded and made notes on a pad of paper. Good. He was paying attention. He looked up at her then and said, "I think I may have a bigger surprise for you. No real answers yet, but something doesn't jibe with one of those store people. It doesn't mean she's guilty of murder, but we need a lot more information about who she is, her background."

Wow. As Maisie had hoped and Vince had indicated before, those in charge of the investigation had been keeping open minds—and that may have led to their focusing on someone else as the main murder suspect. Someone other than Kyle. True? Hopefully Vince would tell her. Maisie had an urge, which she squelched, to stand up and cheer.

Maybe she'd been right in the first place to trust Kyle.

Okay. She needed more information. All she knew so far was that the person in question was a she. Esther, Cora or Beth? She didn't even want to hazard a guess, although Esther had been Greta's partner, and they had been arguing...

"Please tell me about it." Maisie leaned forward, clasping her hands in front of her, and her movement got Griffin's attention. Her sweet K-9 stood up beside her as if expecting they were about to leave. "It's okay, Griffin," she told him softly. "Sit." Which he obeyed, and she stroked his head.

Then she looked back at Vince expectantly. Surely he was going to explain.

"Okay," he said. "Here we are. Now, since you're not a detective, you may not know much about our official procedure as we investigate a case." He leaned forward much as Maisie had, but he clasped his hands on top of his desk as he looked at her with the intensity extending from his brown eyes, behind his glasses, seeming to make his face even narrower.

"Then, tell me," she encouraged, keeping her tone light—but meaning it. Did she ever want to become a detective? Maybe, but only if she could keep a K-9 as her partner.

In this situation, though, she wanted to help solve this case, for many reasons. Including wanting to clear

Kyle, if that was possible. And now there was a hint of a chance that it was.

Nodding, Vince went into an explanation that might be too comprehensive, but Maisie attempted to take it all in since it was enlightening, and it also might be something she should learn. At least in the Chance Police Department, as in most, each suspect in a homicide case was investigated in great detail. Everything possible was scrutinized about their background, and Vince described some of the matters included.

So they undoubtedly knew a lot about Kyle, where he was from, where he'd gone to school, from grade school through veterinary college, and where he had practiced veterinary medicine before. His cop career before that.

And whether there'd ever been any suspicions against him in the past about breaking any kinds of laws— maybe even if he'd gotten speeding tickets somewhere.

Not relevant to this, of course.

"Interesting," Maisie said, meaning it. And those they were investigating besides Kyle? "Did Esther ever own a pet store before?" If she was the one Vince was talking about, maybe he'd segue into telling Maisie more about her possible guilt in this case.

"No, but she was a manager at a major pet store in San Francisco before moving here around eight or nine years ago. She and Greta met at that retail outlet, since Greta was a senior clerk there, and Esther had some relatives who were willing to lend them the money to form a partnership and open this store."

Definitely interesting. But so far Vince hadn't said anything that caused any suspicions about her possibly killing her partner. Unless they'd somehow argued about Esther's family money.

But Maisie didn't ask that.

In fact, she didn't have to ask any further questions then. Vince almost looked amused as he said, "So are you ready to hear our investigation results so far—and our dilemma?"

"Absolutely," Maisie exclaimed.

And was then surprised at the results.

"We're zeroing in, at least for now, on Beth Borrigan," Vince said. "Or whoever she is."

Really? Well, why not? Maisie leaned toward Vince even closer, all her concentration captured as he started to explain.

It turned out that, when the CPD had been at the store asking questions, Esther had assured them about their hiring process and had shown a detective, although not Vince, the files she had on each of the current three employees. Those files contained copies of driver's licenses and referrals from prior employers and sometimes more. Beth had a California license and had last lived in San Luis Obispo, working at a large pet store there that had provided a reference, or at least one of its managers had.

Only, the detectives here were still attempting to confirm that information, but Beth's references—which they'd copied for all the employees, not just her—weren't complete, so they hadn't yet been successful. The picture on her driver's license had even been blurry.

"We haven't discussed any of this with her—yet," Vince said. "We called her at the store a couple of times today but didn't reach her till late this afternoon. Although we did talk to Esther at the same time about wanting to confirm the information in her employee files while we were there. We told Beth we were coming in to talk to everyone tomorrow and wanted to confirm she'd be there along with the others. She agreed to meet with us. But then, a few minutes later, Esther called me and asked what was going on. She said Beth had asked her a few questions then run out of the store."

"What questions?" Maisie asked, enthralled by what this detective was saying.

"She wanted to know what Esther might have told them about her as an employee, and though we'd told Esther not to mention what we said, she'd told Beth we'd been digging into her files. And we'd gotten Beth's cell phone number when we talked with her before, but when we tried calling, it sounded as if the number no longer existed. We've got someone observing the local address she gave. One of the main reasons I wanted to fill you in is your sort-of relationship with the store and its employees. You've met them, talked with them already. That's why I'd like you to go there again before I do since that's not likely to be until tomorrow. You can ask those employees if anyone there knows how to find Beth or anything else that might be relevant. Oh, and you ought to bring Doug and his K-9 along so you'll have backup, too."

"Wow," Maisie said. "I know this doesn't mean she's our killer, but it certainly is suspicious."

"Exactly. Although, have you found anything about Beth that would explain or negate any of this?"

Maisie beamed inside that the detective trusted her enough to ask her opinion. "No," she said. "But I'm really interested in what you found."

Vince nodded, as if that was a given. "I'd like you to get on your way soon. I think we need to pursue this as a lead in our investigation. Maybe it's nothing, but we know there are places where people can obtain illegal driver's licenses. And I've contacted the San Luis Obispo PD and asked them to send someone to the store and ask some questions. Apparently someone there vouched for Beth before, and she's only been here a few weeks, so that person might still be there."

"Got it." Maisie rose, and so did Griffin. "Let me know what you find out. We'll head to the Best Chance Pet Store now."

That afternoon, Kyle was at the downtown clinic, between examinations, when he got a call from Maisie. This time, he was fortunately able to respond right away. He was in his office, sitting at his desk while filling out a report on a cat he'd just examined, when his phone rang.

"Hi, Maisie," he said after checking his screen to see who was calling. It felt good to hear from her, after last night. She was okay, he hoped. But then again, he hadn't mentioned that damn text to anyone, although he really wanted to. As long as there were no repercussions.

And neither had he confessed. Did Maisie want him to, too?

"I shouldn't be telling you this, so keep it quiet," she said, "and I can't go into detail, but there's another person our detectives are now looking into who's got a suspicious background. And although I didn't hear any specifics regarding evidence or motive, that person may replace you as suspect number one."

Kyle hesitated. He wanted to yell out in happiness—but then, again, he should perhaps give a damn about whoever was now in the cops' main spotlight. Someone from the clinic? Someone from the shelter?

Of even more concern, was that person the one who'd threatened to harm someone he cared about—Maisie?—if he didn't confess and save whoever it was?

At least he still had his job here…for now.

And the fact Maisie had called even though she hadn't wanted to see him last night? He was definitely pleased.

"Well, thanks for letting me know," he managed to say, knowing he didn't sound as excited as he should. As much as he actually was, at least on some level. "Do you know when you'll be able to talk about it?"

"Not really. Not till we are able to go after the suspect and place that person in custody. Assuming we find more evidence against that person."

She didn't even suggest which sex that suspect was. Kyle had an urge to shake something in frustration.

"Got it," he said, then added, "I take it you're listening to me and being careful, right?"

"Yes," she said in a dry tone as if irritated he would even ask.

But maybe he should show her that text. "Would you consider having dinner with me tonight?"

"Yes," she said in a light tone. "I'll consider it."

"Or even coffee this afternoon," Kyle added, shaking his head since he realized he might sound desperate. But it wasn't just because he wanted to see her. Although he did.

"Sorry, no. Doug and I have an assignment now, to ask a few more questions at the pet store, and I'm not sure how long that will take."

The pet store. Did that mean one of Greta's employees, or her partner, had now moved to the top of the suspect list? That might make sense, Kyle thought. He'd wondered about it all along.

"Okay. Well, keep me informed, as much as you can. And if you can't make dinner, maybe we can still get together for a drink." He did, after all, have things to talk to her about, like that threat. And fortunately Maisie agreed.

But should he tell Vince first? It might help to clear him. Vince couldn't be the texter. And surely the detective could get other cops assigned to keep Maisie safe.

Kyle remained busy at the clinic, fortunately, so he was able to not think about Maisie...much. He was assigned to take care of a beagle mix who just needed a checkup and some regular vaccines, then a pregnant cat whose owner wanted to make sure the ginger kitty was progressing well, and several other regular kinds of appointments.

He hoped he would get a chance to meet up with Maisie sometime, somehow, before this day ended.

And could he get to the police department to tell Vince?

Chapter 15

It was late afternoon by the time Maisie was done talking with Vince. This time she had been the one to call and tell her brother about their new, immediate assignment, instead of vice versa. She and Griffin probably didn't need any backup now, since they'd both just be nosing around the store and asking questions about Beth. Hopefully, they could do what they needed fairly quickly. But since it wasn't clear what was going on, or if Beth actually was there and hiding—and she was the killer—it wouldn't hurt to have Doug and Hooper along.

Beth. Could it be her? Maisie had seen her at the shelter several times, with Greta and with Esther. She'd seemed enthusiastic about dogs and about the shop. Wanting to do things her own way, maybe, or at least direct others in what to do.

But mentally ill?

Homicidal?

Well, Maisie certainly couldn't rule her out, especially now.

And she couldn't help looking forward to seeing Kyle later. Would she have actual news to impart to him?

Even if that didn't occur, whatever she learned at the store wouldn't prevent her from meeting him later for dinner tonight or, if not, at least a drink. She hoped.

She and Griffin got there first, which wasn't surprising since she'd called Doug while she was on her way. She didn't wait for her backup before parking and entering the store, which had a few customers but wasn't particularly crowded.

Griffin first led her to where another golden retriever, a young female, was sniffing around an area filled with toys. Her owner, a twentysomething woman, laughed and bent to pat both dogs, but then stopped and looked up curiously at Maisie, who of course was in uniform. Griffin, too, since he wore his CPD K-9 vest. "Hi," said the young woman. "Are you here on police K-9 business? And is it okay to pet your dog?"

"We're always on police K-9 business," Maisie responded with a smile, though she had no intention of adding any specifics. "With us, that can sometimes include anything from fetching toys to dog food." And bad guys...or women. "Right now it's fine to pet Griffin, although you're right. Most of the time you need to leave K-9s and service dogs alone. And it's always good to ask, as you did."

"Got it."

The woman peered around her. Maisie heard Hooper's paws on the floor before the K-9 reached her, and she turned to greet Doug.

She lifted her hand to wave at the nice customer she'd just been speaking with, then hurried with Griffin to the end of the row of pet products. Doug and Hooper followed.

"So what's going on?" Doug asked.

Maisie gave an abbreviated version of why they were there since she hadn't explained much when she asked him to join her. Luckily, he wasn't currently on an assignment so he could. He told her he'd cleared it with the station dispatcher while he was on his way here.

Maisie added, "I'm going to try to talk to Esther now, since she's the one who let Vince know about Beth leaving. But just in case, I'd like Hooper and you to look around the store and back room. I doubt she's hiding here, but it's best to be sure. And please be careful."

Her brother, taller than her, bent down and spoke in her ear. "Then that clerk is now the key murder suspect?"

"Unknown, but her actions today require some kind of explanation. And we do need to learn more about her documentation before she began working here."

"Got it. Hooper gets it, too. Come on, boy." Doug began walking back down the aisle with his K-9 but quickly stopped and turned back. "Keep me informed about what you find, if anything, and I'll do the same."

"Of course." Maisie and Griffin started back down the same aisle but veered off at a gap between the shelving rows.

She needed to find Esther.

The first store employee she ran into, though, was Stan, who was organizing boxes of treats in the aisle where Maisie and Griffin now stood. The young clerk's yellow shirt said *Pets Rock*. Would he know anything about what was going on?

Even if he did, Maisie wanted to talk to Esther first. Still, she said, "Hi, Stan. In case you can't tell what Griffin is thinking now, he's wondering what the best treats are here. We've bought some from this store before, but he's always hoping for even better. We'll have to—"

"I'll give him some samples soon, but I'll bet you're not here because of treats. I don't understand what's happening, but Esther's been all confused, and she told me that Beth just ran out with no explanation. Do you know why?"

"No," Maisie said, "but I hope to find out." She paused for just a second while considering how to play this. "Do you know if Beth is okay? If she had a family emergency or something?"

His eyes narrowed, and he ran his fingers through his short, dark brown hair. "I don't know what's going on, but...well, I gathered that Esther might be happy to have a cop like you around."

"Does she feel in danger?" Maisie demanded.

"I don't know what she feels. Except, like I said, confused. I think you'd better talk to her."

"Right," Maisie said and immediately turned, with Griffin, and began to search the store.

She found Esther just returning to the cash counter. She had to ring up a sale, so Maisie waited nearby, allowing Griffin to wander a bit on his leash and sniff whatever was on the shelves.

Fortunately—or maybe not fortunately for Esther—no one else was in line to check out. The store owner soon joined Maisie in the aisle. "Can you come into my office for a minute?" she asked.

"Of course."

It was the small room just inside the storeroom in the back, with a calendar from a pet-supply company on the wall, along with some pictures of dogs and cats. And no sign of Beth as they got there, just Doug and Hooper inspecting the area.

Esther sat on a folding chair beside Maisie rather than behind her desk. There wasn't a lot of room on the floor next to them, but Griffin nevertheless managed to sit down.

"So tell me what happened," Maisie said right away.

"I'm not exactly sure." The heavy-set woman had always seemed middle-aged to Maisie, but right now she appeared even older. Maisie figured it was the stress, which only made her want to know more even faster. "But I'll tell you what I can."

Esther explained that Beth had been spending a lot of time with her and in the store. Maisie, of course, knew that the clerk had come with Esther to the shelter as she had with Greta because she had seen both of them there, but she'd assumed that was Esther's choice—though, she gathered from what the woman said now that it had been a bit much for her. Not even Greta and she had hung out that much together. And Beth had encouraged her to go to the shelter even more often.

"But Beth really seemed to care about our store and about the idea of making even more money by having shelters hold adoptions here and making it a condition that the adopters buy a lot of merchandise, some at a discount, like Greta had started." Interesting. They were somehow making purchases an actual condition for the adoptions? No wonder the prior shelter had backed off from letting their rescues be shown here. "She'd seemed sad and very upset about Greta's death." Her voice choked a bit, and Maisie saw tears in her eyes. Obviously she, too, was sad and upset.

"I'm sorry," Maisie said. "But please go on."

"Well, none of us liked the ongoing police investigation here at the store." She looked into Maisie's eyes, then down again. "I know, it had to be done, even if that veterinarian was the main suspect."

Maybe not any longer, Maisie thought, then listened even more intently to what Esther was saying.

"But yesterday, I got word from Detective Vanderhoff that he wanted more information about me and my employees. He'd already asked about our backgrounds and all, and I'd told him how Greta and I got into the business, and what I knew about our employees. He said he wanted to come in and see the files on each of the clerks, like where they'd come from and what identification and other documents we'd had them supply before hiring them. He said that even though he or his fellow detectives had spoken with all of us before and gotten copies of some of those files, he wanted to verify everyone's backgrounds."

She stopped then and looked at Maisie, who just

nodded. "That's just another layer of caution in our investigation," she said, even though that wasn't done for every criminal search. But there had been enough outstanding questions this time...

"I understand. But I felt—well, it would potentially impose on our employees' privacy, so I let them know. Beth was definitely not happy about it. She was the last one I told, and her first reaction was to tell me no, I shouldn't do that. She mentioned her privacy, too, but I said we'd looked into the information she provided and allowed the cops to look, so it wasn't completely private, anyway. She started yelling, and I yelled back and told her that I had to obey the law and listen to the cops, and if she didn't like it that was too bad. And then, suddenly, she grabbed her purse from the cabinet where employees' personal stuff is stored and ran out of here. I couldn't reach her after that."

Very interesting—and it definitely made Maisie want to know what was in Beth's file.

Esther remained cooperative. Even though she had already given CPD detectives access, she showed Maisie Beth's file both in printed format and on her computer, and let Maisie take pictures of her employee's some-what-blurry California driver's license copy and the information about her references. "I'm just attempting to assist in the investigation," Maisie explained, ready to mention that Vince had sent her, but that wasn't nec-essary.

When she left Esther's office a short while later, she found Cora, who also seemed confused but had no answers.

Time to leave, then, Maisie thought, and follow up on Esther's information.

Fortunately, Doug was ready, too. He let her know that he and Hooper hadn't found anything. "Did you?" he asked.

"Not sure yet," she said. "I didn't learn enough to have a sense where Beth might have gone, and Vince may have someone observing where she lives. Tomorrow may be K-9 time there. I don't know." She had already told Doug that Vince would be returning here with others on the official investigation later.

"It'd be fine with me," Doug said. "We'll see. But as for the rest of tonight, I assume you'll be letting your buddy the vet know what's going on, or at least what you're allowed to, right?"

"You got it," she said. "I'll let you know how things go."

He had walked her to her car, so she and Griffin got in, and she watched Doug and Hooper walk away.

She called Kyle next. "Things went faster than I anticipated," she said. "I should be ready to have dinner with you in about fifteen minutes."

"See you at the Joint?"

"Absolutely." And then, smiling, Maisie headed immediately to the restaurant.

Kyle, waiting for Maisie in the booth that he had gotten along the farthest inside wall, was glad they had decided to meet again at the Joint Restaurant.

Of course, he would have been glad anywhere they had decided to meet.

He told himself it was mostly because he wanted to learn the latest in the murder investigation that had complicated his life. Or at least as much as Maisie could tell him.

But even more…he wanted to see Maisie, to talk with her, especially tonight. No matter what else he had told himself, he had missed her last night.

Would he tell her about that text? Maybe. But not here, where someone could overhear.

The Joint remained the local hangout that it was, popular and busy and with a reputation of being the town's favorite restaurant. He saw only a couple of empty tables, and everything else was full, and the acoustics were lacking thanks to all the conversations.

He would have preferred waiting outside for Maisie but figured he'd better grab a table while he could.

There she was, still in uniform, just walking into the casual dining room with Griffin leashed at her side and wearing his vest, so the dog would be welcome here. Kyle stood and hurried over to them.

"Welcome," he said, looking straight into Maisie's lovely hazel eyes.

"Thanks for being patient. And I do have some interesting things I think I can pass along to you."

"Looking forward to it. We're over here." He showed her to the booth. They let Griffin under the table first, then both sat down.

"So…let's order first," Maisie said, and he had to agree. He wasn't sure how long their dinner would take, but he hoped to invite Maisie over to his place when they were done, for more wine, or coffee, and definitely conversation.

Too bad he couldn't hope for more. Not yet, at least.

They both studied the menus their server, a young guy Kyle had seen here before, brought over. Kyle decided on a roast beef sandwich, and Maisie said she'd take a Caesar salad. They also ordered some wine.

After the server left, Kyle wanted to reach across the table and take Maisie's hand in his...just because. Because touching her might help to calm him—or make him even hotter in her presence than he already was.

It might cause her to start talking about what she had learned today, if anything. Was that someone from the pet store she'd hinted at now more of a suspect to the cops than he was?

He also thought again about the threatening text message he had received—as if it was ever out of his mind. He was wondering even more whether to ask Maisie if he could come to the police station and have some techie cop try to track down the source. But that remained a bad idea, since word could get out, and it had probably come from some untraceable burner phone, anyway.

"Are you okay?" Maisie was looking at him with her head cocked, allowing her soft, short blond hair to move just a bit. She appeared quizzical and maybe amused.

And definitely sexy.

If there was another suspect, if he, innocent as he was, was finally off the hook, maybe he could see if they could start a real relationship.

Only if she also wanted to, of course.

And if that suspect was taken into custody so they would be safe.

"I'm fine. And you?" Most important, he wanted to keep things light now that they were together, not get into any concerns he was feeling today. And if there was anything new Maisie could tell him, he wanted to encourage her to let him know.

"Fine. Curious. Kind of in the middle of things, but not." Maisie's face did appear curious and rather frustrated, but the server brought their wine before Kyle could ask her to explain. With Maisie's okay, they had ordered separate glasses rather than a bottle. He didn't want to stay here long—and he also wondered whether Maisie might still feel too stressed after her day on the job to drink much.

They could always order more.

For now, he asked, "So how are things going?"

"First—" Maisie picked up her wine glass and held it out toward him. Of course he picked up his own and touched it to hers.

"Cheers," he said.

"Oh, yes, we need some cheers," Maisie said. "And if things continue the way they've just been, we might have a lot to be celebrating soon."

Kyle smiled again and took a sip of his wine. Then he said, "Okay, please explain now."

That was when her cell phone rang.

Chapter 16

Maisie pulled her phone from her pocket, feeling Griffin stir near her legs. She stroked him gently with her foot, knowing her black, laced shoes, part of her uniform, wouldn't pull his fur.

"Excuse me," she muttered to Kyle as she looked at the caller ID, unhappy about the interruption. But it was Vince. She'd planned not to answer the call, but she had to, with him. She tapped the Accept button. "Hi, Vince. What's going on?" Something new with Beth? A follow-up to their discussion of her visit to the pet store and Greta's exes? If the latter, she could tell him whatever he wanted tomorrow.

"Hey, Maisie, I thought you'd want to hear where things stand right now in looking into Beth's background." Good. Her first guess had been the right one.

"I've thought about telling Jackson, but I don't want him hunting the woman because he's sure she's his aunt's murderer, though that's still not resolved. I've told my superiors here, of course, and I decided you're close enough to the case to deserve to know—especially since you visited the pet store again, but we haven't discussed the details yet."

"That's right." She didn't say where she was at the moment or what she was doing. "What new information do you have?"

"I had Officer Jones look into this, to help her aim toward a more senior position, and I think she did a great job. And here's where things stand."

She watched Kyle's face as she listened to Vince but didn't, couldn't, let him in on the conversation—even more impossible at a restaurant. Since Vince was mostly keeping the info private, she couldn't just blurt it to Kyle anyway. But would this new information help clear Kyle?

"Tell me," she urged Vince, wondering why he'd decided to call her now but delighted he had. The more she knew and the faster she knew it, the better.

They had done some more digging into what information they had. It turned out that Beth's driver's license was false. Even after further investigation, there was no *Beth*, or *Elizabeth*, or any other *Borrigan* who'd ever lived at that address in San Luis Obispo or anywhere near there. And the California Department of Motor Vehicles didn't have anyone with her name or other information, either.

So why had she taken on a false identity? Why was

she in Chance? Why had she taken a job at the pet store? And had she killed Greta? If so, why?

Maisie's opinion before had been somewhat neutral other than considering everyone who had known Greta as a potential suspect.

Not any longer.

"That's not all," Vince said. "I also had one of my people call the couple of references Beth had supplied. One was supposedly the manager of a pet store in San Luis Obispo where she'd once worked, but the person who answered that call just laughed and said that Rita must have gotten herself in trouble again and hung up. She didn't answer again, and when my investigator looked up the store's number online and called about Beth, the real manager had never heard of her—as either Beth or Rita."

Obviously Beth had lied on her application to work at the Best Chance Pet Store. But why? They'd be looking into who owned that reference phone number, although it most likely was a burner phone with no information attached. But someone from the department would call the San Luis Obispo PD and have them visit that store and see if there was anything they could learn there.

All that Vince said was circulating fast through Maisie's mind. She must have looked concerned because Kyle was frowning at her. She looked away from him.

"So where does the investigation go from here, Vince? And why are you telling me now? Just more of a search into the background of that person?" She didn't feel comfortable using Beth's name, real or not, in front of Kyle, at least not until more was known. And she didn't see where a K-9 officer or her dog would be particularly helpful officially, unless they had an idea where Beth was now and she and Griffin could attempt to find her.

The best thing that could happen next would be to find Beth and ask her all those questions.

"I'm telling you now since you've already gotten yourself involved in this case, and you're probably a good resource to continue with it," he said, making Maisie smile a little toward the table, not Kyle. He then gave the response Maisie had expected. "And we may eventually be able to thank you for being pushy and checking more into the pet-store employees and encouraging us to."

Maisie felt her smile broaden, and she looked back down at Griffin so she wouldn't meet Kyle's eyes again. Not now. Even so, she felt his gaze boring into her quizzically.

She listened to Vince as he continued. "We need to determine a good way to find Beth Borrigan—or whatever her name actually is. And interrogate her to learn more about who she is and whether she could be guilty in Greta Styles's homicide and, if so, hopefully find adequate evidence to convict her. Right now there are too many uncertainties regarding everything about that woman. She's certainly a good murder suspect just because we don't know anything that indicates her innocence, but neither can we prove her guilt."

"Got it," Maisie said as Vince wound down. "And although my visit to the store was interesting, I didn't really learn anything particularly helpful, though I want to do more digging. I'll tell you about it tomorrow. And—"

"Hold on a minute," he said, and then Maisie heard two voices from the other end of the phone. Though she couldn't make out what they were saying—Vince might have been covering his phone to prevent that— she believed one was a woman.

"Good timing," said a familiar voice. It was Assistant Chief Kara Province. "I was going to call you next, Maisie. We need a K-9 officer and dog to hurry to the Chance Animal Shelter right away, but your brother's on another assignment."

Maisie couldn't help blinking as Kyle met her gaze this time. She figured she must look confused, since that was how she felt. But if something involved the shelter, Kyle would want to know about it.

"I'd be glad to head there immediately," she said and saw Kyle's expression grow even more curious. Their dinner together was over before it had really started. But that was part of her being a cop. They could always ask for the wait staff to package their food to go. And she was even more glad now that she hadn't taken the time to change out of her uniform earlier to come meet Kyle. "What's going on?" she asked.

She wished that she and Kyle were alone and she could put her phone on Speaker after letting Kara know, since he'd undoubtedly want to hear what the assistant chief said. Maisie would have to tell him what she could as they headed to the shelter, as she was sure he'd want to go along, too.

"I just got a call from Scott at the shelter," Kara was

saying. "Or, rather, on his way back to the shelter. He'd gone home, but he said he and the managers had started getting calls from some of the staff. They said at first that the dogs inside the shelter areas had started barking off and on a whole lot more than usual. The staffers went to look and saw a few small open boxes of treats just outside the chain link fencing in some of the enclosures. The scent must have gotten the dogs' attention and caused them to bark. Fortunately, none of the dogs were able to get to those treats. We don't know whether they are safe. Scott checked his phone to see what was on the security cameras and saw someone dashing around inside the facility, obviously hiding, but not in any position where he could identify who it was. Quite possibly the person who'd been distributing those treats, although it could have been a staff member pulling a prank. He'll be there soon, and we both figured that having a K-9 helping out would be perfect." The fact that Scott remained an undercover cop would help him, of course, Maisie thought, but probably not enough. He needed help.

"Griffin and I will get on our way now," Maisie said. She was still looking at Kyle, who was now talking with their server. Their meals had just arrived.

"Great. Keep us informed about what you see."

"Of course."

So much for a pleasant outing with Kyle tonight. He clearly recognized she was leaving. He was already requesting that their meals be boxed to go.

She tapped the button to end the call. "I need to go to the shelter. Something's going on there."

"Are all the residents okay?" he demanded immediately. "And the animals?"

"I talked to Vince first, then Kara. Neither mentioned hearing of any injuries or anything like that, but—"

"But I'll head there, too, just to make sure."

"I figured you'd want to," Maisie said. If Kyle had been an ordinary veterinarian, Maisie might have told him to stay away. But he had a cop background. He wasn't part of the Chance PD, and she would do all she could to ensure he stayed out of trouble, but he could possibly help.

Still, she could call Doug and see if her brother and his dog could break away from whatever assignment they were on and come help, too. But she would take a look first and determine if that extra help was needed in addition to her and Griffin—and Kyle.

Kyle had been watching Maisie's lovely face as it tensed and showed concern and emotion, then determination. From what he'd heard, he got the sense that at first Vince had talked about finding some discrepancies in someone's background information that had led them to consider that person more as a potential murder suspect. A good thing, as far as Kyle was concerned.

As long as it was true. He didn't wish what he'd been going through as an innocent suspect on anyone else.

Then things had changed, and he believed Maisie was talking to someone else, probably another cop. He was right. She'd now identified those she spoke with as Detective Vince, and then Assistant Police Chief Kara.

Something was wrong at the shelter, and he needed to know more.

That made Kyle want to stand, take Maisie's arm and Griffin's leash and run out of there.

But they would wait the few minutes till their server brought their food and their bill, as he had requested as soon as he realized that, whatever Maisie was talking about, they'd need to leave quickly. He'd given the guy his credit card to reduce the amount of time they'd have to wait.

For now, he finished drinking the remaining wine in his glass. Then the server returned with their containers. The receipt he brought looked fine and Kyle added a tip. They were ready to go.

"Thanks," Maisie said. "We can even things out later."

He didn't reply, since he had every intention of taking care of it. For now, they wended their way through the occupied tables to the door.

"Why don't you ride with Griffin and me?" Maisie said as they got to the sidewalk outside. "I can tell you what little I know, plus we need to hurry—and I can get away with that better than you in my official car."

"Good idea."

Once they were all loaded into Maisie's vehicle, he was somewhat amused when she turned on her rotating lights on top of the SUV. They definitely were hurrying.

"Okay," he said as they reached the nearest corner, where Maisie turned to head to the shelter. "Tell me what's going on."

Thanks to the parts he'd gathered, little was much of

a surprise. Apparently they had found some discrepancies in the background of one of the store employees. Maisie now let him know it was Beth because of the potential danger at the shelter but requested that he keep the information private for now. Those discrepancies might not mean anything. But the fact that someone—Beth?—may have gotten onto the shelter grounds, left things near some of the animal enclosures and, while seen somewhat on the security cameras, avoided getting caught? Well, that was not only a surprise, it worried the heck out of Kyle. What if those treats were poisoned? At least, from what Maisie said, no dogs had been able to get to the treats.

He was glad he was accompanying Maisie and Griffin, even though he was no longer a cop. But he would assist in any manner he could.

They'd arrived. "Why don't you drive around the perimeter of the shelter so we can take a look to make sure everything seems okay from outside?" Such as no walls shattered or doors left open that could have allowed an unwanted person to get in.

"Good idea," Maisie agreed, and she did as he'd suggested. Everything looked okay as far as Kyle could tell. It was late enough in the day that it was growing dark outside, but the shelter had security lighting all around.

As Maisie parked in the lot near the building, Kyle called Scott. No need to hedge about how he had heard there was a problem. He and Maisie could have been together for a lot of reasons, not just attempting to have an enjoyable evening out.

"Hi, Scott, it's Kyle," he said. "Maisie and I just arrived at the shelter, and we're about to walk in. Can you meet us and tell us more about what's going on?"

"Great idea. And thanks for coming."

"Of course I'd come. I want to make sure the animals are all doing well. Oh, and the people, too." Kyle had wanted to sound somewhat amusing, but what he said was true. Neither of them laughed. "Did you gather all the treats so we can test them?" When Scott assured him they had—or at least all they'd found—Kyle continued, "We'll meet you inside the clinic."

He wanted to go there first to make sure everything looked okay. At the moment, he didn't have any animals in enclosures, but that was his place around here. Besides, even though it was all locked up, he did keep some drugs around and wanted to ensure none had been stolen.

As far as he knew, Maisie had keycards she could use inside the shelter, such as along the reception hallway. But he had cards for all the locks. He now ushered Griffin and her into reception, then through the door that would lead them to his clinic.

Scott met them there. So did Nella. That wasn't surprising. They had a relationship and both were invested in the protection and security of this shelter.

"Things seem to have settled down a bit since we found and removed the treats, but we'd like Griffin to do a walk-around once we fill you in more on what's been happening," Scott said.

"Sure." Since this was his clinic, Kyle led the others inside, where they all took seats in the entry room.

"So tell us what's going on," Maisie said. "I want

to hear firsthand. So far, I've only heard a little from Detective Vanderhoff and Assistant Chief Province."

And Kyle had only heard what Maisie had told him. When Scott began to talk, though, Kyle went inside and checked out the rest of his clinic.

No strangers hiding in there. No drugs missing.

When he got back, Scott said, "I was just telling Maisie more about the strange things our staff members have been calling us about tonight. For one thing, barking dogs are being stirred up at least partly because boxes of treats are left outside their enclosures that they can't get to. There may be other things going on, too."

"I'd like to go see the treats," Maisie said. "Are you sure they've all been removed?"

"Yes, fairly sure," Nella responded. "We don't know whether they're safe. And we don't give our animals that kind of treat, although they appear to be a known brand. But there's no way the staff members could have bought them and brought them in, so we're completely puzzled. Except to assume the person Scott saw on the security cameras, whoever that is, must have done it."

Was it Beth or someone else? Neither of them mentioned the store employee, so Kyle assumed they hadn't yet heard what Maisie had learned. Nor did they refer to anyone else as a possibility.

For once, neither Scott nor Nella was wearing a shelter T-shirt, probably because they'd left home too fast to change clothes. Both were still dressed casually, though, Scott in a black long-sleeved sweatshirt, and Nella in a gray button-down shirt.

"Well, can you show Griffin and me where the treats were left?"

"Sure," Nella said. "You, too?" she asked Kyle.

"Of course. That way, I can do a basic check on how the animals look, to hopefully ensure none has been poisoned or otherwise harmed."

"I'll join you," Scott said.

Once they got to the spot where the treats had been found and Kyle had had a chance to look at the animals, everything seemed fine. No treats there now. But Griffin must have smelled something, since the K-9 appeared to react to more than the scents of the dogs he saw inside the enclosures.

"Let us do a bit of exploring here," Maisie said. "I'll let you know if we find anything."

"I'll come, too," Kyle said, wanting to be there to protect her if necessary.

"No, you stay with Scott and Nella. Griffin and I will scout first and call in backup if it's needed."

With that, she turned her back on him and, K-9 at her side, headed out of the enclosure building and onto the grounds.

Feeling concerned, wishing he'd ignored what Maisie said and joined her, he nevertheless joined Scott and Nella instead as they entered the main dining area for the shelter, where the staff members were now hanging out and talking about what was happening.

The majority of the tables were occupied. He thought he recognized most of the people there, since he had met all the staff members by now. Telma and Camp, the other two managers, were there, too, sitting at separate tables with staffers, as if to attempt to calm them. It was late for them to be there, so they'd probably returned as Scott and Nella had, but both were wearing their work T-shirts.

"What's going on, Scott?" That was Bibi, who stood up from where she'd been sitting but grasped the table in front of her. No evidence of that gap-toothed smile now. "I went with a couple of people, and we grabbed some of those boxes of treats like you said, but how did they get there?"

"We'd like to find that out," Scott responded, taking a step closer to her. "Has anyone seen...well...anything out of place other than those treats?" He seemed hesitant, which was unlike Scott, at least as far as Kyle understood him, though he hadn't known him long.

"Are you suggesting someone's at the shelter who shouldn't be?" Chessie asked. She sounded more angry than scared about the possibility. "Maybe we should all leave."

Kyle had gotten the impression that, even though Chessie was under protective care here, this staff member wasn't entirely happy about all the restrictions. Maybe she had somehow brought the treats in as a way to leave the enclosure for a while? Though, that didn't make sense. As Nella had indicated, how would she have gotten them?

"That would be too dangerous for all of you," Scott said, though his tone was soothing. "For now, you can all go back to your rooms. We have a K-9 who's searching the shelter grounds. And Nella and I are going to stay here tonight to keep an eye out for you."

An eye that would be more directed toward whatever, whoever, else was at the shelter, Kyle figured, than at the actual staffers.

Maybe he would stay here, too, after Maisie and Griffin returned from their patrol: sleep in his clinic if they hadn't found and arrested anyone. Or not sleep, which was the more likely possibility.

Would Maisie and Griffin remain here, too, under those circumstances?

He wouldn't be at all surprised.

Chapter 17

Though it was dark outside, the shelter areas were well lit. The concrete structures beyond the administration and apartment buildings were mostly only one or two stories high, since they just held the rescue animals and, from what Maisie had seen, they all had room for more than those currently there.

Maisie was glad she had such a wonderful, obedient, dedicated K-9 as Griffin accompanying her. Leading her. Well, heck, she adored Griffin, who was part of her family as much as Doug—and Hooper, too, of course.

And Kyle? Well, she knew she'd come to care for him a lot. Too much. Sure, he still hadn't been fully exonerated, although she felt relieved there was another major suspect who now took priority. But more info was needed.

Was he family? No way. Though, she'd appreciated his offer to join her and Griffin, undoubtedly to help protect them. And she would see him here again soon.

But right now, though she allowed her mind to go off on tangents somewhat, Maisie was concentrating. Observing everything around them.

She and Griffin were on their own, scouting the outside areas of the inner shelter, mostly behind the buildings housing the rescue animals. They both were wearing Kevlar vests for safety, anticipating danger. No dogs were barking at the moment, which probably was an indication that the intruder Scott had reported wasn't in any of their buildings, or at least not leaving treat boxes… Strange. But where was he or she?

And she assumed it was a she.

On the other side of the path where they walked was the outside fence, tall and completely covered so no one out there could see anything inside.

Why check this area out? Because even though Scott had seen whoever was lurking in the central area on security cameras, he didn't see that person any longer. They needed to know more about wherever that person had been and where she'd come from. One of the staffers? Not likely. And there were doors into the buildings from this path and at the rear of the buildings, so even though those doors were supposed to remain locked, that person might have found a way inside, sneaked around and left those boxes.

But why? And where was she now? Still at the shelter somewhere?

Maisie occasionally heard a car drive by outside the

fence. When she and Griffin passed the building where all staff members ate, she heard voices and knew that a lot of them, maybe all, remained inside, which was probably good and safe, for now at least.

And Griffin? She hadn't given him anything in particular to smell to attempt to find someone, but he knew the drill. He would let her know if there were any fresh scents around here, at least, of any people he hadn't yet met or smelled. Or anything else that seemed off to him.

For now, he just kept sniffing the path they walked on, interested and alerting now and then but only leading her to the back doors of the buildings. Maisie suspected that was where the treat dropper had gained entry. But when she checked, the doors were locked as usual. Once again, she wondered if their trespasser had a key, or whether it was one of their staff members or someone else who'd gone inside the buildings from the front.

Again, who and why, and what was the story about those treats?

When they'd nearly reached the end of the path, Maisie prepared to take Griffin around the building they stood in front of. She saw the tall, covered and closed gate in the fence, one she knew was an emergency exit, if ever needed.

Griffin hurried over to it, sniffed the ground around it, sat and looked at her, alerting. He obviously smelled something different here. Someone different.

Had a resident left, without there being an emergency?

Or was this how someone had gotten inside?

Maisie assumed it could be either…or both.

The first person she thought of was Beth, of course, after her conversation with Vince. But that couldn't be, could it? All Maisie knew was that Beth/Rita had lied on her job application. And maybe… Well, she could have murdered her boss. But why would she come here?

Of course, she had been here before, but under far different circumstances.

Maisie grabbed the gate and attempted to push it open. Maybe it had somehow gotten unlocked. But if so, it had been locked again, since it seemed secure now.

"Find," she told Griffin, and nose to the ground, her K-9 began walking in the direction Maisie had intended to head, around that last building.

At its end, Griffin turned and walked along the paved path on that side of the inside shelter area, still sniffing the ground.

Who did he smell? Was that person still here, hiding? If so, where…and why?

By habit while in a challenging situation, Maisie let her right hand rest on the gun in the holster at the back of her duty belt. Not that she had any intention of hurting anyone, not even the intruder—assuming they didn't attempt to harm anyone else. Although if she did see that person, she would have no qualms about drawing her gun to get the person to stay still and be apprehended.

But what was this all about?

She thought about calling Scott. The shelter director was an undercover cop, after all. But he was most likely with the staff members, and his primary duty was to protect them.

She could call Kyle instead, since he had offered to help. But why? There wasn't anything he could do, not till she had further information. His former background as a cop could be helpful, but that wasn't who he was now.

Still, it wouldn't hurt to let him know she had a possible lead on the intruder. Was Kyle still in the dining area with Scott? It sounded as if he was, since when he answered her call there was a lot of background noise.

"I just wanted to let you know that Griffin has smelled where the possible outsider got in," she told him right away. "Nothing to worry about, at least not yet, though we're currently following the scent. Whoever it was might have entered through the safety gate in the fence on the left side toward the back of the shelter, since that's when Griffin started alerting. No indication whether that person is still here somewhere. Are you still with Scott or Nella? I need to let them know, too, of course."

"Just Nella. Scott's gone to his office to check the security cameras, I guess." But he'd at least left Nella there to keep an eye on their protected residents, which wasn't a surprise. "He thought he saw something again on his phone," Kyle continued, "but needed a larger screen. Someone inside one of the dog-shelter areas." So Scott had had a good reason to leave them temporarily, anyway. "Tell me where you are right now. I'll catch up with you."

"You don't need to do that," Maisie said, although

she felt a surge of warmth pass through her at his caring nature. "I'm the cop, remember? I'll let you know how things go." She hung up, called Scott and told him what she had already related to Kyle.

"Damn," he said. "I've still been watching the security cameras and got no further insight other than someone was sneaking around, entering the buildings from the central area and leaving those treats, I guess. But I don't see whoever it was now. I'll be coming back down soon to keep an eye on our staffers, hopefully for their protection and not to start pointing fingers at any of them. Meantime, I'd really appreciate it if you and Griffin would keep checking out anything you can."

"Will do," Maisie said, and then, in an abundance of caution, she indicated that there was an identity problem with one of the pet-store clerks and mentioned Beth, since she had been here. "Not sure what that means yet, and there's no reason to think she's your intruder, but I figured it wouldn't hurt for you to be aware of the issues involving her."

Scott thanked her, said he'd keep that in mind as they attempted to locate and identify the intruder, and then Maisie hung up. Then she looked around. She and Griffin were heading in the direction of the front buildings containing the dining area, and her K-9 was still sniffing and moving.

So where was the intruder now?

Or was it an intruder? Maybe that person was with the staff members in the dining room.

She continued following her K-9, who was now getting closer to the main office and dining and entry buildings.

Why? Did he still actually have a scent he was following? Most likely. She trusted her dog.

Just then, the door to the dining area opened, and Kyle burst out—alone. He had his phone in his hand, and he barely looked at Maisie as he turned and headed back toward the entry building.

What was going on? Was there something wrong at his clinic? But how would he know?

Whatever was happening, Maisie was determined to find out.

Strange. Very strange, Kyle thought.

But of course he had to go check the clinic here at the shelter.

He had just received a call from Jada, the receptionist at the downtown clinic. "Are you at the shelter?" she'd asked.

"That's right. Is everything okay? Do you need another vet there immediately?"

"Well, no. We're fine. But the clinic's main cell line just received a text with a picture in it of a wall cabinet that appeared to have been broken into, one that contained drugs, it looked like, with some scattered on a counter. The caption was *Chance Animal Shelter Clinic. Tell Scott.* I tried calling the number, but there was no answer. We can try to have the cops track it down, but do you have drugs there that someone might have wanted to steal?"

"We've got the normal stuff," he said. "And yes,

some, like ketamine, could be used by people, too—who could also OD on it. I'll go look." He'd ended the call.

But why did the text say *Tell Scott*? He'd let him know later, ask if he'd heard anything.

First, he would check on what was happening at his small clinic.

Should he tell Maisie? She was the cop, after all. But until he knew there was actually a problem, why bother her? She was already busy, scouting the shelter with Griffin. And she'd already told him not to join her.

However, was that picture an indication that the shelter intruder had now taken over his clinic?

He'd just have to be careful. And maybe get in touch with Maisie if he needed her help—or Griffin's.

For now, he looked around before slipping into the reception hallway. He stopped inside the door and looked around and listened.

Nothing sounded unusual.

He kept his back close to the wall and slowly edged his way toward the clinic. There, he stopped and listened again.

Still nothing from inside, so he opened the door slowly and edged inside. He stood quietly in his waiting room. Sure, he needed to go inside to the enclosed area attached to the examination room and check on the drugs. But not now. If that person had come in since he was there before and was still around, it might be too dangerous.

Okay, maybe it would be better to check with backup, like Maisie. He started to quietly leave—when he was suddenly startled by a voice.

"Hey, come on in," said a familiar female voice, and someone entered the waiting room from the inside. He knew it was Beth. She was dressed all in black with a hoodie over her head and a safety mask over her face. "Kyle? Where's Scott? I used his name in my text so I figured he'd be here, too."

"Nope, just me." Kyle didn't move. Her hand was behind her back. Was she armed? Or did she just want him to think so? "So what's going on, Beth?"

She took a step closer, and Kyle tensed up. Could he just run out the door?

Maybe, but he'd have to do it quickly.

"Oh, I'm not Beth."

"But—"

"I was never Beth." Her tone was a growl, and she pulled her hand out from behind her. Kyle wasn't surprised that she held a gun—and pointed it at him. "But I changed myself and used that name temporarily, thanks to this lousy animal shelter."

"What do you mean?" Maybe if he kept her talking, he'd find a way to get out. "And please don't aim that gun at me."

He'd had to say that. He heard a noise from behind him in the hallway. A snuffling noise—probably from Griffin.

He had to let Maisie know that the person inside with him was armed.

"Of course I will. Now, don't you want to know why I'm about to use you even more than I already have to get revenge on this damned shelter?"

"Well, sure," he said. Could he get her to admit to

sending that text that threatened, most likely, Maisie? He would in any event protect Maisie from her now.

And could he get her to confess to killing Greta?

"Good. And as soon as I tell you, I want you to get Scott to come here. Unless you want me to kill you." Her emphasis on the word *you* suggested she would kill Scott if he came, so Kyle certainly wasn't going to get the shelter director to join them.

But for now he'd play along.

"Of course I don't. I'll do what you say. But yes, I'd like to hear what this is all about."

She took a step closer to him and waved the gun. Kyle made himself stand still, while looking out of the corner of his eye toward the chairs near him.

Not a good place to hide from bullets, nor could he lift a chair as a shield fast enough. If necessary, he'd need to duck and try to run out the door.

"Well, right now I'm particularly angry that the damned cops are checking to see what Beth's background is—though, of course, they won't find it. Esther told me they were nosing around, and my friend who helped me before told me she'd gotten a call." She leaned slightly against the wall. "See, I'm really Rita Simont. I live in San Luis Obispo. And this miserable excuse for a shelter? It stole my dog from me." She really did look upset, as far as Kyle could see despite the mask obscuring her face. Tears? Maybe.

He already knew to be careful—and more so, since this woman clearly was mentally ill.

She went on to tell him that not long ago she'd owned a beloved shepherd mix named Gravy that she kept trying hard, very hard, to train, but the dog had a mind of his own and was taken from her for alleged abuse. "This damned shelter accepted my Gravy as a rescue dog right after it opened."

And if that wasn't bad enough for her, she was arrested and to be put on trial for the crime of animal abuse but instead accepted a plea bargain where she was put on probation and was never to own a dog again.

Her so-called training must have been hell for the poor dog, Kyle thought, for her to be given that kind of punishment.

"That couldn't be," Beth/Rita said. "So maybe Rita couldn't own another dog, but I could if I was someone else." So she had changed who she was—more than once.

And a little while later, she visited the Chance Animal Shelter with a different identity and appearance after being vetted and accepted as a potential adopter so she could get Gravy back. But he'd already been adopted out.

"So I want revenge, of course. And before you ask, yes, I was the one to kill Greta."

Good. She had confessed. Kyle wished he was somehow recording this, but hopefully she would say so again in a more official setting.

"I'd gotten her to hire me at the store after changing my appearance and identity yet again," Beth continued, "so I could stay in this area and no one would question me. But even with the things I did to get good references and all, she found me out. I had to get rid of her. And I tried to make the shelter suffer a little, too, by framing its only veterinarian." Kyle could see her eyes crinkle, as if she was grinning beneath her mask. "Of course I didn't mind that my coworkers at the store were under investigation, too."

He wanted to rush at her and grab the gun, make her pay...but without being armed himself, he knew better.

"So this time," she continued, "I don't only want to frame you—although I'll do that, too, since you're such a good patsy. I even was able to threaten your job. I assume your bosses heard some pretty nasty stuff about you from the media. I was the one who contacted them as a scared pet owner who was afraid to take my dogs to your vet clinic as long as you, the murder suspect, were there. Did your bosses tell you about that?" She didn't wait for his reply, and her expression darkened. "I gather they didn't fire you, damn it." But then she perked up again. "I was hoping you'd spend all your time here at the shelter rather than there and make things easier for me, but it's working out now, anyway."

"They did almost fire me," he said, hoping to humor her, as well as keep her talking. "I'm on probation, though not the same kind as yours."

Her expression grew sour. Kyle had considered the young woman somewhat good-looking before, but in this black outfit and mask covering nearly all of her except for pale, scowling portions of her face, he of course thought otherwise. And he wondered what she really looked like, since she had clearly changed her appearance each time she changed her identity, with makeup, hair color and styles, whatever.

"Too bad they didn't," she growled. "Anyhow, things

are okay right now. We're here at the shelter, anyway. I really want to hurt this place by eliminating one of its big shots. Oh, I don't want to hurt any of the animals, of course, and not even the people here in protective custody. Just Scott to begin with, since he's in charge. And then we'll see."

Damn. Kyle wanted to get out of there. He wanted to warn Scott.

First, though, he had to ask. "I received a text message the other day and couldn't determine its source. It said I should admit to committing Greta's murder or someone I cared about would be murdered next, and I also couldn't talk about it. Did you send it? And was that person Scott? If you'd back down from hurting him, I could admit now to the murder."

And tell the rest of the story, too, obviously.

"Nah. I meant that cop lady, since I gather you two are buddies. I'll probably still get rid of her later. Right now, I'm after Scott. Although let's see how things go. Maybe you'll be able to admit to both killings." Her grin was pure evil, but Kyle tried to ignore it.

Before he replied to her, he heard another noise outside the door. This time, Beth did too.

"Well, hi, Officer Maisie," she called. "Come on in. Fast. And I'll hold off shooting your vet friend Kyle here if you do."

"Put the gun down carefully, Beth," Maisie said. "I know you're Rita, too, but around here we know you as Beth. Things will go a lot better for you if you cooperate."

But Beth aimed the gun off to the side and pulled

the trigger. It obviously had a silencer, since it wasn't as loud as most guns.

"Nope," she called. "I'm not putting anything down. But the next time I shoot, it'll be Kyle who gets it."

Chapter 18

Damn. Maisie had her gun drawn, too, of course—but out here in the hall she couldn't see how best to use it...if she had to.

She had given down orders to Griffin, and he now lay on the hallway floor—safe out here. Who knew what that woman would do to a harmless dog, even though she'd said she wouldn't hurt a dog or a person under protective custody?

And right now, Maisie had to determine the best way to get in...and help Kyle.

Hearing a sound at the far end of the hall, Maisie turned. New staff member Chessie was headed her way. And she was walking one of the shelter dogs on a leash. Spike, the retired K-9.

Maisie wanted to burst into the clinic, gun drawn,

without waiting, and take down the armed woman inside. But she didn't want anyone else hurt.

Certainly not Kyle, who might already have a gun pointed at him. And now, another civilian who could get in the way?

But Maisie knew, for Kyle's sake, that she did need to enter the clinic, since she'd been ordered to by Beth. Maisie would do all she could for Kyle's sake. As much as she'd been attempting not to let herself get too involved, she cared for him. A lot.

Allowing him to get hurt was not on her cop agenda.

But she also wanted to get Chessie away from there. That should be easier. She hurried down the hall toward her.

"You need to get out of here," she told the resident softly but in a voice that she hoped brooked no argument.

Chessie looked down at the gun in Maisie's hand, now pointed at the floor. "It's Beth in there, isn't it?" Tears were running down her face. "This is my fault. We'd been talking when we could, including about the real nature of this shelter, and she promised to help me get some away time from here if I let her in...and so I did. I know she started scattering treats around, but she said that was just to distract all the people and dogs. They weren't dangerous. And she said she especially wanted to get Scott to look for her and where those treats came from, though she didn't say why. But I got worried, so I brought Spike with me. What's happening?"

Okay, Maisie had some answers now, though they didn't do her much good. Only, she knew what a wonderful K-9 Spike was, too, like Griffin.

"You'll hear later," Maisie said. "For now, leave

Spike with me and go tell Scott to call the Chance PD and let them know that the person who killed Greta Styles now has a hostage in the veterinary clinic."

"Oh, no," Chessie cried, although fortunately she still kept her voice low. "I didn't know. I—"

"Give me the leash," Maisie ordered, and Chessie complied. "Now, go."

Thankfully, she did.

But how was Maisie going to get in there with the two K-9s as assistants, keeping all of them, and Kyle, safe?

And whatever she did, it had to be fast.

"Okay, Beth," she shouted toward the door. "I—"

"Have you called for Scott to join us?" the woman yelled. "That's who I want to see. And if you've called for other cops and they show up, I'll just go ahead and kill this worthless vet instead."

Instead? Instead of Scott? Maisie assumed that was what this woman wanted—not just for Scott to join them but to kill him.

And Kyle, too? He was anything but worthless. Maisie assumed, with his cop background, he was working on ideas for getting control of the woman threatening him.

The fact that he hadn't yet was somewhat scary. In fact—

"You had better let me talk to Dr. Kornel, make sure he's okay, before I come inside," Maisie called.

After a moment, Beth perhaps nodded to Kyle to talk since Maisie heard him. "I'm fine, Officer Murran. But you and Griffin had better leave—and not call Scott. Beth does have a gun pointed at me, and she showed me a knife just like the one she used to kill her boss Greta. She has it in a pouch on her belt. And—"

"Shut up!" Beth screamed, and Maisie half expected to hear muffled shots ring out.

But Maisie did have an idea. "Tell you what, Beth. I'll come in with Griffin, and you can keep us as hostages and let Dr. Kornel go. Then we can carefully walk our way out of the shelter. Have you thought otherwise about how you'll escape after you kill one of the managers here, or anyone else?"

"Yeah, I'll kill anyone who gets in my way."

Unstable? Definitely. "Well, you can't frame someone else that way. And there's likely to be too many people around for you to hurt them all. Think about it. Don't you want to just leave and go somewhere else? Come with Griffin and me, and you can."

Silence. Maybe she was thinking, or at least trying to. And Kyle hadn't attempted to interrupt and say something protective of Maisie, which concerned her. Had the woman done something to him?

"Okay. But on my terms," Beth finally said. "This damn vet is coming with us. That way, I'll leave, and no one will know I was here—till I let you both loose."

As if she planned to do that. And others would know she'd been here. But Maisie's sense of potential optimism was rising. Would Beth come out here with Kyle with the intention of leaving? She'd have her gun aimed at him, yes—but with his cop knowledge of how to protect himself, and the two dogs for help, Maisie would hopefully have a good chance of bringing her down before she hurt him or anyone else.

And Beth didn't know that Chessie had been here and had gone for help.

"I understand," Maisie called. She geared up quickly with the things she had in her duty belt, then just waited. And waited.

What was Beth doing?

Maisie heard a strange noise from behind the door. Kyle groaning? Surely the woman wasn't hurting him after saying she was bringing him along.

Suddenly, the door swung open. Kyle started walking out of the clinic with Beth, or at least a woman dressed so as to be unidentifiable with a dark hoodie and safety mask on, at his side. He was hunched over—and the woman held a large knife at his throat.

Yes, one that looked like the same kind as the murder weapon.

She held a gun in her other hand, but it was pointed toward the floor.

"Now get out of the way and follow us," Beth said, and Kyle shuffled slowly into the hallway.

He glanced at Maisie and nodded almost imperceptibly. Nodded? He definitely didn't have this under control. But he probably was telling her to do what she needed to do to stop this woman.

Which of course she would. She and the K-9s.

Aiming her gun at Beth, she immediately yelled, "Attack," and both Griffin, who was standing on alert, and Spike lunged toward Beth.

A knife at his throat. Kyle felt it dig in—but not too far before Maisie sped around to the side of the dogs and, now wearing her thick neoprene police gloves that Kyle remembered well from the old days, reached beneath the knife at his throat and pulled it back, away from him.

Okay. His throat had been cut, but not deeply. There was a little blood involved, and it felt a lot better when Maisie hugged him hard with one arm as she held her weapon in the other hand and carefully watched as both dogs, growling, attacked the woman, knocked her over and bit at her throat.

His turn to help. Kyle pulled away, grabbed Beth's arm that was flailing with the gun and pushed it to the floor, standing on her wrist till she let go, then did the same with the hand holding the knife. He turned her onto her stomach and yanked her hands behind her back. The dogs backed off but stayed right beside them, obviously willing to jump in again.

"Cuffs?" he asked, looking at Maisie.

She grinned, and why not? He figured she had recognized that this one-time cop still had it in him.

She reached to her side and took her cuffs off her belt, then knelt down, too, and snapped them on Beth. "Rita, or Beth, or whoever, you are under arrest for the murder of Greta Styles and felony battery of Dr. Kyle Kornel, and I'm certain there will be a lot of other charges against you." She then stated the woman's Miranda rights.

She got a phone call then and looked at her cell. *Doug,* she mouthed toward Kyle. She listened for a moment and said, "Yes, it's okay to come into the clinic now, bro."

Kyle wasn't surprised to see Hooper join them in the hallway as Maisie's brother entered, and in a minute Scott and the other managers, and a reluctant Chessie, entered from far down the hall.

It was over.

Well, not entirely. This veterinarian couldn't help hugging the K-9 cop again who'd helped to clear his reputation, and who had done her damnedest to save him.

As Doug took over the custody of the woman they still thought of as Beth and also recited her rights, Scott came over to them. He bent and petted the three K-9s, then stood again.

"So what was this really about?" he asked.

"Well…" Maisie hesitated, glancing toward Doug, who, with Hooper, gently pushed the cuffed person they now had in custody out of the hall and into the reception area. Maisie was glad to see that backup had already arrived, and another officer helped Doug maneuver Beth out the door where police cars were undoubtedly waiting. Others came in to take care of the evidence. "You were apparently a bad director," she finally said to Scott. "This was revenge because this shelter took her dog in last year after the authorities told you he'd been abused—by her, his owner, as it turned out. And by the time she came to get him, he was gone, adopted by someone else, and she blamed you."

"What?" Scott looked confused. So did the others. "I think we need to hear more about this story," he said.

"Sure," Maisie agreed.

"And…and I need to tell you what I did," Chessie said, once again crying. "I let her into the shelter."

Scott glared at her. "I want to hear more about that, too—and then we'll have to decide if you can stay, after breaking some of our most important rules."

"I understand. But I know I was wrong. No matter what I said or did, I love this place and how it makes me feel safe. I really want to stay. Please."

Kyle wondered how that would turn out. Especially since she suspected that not only had Chessie let Beth come in but had somehow managed to get her a keycard.

For now, though, Maisie said to him, "Let's give a quick rundown to Scott about what happened. And then we should go to the station and give our official statements."

Things after that worked fine. Maisie couldn't have been happier.

First, veterinarian that he was, Kyle checked over both Spike and Griffin in his clinic at the shelter. He said he wanted to make sure that the little bit of blood he'd seen on Griffin was his own, from when Beth nicked him with her knife.

Fortunately, it was just a slight cut on his neck that he cleaned and stuck a bandage on. It could have been a hell of a lot worse, but it wasn't.

Maisie was relieved. And glad she'd been able to help save him.

Then Kyle made it a point to go to the storage area where animal food was kept and gave both skilled and wonderful dogs some special—safe—treats.

Maisie couldn't help laughing and cheering him on. And…when they were alone, she kissed him. As he kissed her. Close and hot, suggesting that now that he was no longer a murder suspect, they might have a chance at…well, some nice, sexy fun at last. And even more. A relationship.

She hoped.

Later, at the police station, Maisie was glad that Kyle joined Griffin and her in a meeting, despite the late hour, with Chief Andrew Shermovski, Assistant Chief Kara Province, Detective Vince Vanderhoff, K-9 Officer Doug Murran with Hooper, and several other high-ranking officers.

She shuddered as Kyle described how that woman had burst into the vet clinic when he was there, confronting him, telling him that she had in fact killed Greta and why. That story was as ugly as Maisie had anticipated. For one thing, Greta had figured out what a liar Beth was and was using it against her as a shop employee, cutting her wages and forcing her to work lots of hours.

But that wasn't the only reason Beth killed her. She had decided that killing Greta, and framing a member of the shelter staff for the murder, was only her first step in getting revenge for the fact she hadn't been allowed to re-adopt her abused dog months ago, notwithstanding the fact, as part of her plea bargain, she had agreed never to own a dog again. Of course, she had already taken on a new identity by the time she had tried. One deciding factor, though, had been that her dog had already been adopted by a loving and kind family.

But none of that had affected the woman's determination to exact revenge against the shelter. She'd said she intended to kill some of the managerial staff who had prevented her from retrieving her dog and frame Kyle once again.

From what Kyle indicated, now that others in charge could hear it, too, she had done some other nasty stuff, such as when she had contacted the media and told them things to encourage them to contact the downtown vet clinic in a way that wound up jeopardizing Kyle's job. And then there was that text from an unidentifiable source demanding that Kyle confess to killing Greta or someone he cared about would be killed. The texter had been Beth. She'd admitted it to him.

Kyle now told them all about it and explained why he hadn't mentioned it before, thanks to the additional threat if he let anyone know about the text.

Maisie was upset he hadn't at least told her, although she understood he thought he'd been protecting her. And her fellow cops didn't seem pleased about his secrecy, either, despite acknowledging he had a reason to stay silent.

"I know I can't prove she was the killer or anything else she admitted to me," Kyle then said, looking at Maisie with apparent frustration, "but—"

"But our department will do some further checking," Maisie said, "and use whatever they find against her when she's prosecuted for the assault and battery, murder and more. And you'll have the fun of testifying about what she said."

The frustration on his face lightened and he smiled. "Oh, I'll look forward to that. And—" he looked from Sherm to Kara and back again "—you should also hear about all that K-9 Officer Maisie Murran did to save my life." He pointed to the bandage on his neck and described how she'd come into the clinic and attacked Beth.

"That wasn't me," Maisie said. "Not entirely. You need to commend Griffin, here." She bent and stroked her K-9's neck. "And the retired K-9 now living at the shelter, Spike."

"Yeah, good dogs," Kara said with a smile that Maisie mirrored.

Soon, the meeting was over. Time for Kyle and her, and Griffin, to leave.

To part for the evening and longer? Maisie certainly hoped not.

"Feel like joining me for a drink tonight?" she asked as they went outside through the station's door, to where they'd both parked their cars. After all, they'd left the restaurant before without eating their dinner.

Surely they wouldn't each just go their separate ways now that this memorable day was ending, would they?

At a minimum, Maisie still intended to visit the shelter often with Griffin and figured that Kyle would be there some of the time, too.

"I'd enjoy that," Kyle said. "I think that, even with this cut, I'll be able to swallow."

Maisie laughed. "Oh, you're going to do all you can to get sympathy, aren't you?"

"Will it work?" he asked.

And then, though they were still outside on the sidewalk in front of the police station, he reached out—and she went into his arms, only somewhat concerned whether they'd be seen kissing—with her still in uniform. She continued, of course, to hold Griffin's leash, but her K-9 didn't seem at all upset when they kissed.

Kyle joined Maisie at her house that night. They had gone to a popular Chance bar first and each had a glass of wine. She had remained in her uniform, and Griffin joined them. Which suited Kyle just fine. That wonderful K-9 had helped to save his life. As had Maisie.

Then they headed to Maisie's home...and engaged in the wonderful celebration he had hoped for since he had met her.

She always looked great in her uniform. And without it? Fantastic.

In her comfortable bed, with Griffin sleeping on the floor beside them, they had engaged in the most delightful sex he had ever experienced. Celebration? Oh, yeah. And a lot more.

After the first time, Maisie had lain there beside him, naked and gorgeous and smiling widely. "Till I met you, I never considered sleeping with a murder suspect."

"And was it worth the wait until you felt certain I was innocent?" He was grinning, too, and he moved closer so her body was against his. Warm and curvy and everything he had anticipated. And this position made him want her again.

"I think the waiting sparked this into something I'd never even considered before." And with that, she reached down and began stroking his erection again—not that it necessarily needed any encouragement—and that caused him to start kissing her...all over.

And not for the last time that night, either. In the morning, he had to think hard to determine how many times they'd been fabulously joined.

But they both had to report to their jobs. After a quick breakfast together, they made plans to see each other again that night.

He just hoped that day went fast.

Maisie was exhausted and exhilarated as she headed to the station that morning. Saturday morning. Often one of the two days a week she had off—but that was flexible. And right now, she needed to go to work.

And didn't even try to keep her mind off the wonderful night she had just enjoyed.

Sure, on some level, she had hoped that she would have the experience of sex with the handsome veterinarian who had been occupying her thoughts so often lately, in both good and not-so-good ways. But the reality of it had been even more amazing.

"I think you like him, too, don't you, Griffin?" she called to her dog in the back seat as she drove. Her wonderful K-9, who'd helped to bring yesterday's dangerous situation to a perfect conclusion, sat up and made a small woofing noise that she took to be a yes. Right. He was most likely just acknowledging that she was speaking to him, but that was fine.

She soon parked and got Griffin out of the vehicle. She was delighted that he no longer appeared to be favoring his sore paw, although, with Kyle's help, she had cleaned it and put on his bandage for the last time before leaving home that day.

When she entered the station, Officer Jones was at the reception desk, as usual. She stood and grinned and clapped as Maisie and Griffin walked toward her, and so did the few other officers who happened to be gathered there, including Officer Glen Kreake and even Officer Jackson Styles, and also a couple of civilians who seemed to be waiting to see someone. "I heard what happened yesterday," she said. "You did it!"

"With help," Maisie said.

"Some, I gather," Penny agreed. "Anyway, I was told to send you right to our chief's office as soon as you got here. There's a meeting going on to recap what happened last night."

Maisie hurried to his spacious office, where Chief Sherm, behind his large, neat desk, stood at Maisie's entrance with Griffin, as did those facing his desk: Kara, Vince and even Doug, who was already there with Hooper.

"Great job, you two," Sherm said right away, looking at both Maisie and her dog.

"Yeah," Vince said, as Doug came over to give her a hug. That made her eyes tear up a little, but she hid it as best she could. "You want to hear what our overnight interrogation of our suspect revealed?"

"Absolutely," Maisie said, taking a seat as the others sat back down, too.

Clearly, Beth had admitted to everyone, not just Maisie and Kyle, her murder of Greta. She'd come prepared to do just that on the night she had killed her boss, carrying the knife and a large medical gown of thin plastic that she'd donned over her outfit so the blood would get on it rather than her clothes. Afterward, she had squished the gown and hidden it in a heavier plastic bag and shoved it way down in the large purse she often carried, so all its other contents hid it. Knowing there were K-9s around, she'd also used some insect repellant on it to cover the odor. Maisie was a little surprised Griffin hadn't alerted anyway, but from what Vince indicated Beth had said, she'd done some research until she had found something that had apparently worked to fool K-9s.

She had tossed that evidence away, but the investigative team would attempt to find it.

The rest Maisie pretty well knew: Beth's motive, to attempt revenge against the shelter and to frame the shelter's veterinarian. And how she had befriended Chessie to get her to let Beth into the shelter when she wasn't supposed to be there. And more, including the fact that the knife she'd had with her yesterday was one she had bought at the same time as the murder weapon—far from here, and identical to it.

"We've recorded it all," Vince concluded. "And we'll want to get your statement recorded, too, to use against her at her homicide trial. Great job," he repeated. "And we'll of course keep her in solitary, although we're not sure how much she knows about the real nature of the shelter."

The meeting was soon at an end, and Maisie was glad to return to their office with Doug. She also felt herself beaming under her brother's praise.

"So...what's next for you and Dr. Kornel?" Doug

asked, grinning at her as they both sat at their desks, their K-9s at their sides.

Maisie felt herself redden and bent down to pet Griffin. "Don't know yet," she said.

"Something good, I bet."

And because Doug was her brother and knew her well, she admitted, "I hope so."

She spent much of the rest of the day working with Vince to provide her statement. But she did manage to leave the station a little early and head for the shelter, where she had already confirmed Kyle was on duty.

Parts of the shelter remained behind police tape since the investigation was continuing into where Beth had gotten into the facility, with Chessie's help, and how the intruder had dropped off dog treats before hunkering down to wait for Maisie.

They had confirmed with Esther that those treats had been stolen from the store—not very wise on Beth's part, Maisie mused, since that would have added to information confirming who had been there, if there had been any question about it.

But part of what the authorities had learned from Beth was that she'd attempted to create a major distraction at the shelter—one that would attract the managers' attention, and particularly Scott's, so she would be able to get him alone there. And kill him. That was also why she allowed herself to be seen on the security footage even in disguise, she'd said, although she might not have been able to prevent that, anyway.

And Kyle showed Maisie that security footage after he let Griffin and her in and they walked around the shelter together. Maisie had wanted to hold his hand, but she was still in uniform.

She anticipated what they would do again later, when she could take it off.

Similarly to how it had occurred at the police station, Maisie was applauded by people at the shelter, by both managers and staff members—as was Kyle.

"Thanks so much," Scott told her, shaking her hand. "Things could have been a lot worse around here without you."

"Thank Kyle, too," she told him. "His life was on the line, and he helped to bring our suspect down."

She asked about Chessie. The staff member had apologized over and over, and was permitted to stay, at least for now, on a sort of probation. Her ex still hadn't been located, but the authorities would continue to look for him.

It was getting late, and Maisie and Kyle soon were able to head to his clinic for him to close it up, Griffin beside them. When they were in private, door shut behind them, they immediately got into each other's arms.

Their kiss was hot and long and tempting. Maisie enjoyed the feel of Kyle's hardness against her as they drew even closer together.

Eventually, Maisie suggested breathlessly, "Would you like to come home with me now? I think I can put a decent dinner together for us."

"Well, I am hungry," Kyle said against her lips. "And we can eat whatever later, when we're both sated."

Maisie laughed.

"And depending on how we're feeling then," he continued, "no need for you to cook. In fact, I'd like to go to dinner someplace more special tonight than the Joint. I want to celebrate."

"The capturing of the real murderer?"

"Yeah," Kyle said, taking her hand and staring down into her eyes. "Now that you have no reason to think I'm a murderer, maybe we can consider a future together."

"Oh, yes," Maisie said breathlessly. And then, almost as if she couldn't help it, she blurted, "Now I feel free to tell you that I love you, Dr. Kyle Kornel."

He laughed and kissed her again. "I love you, too, K-9 Officer Maisie Murran."

They kissed again. Soon, they left the vet clinic, Griffin at their side as they walked slowly down the hall, their hands clasped, Maisie's shoulder close against Kyle's.

And she couldn't help thinking about their wonderful future.

* * * * *

Look for Her Undercover Refuge*, the first book in Linda O. Johnston's Shelter of Secrets miniseries, available now wherever Harlequin Romantic Suspense books are sold!*

WE HOPE YOU ENJOYED
THIS BOOK FROM

⊕ HARLEQUIN
ROMANTIC
SUSPENSE

Danger. Passion. Drama.

These heart-racing page-turners will keep you guessing
to the very end. Experience the thrill of unexpected
plot twists and irresistible chemistry.

4 NEW BOOKS AVAILABLE EVERY MONTH!

#2183 UNDERCOVER COLTON
The Coltons of Colorado • by Addison Fox

Sami Evans has long suspected her father may not be entirely aboveboard. So she's not surprised when her one-night stand turns out to be an FBI agent. Dom Colton needs to get closer to Sami's father, but when Dom and Sami fake an engagement, he's realizing his feelings might be more than a cover.

#2184 CAVANAUGH JUSTICE: DEADLY CHASE
Cavanaugh Justice • by Marie Ferrarella

Embittered and broken detective Gabriel Cortland is forced to pair up with an optimistic partner to take down a prolific serial killer—the one who killed Gabriel's pregnant wife. Gabriel is determined to work alone on this, but Shayla Cavanaugh knows how to break down his defenses. But with a killer on the loose, Gabriel's new lease on life may not last very long...

#2185 COLD CASE COWBOY
Cold Case Detectives • by Jennifer Morey

When she finds refuge at his ranch, Indie Deboe struggles with her feelings for Wes McCann. She's lost everything before—to the same killer who could be a threat to both of them now!

#2186 HOTSHOT HERO UNDER FIRE
Hotshot Heroes • by Lisa Childs

Hotshot firefighter/paramedic Owen James is in danger—and not from firefighting. Someone is trying to kill him, and he finds himself falling for the prime suspect!

He winced. "Yeah, I remember…"

A smile tugged at the corners of her mouth, pulling up
her lips. "Don't go looking for any flowers from me as
an apology."

"There's something else I'd rather have from you," he
said, and the intensity of his blue-eyed stare had her pulse
racing. Then he leaned forward and brushed his mouth
across hers.

And shock gripped her so hard, her heart seemed to
stop beating for a moment before resuming at a frantic
pace. He'd kissed her before, but it still caught her by
surprise. Not the kiss so much as the passion that coursed
through her. She'd never felt so much desire from just a
kiss. And why this man out of all the men she'd dated
over the years?

Why Owen James, who'd hurt her in high school with
his cruelty? Who hadn't saved her mother?

Why would she be so attracted to him?

It wasn't just because of his flowers and his apology. She'd felt this passion last night before he'd come bearing the roses and his mea culpa.

She'd worried about him yesterday, but just like in high school, she didn't believe it was possible that he really cared about her, that he wanted her. Was he up to something? What did he want from her?

His mouth brushed across hers again. Then his lips nipped at hers, and a gasp escaped her. He deepened the kiss, and she tasted his passion.

He wanted her as badly as she wanted him.

And that was bad…

Very bad.

Because she had a feeling that if she let herself give in to her desire, she would be the one who wound up hurt next…

Don't miss
Hotshot Hero Under Fire *by Lisa Childs,*
available June 2022 wherever
Harlequin Romantic Suspense books and ebooks are sold.

Harlequin.com

HRSEXP0422

Love Harlequin romance?

DISCOVER.

Be the first to find out about promotions,
news and exclusive content!

f Facebook.com/HarlequinBooks

🐦 Twitter.com/HarlequinBooks

📷 Instagram.com/HarlequinBooks

📌 Pinterest.com/HarlequinBooks

You Tube YouTube.com/HarlequinBooks

ReaderService.com

EXPLORE.

Sign up for the Harlequin e-newsletter and
download a free book from any series at
TryHarlequin.com

CONNECT.

Join our Harlequin community to
share your thoughts and connect
with other romance readers!
Facebook.com/groups/HarlequinConnection

HARLEQUIN

HSOCIAL2021